LITTLE CRANE

DARKEST DESIRES

JORJOR BATTLE

Copyright © 2025 Jorjor Battle

All rights reserved. No part of this publication may be reproduced, stored or transmitted in any form or by any means, electronic, mechanical, photocopying, recording, scanning, or otherwise without written permission from the author. It is illegal to copy this book, post it to a website, or distribute it by any other means without permission. It is also forbidden to use this book for AI learning/software in any way. If it is discovered that you have violated this agreement, Jorjor Battle reserves all legal rights to it, including pursuing legal action for breach of contract which may claim damages including, but not limited to, lost profits caused by the violative distribution.

This novel is entirely a work of fiction. The names, characters and incidents portrayed in it are the work of the author's imagination. Any resemblance to actual persons, living or dead, events or localities is entirely coincidental.

Jorjor Battle has no responsibility for the persistence or accuracy of URLs for external or third-party Internet Websites referred to in this publication and does not guarantee that any content on such websites is, or will remain, accurate or appropriate.

Designations used by companies to distinguish their products are often claimed as trademarks. All brand names and product names used in this book and on its cover are trade names, service marks, trademarks and registered trademarks of their respective owners. The publishers and the book are not associated with any product or vendor mentioned in this book. None of the companies referenced within the book have endorsed the book.

DEDICATION

To the silent hotties who love hard.

I see you.

CONTENT WARNINGS

This book is a dark romance. It explores dark themes that can be triggering. Please check over the list of content and triggers, if needed, before reading.

Familial abuse, murder, death, sexual content, trauma bonding, mentions of trafficking, child abuse, grooming, mentions of suicide, self harm, mentions of SA (off page).

Playlist

Mortes Ostium Society

Founded by Jack the Ripper, the Death's Door Society has been shrouded in mystery for centuries. Built as a sanctuary for serial killers to practice their craft, the Society provides care and resources to it's precious members in whatever form they need.

Only the best of the best gather for the Mortes Ostium Masquerade Ball. Once a year, killers from every corner of the world descend on Paris for a weekend to connect, reminisce, and compare their achievements of the year.

Each book in the Darkest Desires series centers around the grand ball, and the love that the members of the society find along the way.

cordially invites you to the

Masquerade Ball

Musée de la Chasse et de la Nature
Paris, France

███ to ███ | June | ███████

Black Tie

Accommodation Provided

RSVP
Member ☐ ☐ Plus One

PROLOGUE
Diora

"There's a light in children's eyes that you just don't have, dear."

My mom's words ring in my ears as if I am hearing them for the first time. I am only six, but it didn't seem to matter to my mom. Six years was more than enough to develop the light, according to her.

If I ever had the light, it died this day. It died the moment my mom gave up on me. It died the day they separated my sister, Juliet, and me.

Now that I was six and Juliet was eleven, Mom and Dad said things had to change. Juliet is excited about getting her own room. It's a sign that she is now a big girl. Older. More mature. She didn't know the real reason we were being separated.

I did, though. They didn't want Juliet to be tainted. *"Juliet is the last good thing to come from my womb."* Juliet had the light Mom was talking about. I didn't. I could wear all the light pastel colors I wanted. Brighten any room with lamps and lights and I would never have the same light that Juliet does.

My princess pink blanket crumbles under our weight. All the work I did to make the perfect bed is wasted as my mom comes into my room saying she wants to talk. Who has talks with a six-year-old?

I sit beside her, and even then, I see the recoil she tries to hide. My smile falls as she stares at me. Eying me like a prey watches a predator. When the bedroom door shuts, Mom can be her true authentic self. The disgust, the fear, can shine through her facial muscles, and the honesty I wish she'd kept hidden for longer soaks the air.

"Mommy?" I ask as she carefully lays a hand on my head. She sighs as tears fall down her face, one by one. I wish I could make the fat tears go away, but I know I am the cause of them.

"You love your sister, don't you?" she asks. Patting my hair. Getting harsher with each pat. She slowly rocks herself back and forth, as she normally does when it's just me and her. She cries when it's only me and her. She says mean things when it's only her and me.

If Mom hates me so much, why is she only her truest self around me?

"How could you? Do you even know what love is, honey?" she mutters.

"I do," I say. "I love Juliet."

"Then why don't you be normal for her? If not for me, then for her?"

"What's wrong, Mommy?" I ask, reaching for her hand. Her skin is always soft, smooth, a luxury she doesn't let me touch, and yet I try, anyway. She snaps her hand away from me.

"Don't touch me, Diora," she quietly barks. *"Don't spread your evil."*

I shake my head, confused, yet not confused at all. It's as if I need to hear her say it again and again. The constant reminder that I'm not good. I'm not light. I'm not Juliet.

"I'm not evil," I say, and my voice breaks. I know it's not true. That I'm not normal, but I thought, maybe, if Juliet loves me... If Juliet loves me, why can't Mommy?

"What do you call playing in a dead child's blood, Diora? *Evil, bad spirited.*"

I swallow my words, not wanting to argue with Mommy. I stare at my mommy. Meet her scared eyes.

It wasn't. I wasn't. I shake my head as Mom's tears roll faster down her face. I wasn't playing with blood. I wasn't playing.

My mind jumps back to yesterday. The smooth consistency of the red liquid spread around my classmate, Darcy, when she jumped off the school play set and hit the cement.

Blood is bad? I blink as my mind races with words I can't speak. Mom won't believe me. She never does.

Blood is messy. I was trying to clean her up. Once I got there, once I got to her, I tried to put it back. I wasn't playing with her blood. It was soft, smooth, in my hands, but I was trying to help. I swear I was.

Mommy wouldn't believe me. Neither would Daddy. Or the play guard. Or Darcy's parents, who screamed in my face at the school's front office.

I knew this.

And yet, I still tried to help Darcy. That's what Juliet would have done.

But that doesn't matter.

They've written me off.

They've given up.

I watch silently as my mom's tears stream down her face, and her silent sobs wrack her body as she pats my head. She wraps her frail arms around my body and pulls me in for the last hug I'll ever get from her.

Her shirt is soft and wet from her crying. But I... I like the warmth her body gives me. I want to wrap my arms around her like I would when Juliet hugs me, but I don't think Mom will like that.

"Oh, baby, my little baby Diora. You're a monster."

A monster?

"You have to stay away from Juliet. You mustn't taint her, Diora." Her words come out sharp as she grips my head. She rocks me back and forth with her. I don't know what to do. Mommy is sad. I didn't... I knew... I wanted to... I don't know.

"Monsters are bad?" I ask. Her grip starts to hurt. My skin pulls in her tight grasp and my eyes hurt. I close them. The strain behind them intensifies. It hurts. It actually hurts this time.

"Monsters are bad, Diora," she says.

"I can't be a monster. I love Juliet, and I love you, too, Mommy." I wanna fix this. Fix my mommy, fix me. I try to look at her, but she won't let me move my head. She sobs out loud this time, and her tears wet my hair.

"I'm so sorry. I'm so sorry," she cries, and that's when I sense the sharp kitchen knife at my wrist. She slices vertically up my forearm and it burns. It hurts. I can feel it.

"I can't love a monster, baby."

"Mom!" I hear Juliet's voice on the other side of my door as that same smooth, creamy blood runs down my arms and onto Mommy and my bed. She's loudly crying as Juliet pounds on my door. Juliet starts crying, as if she knew.

My dad's footsteps are loud as he storms in with tears down his own eyes. I've never seen Dad cry. He rips the knife from Mom and swallows *her* in a hug. Her. Mommy. Not me.

My arm grows numb, and my princess pink bedding gets ruined. Messy. Bloody.

I blink, a single time, and I feel Juliet's little arms wrap around me. Mommy tries to grab for her, but Juliet dodges her. My blood smears on her arms as she hugs me. I enjoy Juliet's hugs. Juliet's hugs are soft and warm. I rest my dry cheek on her shoulder as she sobs into me.

I can't be a monster. If I'm a monster, Mommy will take me away from Juliet. I have to be good.

For Juliet. I'd do anything for Juliet.

Chapter 1

Diora

I like the texture of dirt and plants under my nails as much as I like skin and blood. Watching the four officers from the corner of my eye, I lift the hot kettle from the hot pot on my workstation and pour boiling water into four antique tea cups.

The four officers sit in metal chairs, designed to look like old fashioned dining chairs, around my round, stained glass table. They are gagged and bound, with nothing on except their t-shirts and underwear.

They thought they were flirting with a meek girl in a bar full of rowdy drunken men.

They didn't know the meek girl in front of them had been working on their capture for six months now.

I've been picking each of them up from their favorite after work bars for four weeks now, one at a time, keeping them drugged in my greenhouse in the forest on Laker Street.

My white gloves are covered in dirt smears as I pick off a few flowers of foxglove. I crush the pendulous bell-shaped flower into tiny pieces. The pretty pinks and purples make me smile as I sweep the crushed flowers into small tea packets.

Foxglove is a beautiful plant that has many uses, both as a poison and a medicine. It's one of the most beautiful poisonous plants, subjectively, and therefore, it is my favorite to use.

My scar from... from sixteen years ago now, shows on the inside of my forearm as I prepare the tea. I drop a tea bag into each mug of boiling water, letting the water soak up the properties of the plant. I inhale, feeling the chemicals from the plant sting my nose. This dose of poison is deadly, even to those in optimal health.

These officers are in perfect health, according to their last required physicals. How convenient is that?

How convenient was letting the perpetrators of my sister's nightmare free?

Doesn't seem so convenient now, does it?

Hearing a grunt, I turn around with two saucers with teacups on them in my hands. The officers wake up, the chloroform wearing off. It's not my favorite weapon of choice, but in a pinch, speed and effectiveness must come first. I had to get four largely muscled male bodies from the shed behind my greenhouse to the scene of their final show: my first crime.

Their murder.

"Hi, gentlemen," I say, setting everyone's teacups in front of them, including one in front of me. They struggle against their restraints, but they're too weak to break them. I made sure.

"I figure you must be confused, angry, maybe even upset, huh?" I ask, swishing my tea with a tiny spoon. "So was she."

Their grunts and heaving sound gross. I grimace as I glance at the clock above my work station. Two a.m. Hmm, I guess starting the show now is fine.

"You must not remember our first meeting at the police station, since most of you approached me first, kind of... Well, that's not important. What's important is that you know why your wives and children are going to miss you," I say, taking a sip of my own foxglove-filled tea. I let my own tea soak longer, since I prepared it earlier than theirs, though I won't be drinking as much as they are. It's unfair to be bad without punishment.

Being bad cannot go without punishment, even if it is only in reaction.

Murder is wrong. No matter how much I'm itching to do so. No matter what reason I muster up to justify why I'm doing what I'm doing.

Sipping on my tea, my breathing changes as I consume the poison. Though, I know I'm not dying today. I've just started my vengeance for my sister, Juliet, and I will not die before I've got my greedy hands on the woman who orchestrated the worst night of Juliet's life.

Getting up, I ungag each man, letting their slobbered white rags pile in the mini black fireplace by my workbench. They cough and gurgle as they regain the power of speech.

I stumbled upon this greenhouse when I was a kid, and have been rooted in these four walls since. It's big enough to have a few rows of plants I've accumulated over time, with floor to ceiling arched windows. The intricate designs on the windows and ceilings give the little house an ethereal vibe.

Like an old haunted house, with crown molding and sculptures, this greenhouse has become my safe space. Even with all the windows, I'm not worried about being caught. This is the one space I can unleash my urges, and now I've found the perfect victims to satisfy my craving for death.

"You all are gross," I say, conscious of the contaminated heat mixing with their bodies' smells and germs that touch my skin. Cold nights remind me of my sister. How she loves cold nights. She loves bundling up in blankets by the fire watching TV. I love spending time with her, so I let her wrap me in her softest blankets, too.

Juliet is the only person on this earth who loves me, and *they* dared to hurt her.

I failed to protect her.

That won't happen again.

"What the hell are you doing?" the tallest man spits. His name is Josh Panko. He's been on Litchfort's police force for over twenty years. Has a wife and two kids, aged seven and eleven. His hobbies include watching football and going to the bar. Anything but spending time at home with his wife and kids.

"Don't you hurt my fucking wife, you fucking bitch." Now, Kyle is different. Kyle loves his wife, and he has no kids. His hobbies include sitting on his back porch with a beer and a book in his hands that he never reads.

Growls and yells never bothered me. They don't process in my brain like they do my sisters. She gets scared when people get mad. It's why I never get mad. Their anger would scare her into these men's submission. That's why I'm here and she isn't.

"I'm not going to hurt your wife or your children—not physically."

"Of course you're fucking not. Untie us and maybe we'll let you off easy. Kidnapping officers is a high offense," Josh Panko says, trying to bargain with me. I turn around to face the four men. They look a mix of pissed off and amused. As if something is funny.

Maybe this is funny to them. A girl like me kidnapped four men like them. I'm not necessarily strong, and they weigh about two-hundred pounds each, and yet, what they have yet to realize is that, even with all the odds against me, I still got them here, bound and gagged.

"I'm not hurting your wives or children because they are good. I'm killing you because you're evil."

"Won't killing us make you evil, too?" Josh asks, though, I've already thought this through.

"No, it won't," I say, taking my seat again and sipping my tea.

"How in the fuck would it not make you evil, too?" Kyle Montery asks, spitting as he's talking. Fear is clouding his thoughts. He's unable to keep a cool head in any situation, so it doesn't come as a surprise to see him slipping first. His anger is causing his chest to heave, his pulse decreasing with his increasing breaths.

The foxglove in the air is already working on him. It slows the pulse, and I see by the effort he exudes, he's working overtime to control his breathing.

"I can't become evil. I already am," I say. My single strand of pearls around my neck becomes hot and heavy as the room's temperature rises, aware of the next stage of my plan taking place. My windows begin to fog. I can't contain my smile.

"Be good, then. Let us go," Josh tries. He must think he's playing me. He's an annoying kind of blond—not golden enough to appear soft, but bright enough to make my eyes twitch. His blue eyes irk me, too; they're too blue. The kind of blue that appears right as lightning strikes, on the verge of being white.

I hate it.

I hate him.

"You want to leave before you know why you are here?" I ask, not making a single move to untie my guest. My own chair is made of the same metal, painted white to help create the tea party ambiance.

"We don't give a fuck," Kyle barks. His eyes move rapidly back and forth as the sweat drips down his forehead. I prefer Kyles over Joshes in this world. Kyle is true to human nature. No one is calm when their lives are threatened. He's showing me all his cards, and exactly how he feels, while Josh is hiding. He hides behind the facade of control.

"Okay," I say, shrugging my shoulders. I rise from my chair, my white t-shirt stained with plant stems and sweat clinging to my chest as I move to stand behind Kyle. His brown hair stinks, and he shakes violently, yelling incoherent curses. Still, I lace my fingers in his hair and lay my head over his greasy hair.

My cheek itches with the nastiness that is Kyle's greasy hair, but I persist.

"Hmm, well, the least you could do is let me give you a name," I say. I grin as my eyes meet my silent captive. Lewis Karplie. He hasn't uttered a word, and I think he may be the only person to recognize me.

He hadn't recognized me when they approached me in the bar, but I think he does now.

Lewis Karplie is the only Black officer here. As much as I wanted to give Lewis a pass, an excuse for a fellow Black person trying in this world, I can't.

He has three kids and a wife, who all strive to do their best in their own pursuits of life. He spends the most time with his family, game nights, movie nights, dinners, he makes those.

He's a seemingly good dad, like the rest of these officers, doing the bare minimum to have a family. But then, the lights go off, and we see the truth.

The shadows that reveal the darkest truths of every single person in this room, including me. We are not good. We are evil. We've done bad things, and now we must pay the price.

Lewis jumps back in his chair when his eyes meet mine. He is the one person I debated excluding from tonight's show. Lewis had hesitation that night. When my sister and I came to the police station to report her rape, he had the nerve to give us hope.

All that pity withered away the moment the politician's name left our lips and suddenly, Lewis Karplie's face turned to stone. He refused to help us any further and ripped the report to shreds.

"You know, Lewis. Why don't you share with the class?" I command as my grip gets tighter in Kyle's hair to keep him still. Kyle's calmed down now, still shaking like a leaf, realizing he can't break his restraints. He's getting weaker. They all are, whether they know it or not, as the poison works in their systems.

The steam from the tea has been filtering in their systems quickly, since I placed their cups directly under their noses.

Lewis begins to convulse, his locs shaking as he shakes his head no repeatedly. Wide brown eyes pierce into mine for a split second before Josh gets the man's attention.

"Lewis, what do you know? Lewis, say it. Now."

"I-I don't, I can't believe—" Lewis chokes.

"Lewis, if you don't tell your partners why they're here, I'll slit Kyle's throat right now," I say, letting Kyle's hair go with one hand and pulling the dagger from my belt holster. It was situated behind my back, like how they turned their backs to me, to Juliet.

"Lewis," Kyle hisses as the sharp end of my dagger traces the side of his neck.

"Okay, okay. God," Lewis pants as dread covers his skin. He shivers, and he meets my eyes again and mutters the name I wanted to hear. "Juliet Moss."

"Ahh, yes, Juliet Moss. You are right Lewis. Ring any bells, boys?" I say, moving away from Kyle and to Lewis. I stand behind him now, wondering if giving him mercy is worth the pain they helped cause that night.

A quick death for answering my question.

Or a slow death for turning my sister and me away?

"Juliet?" The fourth and final member of our party speaks. Orlando Jones. He had been quietly muttering to himself until the reason they are here was revealed.

Orlando Jones is the fourth member of this clique. These four are famous on Litchfort's force, for being Yara Holdings favorites. A.k.a. her minions, cleaning her dirty doings up.

Orlando doesn't have a wife or kids. He lives alone in his apartment on Monroe Street. He often sits in the dark; for what, I'm not quite sure. He always lets the TV play in the background, but I can tell he doesn't watch it.

Not that I cared that these could be completely innocent men who made a mistake. A mistake of brushing off the crying girls trying to report the most powerful politician in Michigan. A battle we won't want to fight, they'd say, as they turn us away.

Even then, they'd be sitting in this greenhouse filled to the brim with poison and my need for vengeance and repentance.

"My sister, of course, it could be hard to remember one of many victims who have tried to come forward against Yara

Holding's crimes, but..." I inform them, letting my sentence drop off as realization of what they did to end up here sparks to life in their minds.

Yara Holding is working her way up to a powerful seat in government—the senate majority leader. Currently working as a lawyer, she builds connections the quickest way she knows how: giving powerful, hungry, greedy men already in power what they want most: a night without consequences.

She has these men's jobs on the end of her whip. Instead of protecting people, the whole point of their jobs, they let Ms. Holdings' crimes be swept under the rug.

It's fine, though. Cause I'm here.

Deciding that Lewis Karplie will be dismissed from this party first, I release my hold on Kyle. Lewis shakes in his chair as I approach him. Bringing a tea cup up to his lips, I force a drink down his throat, jerking his chin upward, so the only way the drink can go is down, and he swallows the foxglove like a champ.

Despite the shaking and the burning and his body's instinct to gauge the drink back up, I seal his lips closed with my hand. Regardless of how much seeps through, I've got enough in his system for the effects to finish him.

The men shout, and Orlando Jones even cries at the sight. Even then, nothing has changed my desired outcome. Lewis Karplie's body begins to shut down. With my hand so close to his neck, I can feel his pulse slow tremendously, and his pupils become smaller as the foxglove takes down his body with each second that passes.

He stares right into my eyes as he dies. He doesn't say anything. Maybe he'd accepted his fate long before I walked over. Maybe he realizes you can't argue with evil when you're evil yourself. Maybe he knows, deep down somewhere, that he deserves this.

Life drains from his face, and he goes slack in my hands. Letting his head drop, I walk back to my seat, taking a deep breath before sipping my tea, letting the burn in as I stare at Lewis Karplie's dead body. I wonder if everyone's first kill is like this.

I gaze down at the light pink liquid in my cup, unable to hide my smile any longer. My black, frizzy hair covers the sides of my face as I stare down. A giggle slips past my lips, and that's what gets the men to quiet down.

I look up, meeting each of their eyes as fear drips into them. Understanding their situation now, pleads of mercy fill my little house. The sounds bounce off the arched windows, and despite how cold it is at this time of night, it's boiling in here.

I watch as the foxglove I've injected them all with prior to them waking up speeds its effects as their bodies fight harder. They'll die faster without me having to lift another finger.

"I'll fucking kill you," Josh whips at me, cracking his calm boy persona.

"You're already dead, Josh. All of you are," I inform as I stand to pick up each of their teacups and dump the liquid over the remaining three officers.

Those were more for set up. I didn't know who'd figure out why they were here first, so I placed a teacup in front of each of them. "I injected a lethal amount of foxglove into your systems about an hour before you all woke up. With the combination of your panic and the chemicals from that plant and many others, it's only moments before you drop dead, like Lewis."

Splashes of the now lukewarm tea hit my exposed feet and their faces as they spit and scream in surprise. Their anger has changed to pleading as the weakness in their bodies registers in their minds. Their pleads anger me further, proving why Lewis deserved the quick death I offered him.

"Hurting yourself too is an unusual style of dealing with guilt, my dear Diora, but I must say, I'm impressed with what I've seen," a slick, aged voice speaks. The sudden sound makes me jump from my seat, reaching for my dagger.

Who the hell is here?

I'm not the biggest fan of blood. Using knives and daggers isn't my specialty, either, but I've trained in using multiple weapons since the start of my vengeance mission.

"Help! Please help us!" Orlando shouts, drool spouting from his mouth. The woman grimaces before pulling out what appears to be a Ruger LCP Max, but to be honest, I'm not sure. I only know how to shoot a gun, and the one she has is small enough to fit in her white tweed purse.

I'm more concerned with why she's here. I glare at the unknown woman. Doesn't she see I'm in the middle of something?

"I'll shoot right between your eyes if you speak out of turn again, Orlando," she says, keeping the weapon trained on him. Her attention snaps back to me as she steps into the light. She's an older Black woman, maybe in her fifties or sixties, in what could be her Sunday best. Her tweed dress fits impeccably, and she slinks into the room with kitten heels on. Her hair is dyed brown, with a few grays peaking out, and her eyes are brown and sharp, setting me on edge.

I'm pissed she interrupted my night. It was going exactly how I planned, and here this woman comes. Now I have to kill her, too.

Rolling my eyes, I watch the new player on the scene.

I can't speak unless she speaks to me, that much I know. She has the gun, so she has the power at the moment.

I don't know if she's on their side, acting as their savior, and that is my biggest concern. It looks to me she knows them, yet threatening to kill one of them makes me unsure about why she's really here.

I can't have her messing this up. I spent six months planning tonight, and I will not let her ruin it.

Orlando's body shakes harshly before slumping over, his head hitting my delicate watercolor inspired tablecloth, death finally taking him. Now, all that's left are Josh and Kyle, who is still spitting out curses and thrashing in his chair nailed down to the floor.

Josh's eyes have gone dark, as the hope of besting me has died. I didn't think much more would make me happier but this realization from the man who turned my sister away from reporting her sexual assault and making her feel dumb because "how can a woman sexually assault another woman" is the perfect icing on my cake.

Juliet Moss deserves justice. She deserves the world, and I'll give that back to her.

"Two to go and you've barely touched these men, Diora. Darling, you're destined for great things," the woman says, coming to stand closer. She only takes a few steps, but her smile—it's her smile that has me flinching.

Friend or foe is the question blaring in my mind, and I can't make the determination. I stand this time and make a show of my weapon. My knife now comes in front of my chest, the blade facing away from me. It pisses me off that she's made me do this. Hold this knife.

The poison in the air isn't enough to take someone with as much energy as her.

"Who are you?" I ask. Her smile doesn't falter as she sees my weapon, and from the way my arms line with goosebumps, I get the sense that she's stronger than me. Way fucking stronger.

"I'm Mrs. Jay, soon, you'll be calling me Mother," she says, tilting her head with a sickly sweet smile. "What's the plan, darling? What's next in this lovely show you're orchestrating?"

"Why would I tell you?" I snip. I don't know this woman, and yet here she comes, guns blazing and asking me for answers.

She moves the gun toward me this time, and I huff before answering.

"Let the poison kill them," I say, not entirely sure why I'm offering such information to her. If she kills me, then she could let the rest of these pigs free, and I will not let that happen.

But if she's here to... watch, maybe I can finish out this plan before she kills me.

If she kills me. I sense that's not in her plans tonight. If it was, she'd have done it already.

"Mmm, that's why you've planted the plant in all their yards. Hmm, you plan to dump their bodies close by, make the deaths seem like an accident. A coincidence?"

How did she know that? She didn't need me to tell her anything. She must have been here the whole time.

"One Google search would tell anyone the plant was poisonous. Have you thought about that?"

"Why Google what you don't know?" I ask.

"Hmm, well, I can't interfere. That would be against the rules of Mortes Ostium, but I'm getting the feeling you won't have a problem with meeting their requirements," she says, standing by the table now. "Do you have an extra chair? I'd love to watch."

Who the hell is this woman, and what the hell is Mortes Ostium? The confusion makes my skin itch uncomfortably. My eyes dart between each living being in the room. Do I take the chance to trust this person, or do I kill her now? Could I kill her now?

"Darling, I've been in the game for thirty years; you're not beating me today. Now, please," she says, waving her hand to the lack of a chair behind her. I drag the stool from my workstation for myself and give her my height appropriate chair. She sits, smoothing out the skirt of her dress before clasping her hands under her chin and staring at me.

I've got the height advantage, but it doesn't feel like I have the advantage. She's completely at ease, even staring up at me.

"What the fuck is going on?" Kyle shouts, seeming not to operate on any other voice level other than loud. Maybe I should move this along and kill them quicker—no. I have to stick to my plan.

"I don't know," I mumble, keeping my eyes on the threat in the room.

"I figure now is best to talk, Diora Moss. I'd like you to join me."

"Join what?" I ask, scrunching my eyebrows. Is she talking about that Mortes group? What could this lady possibly want with me?

"My company, Haven Corporation, honey. I've been trying to spark creativity in my life, and I think you are the perfect fit," she says, booping my nose with one of her perfectly manicured nails, which causes me to flinch back and glare.

Does this woman have no fear? How has she gotten to such a state where she boops a person's nose who is in the middle of committing four murders?

"Perfect fit for what?"

"Killing people, of course. After thirty years, the act gets boring—dull even—until you find that spark again and I believe you to be my spark, Diora." The woman says as she digs in her large purse. "Here's a phone, once you've decided to join, give me a call, my contact is under Mother, and I'll give you future instruction," she says, sliding a compact flip phone on the table toward me.

I catch it, tossing it on my workstation. My brows furrow in confusion as I accept the phone, but I know there's not much I can do. She's killing people, I guess, but who? And why? Will I have time to complete my own mission if I link up with her? Do I have a choice?

"Haven is my personal company, but Mortes Ostium is a separate society for people like us. I have no say over whether you'll be admitted into that," she says. Her words still don't clear any confusion I have as the names get muddled in my head. "Collect a sample of each of their blood on microscopic blood slides for safekeeping, and don't forget I know that you're who killed these four men, and I know where you did it, so think wisely before deciding whether to call me or not."

Her face drops the lovely smile she had into a sharp glare. I watch as she remains seated at the table and Kyle and Josh attempt to blink away their blurred vision, which won't work.

The woman also sets blood slides on the table, carefully this time. As I take the four of them from her, my brows furrow.

"Go ahead, get a drop of blood from each dead person here." She smiles encouragingly and motions her hands toward Lewis's dead body.

Slowly rising from my chair, I take my knife and slice Lewis's arm, letting blood drop onto the slide before closing it up and setting it on my workbench.

My gaze flies between my captees and her as I collect their blood and place the slides on my bench.

"Let us fucking go, you bitch," Josh tries to demand. His voice comes out weak and shaky.

"No," I say, sipping on my cold tea as I watch the mysterious woman. "Not until you die."

I wait till Josh and Kyle's heads hit the table before I collect the blood from them. I have no idea what I'm going to do with these slides, but it seems better to do what the crazy lady says.

"How fun was this?" the woman says now that it's just her and me here. "Keep these, and someone will come to collect them and put them in your file with Mortes Ostium. Remember that, and I'll be expecting your call to work for me soon, darling."

She leaves with one final glance at the room filled with death.

Now it's just me, four bodies, and a mountain of confusion.

Chapter 2

Diora

The dirt under my fingernails itches, but not nearly as much as the phone burning a hole in my pocket. The sky is bright and the sun is shining by the time I get home, their names circling in my head as I unlock my apartment door.

Josh Panko.

Kyle Montery.

Lewis Karplie.

Orlando Jones.

All dead in their respective backyards, with a little gift from me. A foxglove plant planted in each.

I'll admit, my clean up isn't the best, but it's enough to get the job done. Sliding through the front door of my shared apartment, I try to clasp the door handle into place without signaling I'm home.

I freeze at the door as I silently close it behind me.

Juliet is awake.

I can tell by the noise of the news station on the TV and the soft patter of her slippered feet across the fake wood floors. Of course, they are freshly mopped, and I thank my brain for getting rid of my shoes in the trash a few blocks down.

My dollar store flip-flops saved my feet on the trek through Litchfort, Michigan in the muggy heat of the spring.

My eyes dart around the entry of our apartment, trying to see if I can sneak around Juliet and head straight to the shower. As her footsteps sound closer and closer, I know that the possibility of getting past her is dying.

Her hearing is as good as mine. For different reasons, of course.

My hearing came naturally, as a side effect of the itch I have to kill.

Hers came as a result of someone else's itch to hurt her.

"Dee, you're dirty," Juliet says as she comes into my view. She wears a cozy two piece set. Cream colored, as if the lightness of her outfit will ward away the grime on her perfectly clean body. Her brown curls are neat and pulled back in a slick bun, and her ochre brown skin shines with body oils and lotions.

Juliet has deep brown eyes like I do. Hers, of course, have the light my mother always talked about, and mine still don't. My sister is older than me by five years. We both have round, down-turned lips, but my lips are more pouty. We're similar in appearance, but our height difference makes me look like I'm the older sister, since I'm about three inches taller than her.

"I was at the greenhouse," I say and hope that's all the explanation she'll need. It's not a lie, therefore it shouldn't feel like I'm lying to the one person I care about, but omitting the whole truth lights a twinge of guilt under my skin. Juliet's safety means more to me than the guilt I have from lying to her, though.

Nothing matters more than her safety.

"Is that blood, Diora?" she nearly shouts. The sound brings a smile to my face. Hearing emotion from her will always be a win for me, even when it's drowned in disgust. Something is better than nothing.

"Many plants have thorns, Juliet." This blood isn't mine, of course. I don't know why I listened to that woman, Mrs. Jay, when she told me to collect blood samples of my kills, but I did.

Being good is simple, while evil is more than just evil. Evil has rankings, levels to it that even monsters can recognize. Mrs. Jay carries the presence of a leader, the monster of monsters. I can't risk poking that beast. Not when I have someone to lose.

"Then you need to make sure those thorns don't prick you," Juliet says, reaching a hand out to me but stopping right before she makes contact. She's already had her shower. She's clean. She's content in her cleanliness, and I understand, for her sake, she can't mess that up.

Since that night, she has a focus on cleanliness. She believes that night made her dirty. Unlovable. Undeserving of anything.

I can empathize with my mom's depression from the lack of light in me, but seeing that light die, seeing that light die in *Juliet,* was so much worse. It would kill Mom. I know it would because it nearly killed me.

I never understood the light, the goodness in a person, until Juliet. She was everything to Mother, everything to me. When that light died, I vowed to get her light back.

"I need a shower," I say, sliding past her without making contact. Since that night, Juliet does not like to be touched. I ensure that I don't initiate contact, even by accident. She deserves that from me and more. So much more.

I don't know if it's PTSD or anxiety that's made her so attached to cleanliness, but I respect it. I accommodate her the most, and that's why she lives with me and not back home with Mom and Dad.

They weren't there. They didn't see the light slowly fade out in her eyes like I did. They noticed it was gone, but it's not the same as watching it die.

Down the hall to the bathroom, I quickly strip and run the scalding hot water. As much as my older sister is on my mind, Mrs. Jay's offer makes its way front and center. What did she mean by spice up her life? She is a killer, like me, I assume, so did she want to teach me to be a better killer, maybe? Why does she kill?

I kill for Juliet, but more so for the itch I get. Like the stretch of a petal on a flower, I feel the incessant stretch to harm. I've never acted on it till tonight, contrary to belief, and I've never felt as comfortable in my skin as I did tonight.

I can feel the wrinkle of my eye as I sigh in complete happiness. I killed four men tonight.

Four men lost their lives, and it's all my fault.

Four men died, and now Juliet can rest easier.

How good it is to be evil.

Finishing my shower, I step out of the bathroom in a pink sleep set and meet Juliet in the living room. Juliet must have been up all night again. She used to be a morning person, working at the Litchfort newspaper. She'd be pouring her coffee in a to-go cup right about now, as she would be close to walking out the door.

I sit on the opposite side of the couch as she sips on her nightly glass of wine, watching the news.

"At what point is something tainted?" Her question startles me, not that she could tell. Her eyes stay trained on the news story about a fire on the other side of town. Though, by her glassed over eyes, I can tell she isn't paying attention. In fact, she rarely pays attention. She's always waiting for something. Maybe waiting for a story to make her feel less alone.

I'll create that story for her. She'll see that, one day soon, she'll be free of that night.

Because everyone involved will be dead.

"Tainted? You're not tainted, Juliet," I say, shaking my head at any thoughts of Juliet being evil. It's impossible. She can't be. She's not. She's good, she's perfect; she's just as she should be.

"How many bad thoughts makes someone bad?"

"Thoughts are not the same as actions," I say matter-of-factly, as if I have any right to comment on being good and bad. I watch her from the corner of my eye. Her guilt must be getting to her right now.

She asks me this often. It's part of our routine. She's told me she feels like the dirt on my plant stems after I take them out of the ground. The dirt often sticks to the stems and is hard to get completely off. The dirt doesn't make the plant ugly, yet people shy away from it because they don't want to get dirty. She shies away from herself because no matter how clean she gets, she is still dirty.

In my world, Juliet is good. Down to her core, she is good, and this world has planted the seeds of her doubt in that. I have to fix that. She has to know.

"I am bad. Though, I can be good, but I can be bad, too." I hate that she says that. I hate that she believes that she is bad. She's not. Not in this world or even in this universe. Juliet Moss is the good-est person I know.

I'll be as evil as I need to be so that she can be good.

"Tea?" I ask, but more like, tell Juliet. I rise from the couch and turn the kettle on. As I wait for the water to warm, I grab my home stash of ashwagandha root and crush it by folding and rolling it with a rolling pin.

Once it's crushed into small enough pieces, I drop it in her mug and fill the rest with water. I make this tea from scratch every morning and night. It's the only way I've found to get Juliet calm enough to get through her day, her night, her life. It doesn't taste the best, but it gets her to relax enough to breathe normally.

It gets her to function more like her normal self. Not the obsessive hurt lamb. I make some for myself, too, still incredibly hyped up on tonight's kills.

Though it's ten in the morning, we both need to relax. Setting her mug on the coffee table, I take mine to my room. Setting it down on my nightstand, I pull out the flip phone Mrs. Jay gave me.

It lights up as I open it and select her contact name. It's Mother on the phone. Air can't escape my nose fast enough as I lift my fingers to type out my message.

I'm in.

Two little words that will probably change the course of my life, but I'm not dumb enough to let a potential opportunity to learn as much as I can from this monster.

I'm a child compared to her.

She's been killing and getting away with it far longer than I have. Thirty years is a long time to be "in the game", and I have a feeling I'll need all the help I can get.

I have to be the evil that Juliet needs so that she can stay good.

Mrs. Jay wasted no time. She wanted to meet in my greenhouse again. Mrs. Jay practically glows as she swishes around the room, studying my other plants. She looks but never touches, knowing better than to touch them.

My love for plants started with the beauty and silence that came from the flowers in my backyard growing up. Those "flowers" later became known as weeds that my mom hated and tried to kill, but that didn't change their beauty to me.

Mom could hate them, glare at them, spit at them, mow them over, and it wouldn't change their beauty. Yellow dandelions were my first comfort as a kid. Juliet had a light brown teddy bear with big round eyes and pink blush on its cheeks, and I had a bright yellow dandelion that grew brown from being separated from the ground.

My greenhouse contains rows of plants with skinny walkways between them. I don't grow much since the abandoned greenhouse isn't in the best shape. But it's mine, for the most part, so I'm content.

It's off putting for someone else to be in my space. Mrs. Jay has yet to say anything beyond a hello and is busy studying my safe space. I should have the advantage here, but it doesn't seem like I do. I know this place like the back of my hand, with my eyes closed, yet she moves with such grace and power I don't think I'd win a fight against her. Maybe I never will.

She stops over my newest project. The plant that has grown but has months before it'll bloom. This tree doesn't quite have a stump, but the stalks are holding up as it grows.

"It'll grow into an Angel Trumpet tree, hopefully," I say, pointing to the sign I have in front of the potted plant. I watch as her eyes gaze at the plant and then swiftly move on to the next one that piqued her interest.

I didn't know killers could appear so... so normal. It's so obvious on me. My parents clocked it the moment I was born. It's as if it's written across my forehead, but with her, it's an aura you can't pin down one hundred percent. The way her eyes cut you or the grasp of her hand on yours. You couldn't pin a murder on her. Her aura comes off as a question, not a statement.

She obviously could teach me to be a killer. That isn't a doubt I have. With Mrs. Jay's training, I could make these kills so much more effective to my cause.

Mrs. Jay is a monster. She can try to hide under the Chanel suits and pearls, but she's like me. I wonder if she gets the itch like I do. I wonder how long it took her to fall to the itch.

That's what made me text Mrs. Jay last night. I can only accomplish so much, but six months with a monster like Mrs. Jay, I could be unstoppable.

I also don't doubt she'd rat me out for killing those officers last night. She wouldn't have approached me with insurance.

"What am I here for?" I ask. She slows to a stop in front of me. As tall as me, she meets my eye directly.

"You have great potential, Diora. I can see it, and I hope you can see it, too, with me. I need a feminine touch, and I think you'd be the perfect fit."

"Perfect for what?" Scrunching my eyebrows, I watch as she sits at my little round table where I had the officers tied up last night. She crosses her ankles and rests her hands in her lap as she smiles up at me.

She nods her head toward my kettle and raises an eyebrow. "Every meeting needs tea, don't you think?"

I start it and turn, so my back isn't to her. She waits silently as I prepare our drinks. Grabbing two teacups, I set them on my workbench and turn back to look at her. What kind of tea would she like?

I only have three non-lethal teas. Black, green, and rosemary. What will happen if I get this wrong? Will she kill me? Is this what fear is? It crawls up the backs of my arms and creates a home at the base of my neck.

Hmm, I think I'll like hanging around Mrs. Jay. I pull the black tea. And drop the bags in the mugs before turning to face her.

"If I was a fearful woman, I'd be scared to drink anything from you, sweetheart." She laughs as she accepts the drink.

"So, why me?" I ask again, settling across from her at the clean round table.

"I can't tell you that yet, darling. I can't trust you," she says with a wink, as if I am supposed to know what that means.

I leave my silence to answer her. I'm confused why she even bothered with blackmailing me into joining her, yet she won't tell me what exactly I'm joining her for. She releases a sigh, looking as calm as ever even after she saw me kill four officers last night, and yet, she seems like the more dangerous one.

"Well, let's get started. First, I need to see your physical abilities, as well as your mental abilities. We'll work together, and we'll see if you pass the initiation, and once you do, the real fun will begin.

"What will we start with?" I ask, trying not to show any hint of excitement or nerves. I can't give her any more power than she already has.

I'll never figure out what she wants unless I play her game. Why I even give her the chance to play, I don't know, but I can't help but want to know what she sees in me.

"Tell me about every single plant in here and how you could use it to kill someone, even the non-lethal ones."

Chapter 3

Elliot

Three Months Later

Hearing the light chirps of a few bluejays, the corners of my lips turn upward as I slip onto the balcony on the second story of my target's house.

Getting up here was a bitch and a half, but the thrill of the kill outweighs the burn in my shoulders from hoisting my 220 pound body up here. Having muscles has never felt so fucking heavy.

My target left the doors cracked open, enough for the nice breeze of a private estate to come in. Maybe he thought he was so high up he'd be safe, or maybe he didn't think at all. It's people's greatest weakness: not thinking things through. Not planning enough. It works to my advantage.

The boy's father truly made this too easy for us. It truly makes me wonder why he bothered hiring one of us instead of doing the kill himself.

Maybe he didn't want to kill his son himself? I'll get the job done regardless, but I can't lie and say it doesn't pique my own interest.

Mother put me on this assignment, and I know exactly why. She thinks since I killed my own foster father, familial ties don't bother me. It's ironic, really. Cause she couldn't be further from the truth.

Familial ties are the only reason I haven't slit her damn throat.

It doesn't matter if she's wrong or not. It doesn't matter what I feel or shouldn't feel. Whatever Mother says, I do. She says to kill the son of a man with more money than most tech giants could ever dream of, I do it. If she wants me to do it at lunch, in broad daylight, that's what I do.

It's been like this since she found me. It's been twelve years since Mother took me in as one of her Strays. Not once have I disobeyed her order or stepped out of line, despite the absolute hell she's put me through.

In twelve years, I've made twenty-two kills, and with being part of her corporation of organized hired killers, I'm sure my stats will reach the hundreds before I age out of the game.

Mother took me in when I was on the run after my first kill. Age is no feat for Mother; she's still going strong in the game of killing with forty-nine kills. I've got almost half her kills in nearly half the time, but I doubt she's training any of us to be stronger than her.

I listen for footsteps as the bird chirps become quieter, the flap of their wings flying away. There must be someone coming near. He's coming. My target is the only other person in this house from the times of twelve to two today. The staff was treated to an impromptu lunch surprise by Mr. Marks, my target's dad, and of course, the brat didn't want to go. Fucking dumbass. Lunch could've given him one more day to live.

I listen to his loud ramblings about a poker game he must have played recently, and my favorite wire burns in my back pocket. He's here.

"What the hell are you doing?" I hear the obnoxious brat yell as he pops into his room to do gods know what. He looks like a rich man's son. Brown short hair, fake tanned skin, slim, but not strong whatsoever. White shirt, swim shorts. This is too easy. No sense of awareness, survival, nothing.

I smile, leaning against the open balcony door.

"Your daddy sent me," I say. The simple reveal of relation allows me to move more freely. Like the staff of guards and staff suddenly disappearing hasn't raised the boy's survival alarms already.

"Oh, well, guards stand discreetly, not so—so—I don't know, just don't leave your fucking post again," he says, waving his hand, trying to dismiss me.

A moment, a moment is all I have to decide. A kill isn't as thoughtless as people may think. Not for me. Not for serial killers. People who kill not just for the thrill, or protection, or liabilities, but because of the urge. The need, the craving of blood spilled or lifeless bodies.

Everyone justifies their kills in different ways. I paint myself to be some sort of vigilante. I kill people I deem worse than me. As bad as me. But this kid, he's not as bad as me.

He sells dope. I kill people.

I kill people, not just for myself, but because I'm told to. I follow her commands like a fucking dog.

I shouldn't kill Kal Marks.

"I'm not a guard, Kal," I say, stalking up to him. He gives me an incredulous look before he spits at me. I smile as I wipe the spit off my face. He fed drugs to little kids under twelve. Kids. I have to remember. He's as bad as me.

We don't deserve to live.

Too bad no one is strong enough to kill me.

"I'm here to kill you, Kal," I say. His eyes widen before he breaks out in a laugh.

"No, you're not." He laughs again. The damn twerp walks past me. Swiping away on his tablet.

I sigh as I watch as walks past me. I see that his brown hair ends at the base of his head, leaving his neck wide and clear for me. Like a present. I grab the wire from my pocket. A two strand wire, meant to cut through bone, attached to two wooden blocks used as handles.

"Indeed I am," I say and wrap my wire tight against his neck as I drag him to the dresser with the huge mirror attached. His body is forced forward as we move to the dresser, the wire cutting into his skin as confusion fills his facial features, the pain from the wire saw wrapped around his neck.

Dying is one thing, but seeing yourself being killed. Wow, that's another level of terror, which I can feel as he pisses himself. Slashing his throat as he fights my hold, making his situation worse and mine easier.

"Daddy's little failure needed to be tucked away before he got caught selling dope to children. When Daddy's little failure couldn't stop, no matter how much Daddy threw at him, Daddy gave up hope his little failure could be redeemed. So, he called me."

"Fucking let me go," he roars. His hands come up to the wire to try to relieve the pressure from the cut of his skin, only for it to sear his hands, and he drops them. Being taller than him isn't to my advantage. Forcing him to bend back would've sweetened the deal, but seeing his neck drenched in blood satisfies a deep hunger only this fool could fix.

"Do you know how much your life is worth, Kal?" I ask as he spits, saliva and blood mixing in a glob that lands on the dresser. "One-hundred million, Kal. Daddy paid me one-hundred mill to kill you and clean up your mess." That one-hundred mill also goes toward killing Kal's associates, and a personal part of my cut will be sending those kids to a recovery program, but still. The rest goes right back into the corp. This is the most expensive job we've had; probably another reason Mother put me on this job.

Kal's blood and sweat soak my black t-shirt. His feet scramble under himself. He practically does all the work. I wanna say this is my last time taking a rich, spoiled boy assignment, but I know that won't be the case. The moment the complaint is uttered from my mouth, spoiled rich boys are all I will be assigned to for months.

I squeeze the wire tight, halting his terrified screams to silence. A perfect silence that cures something in my brain. All I hear is the rip of his skin, feel the sag of his head as he dies in my wire, between my hands.

As I loosen the wire, his body hits the ground, splashing in the pools of blood beneath us.

Fuck. That was nice.

His life slipping from my hands is one of the best feelings in the world. That sense of power can't be replicated in any other way.

I pull out my phone, dialing the number for Haven Corporation. "Get the cleaning crew here."

I step over Kal Marks' body. His head is barely attached to his body, blood spreading everywhere on the cream carpet. Slipping off my shoes, as not to track blood, I walk in sock covered feet back to my car. I put the camera on a loop about fifteen minutes before I got here, allowing me to park right in the front.

Glancing at the clock on my dashboard, I watch as noon hits. This is Mother's shopping hour.

Which means I have an hour free to meet with Mortes Ostium.

The spring heat means that Michigan birds are back, making this my favorite time of the year. My dress pants crease as I lean back in the white frilly metal chair, and my book on wild birds slides in my lap while birds sing and fly around in the trees nearby.

The metal tables are tarnished with rust, since Michigan experiences all four seasons, but I don't mind. I'd take the random bits of orange rust on my clothes than sit inside where everyone else is.

Mallory's Coffee Shop is tucked away on a corner street, which makes it the perfect spot for people who want a space away from the bustle of downtown. Being a college town makes it the perfect mix of busy, but not too busy. Enough people to get lost in, but not too many to get drowned.

This shop is too "low profile" for Mother to enjoy, which is why I chose to be here. I also set this as the place to meet with Mortes Ostium today. I got the call this morning that Mortes Ostium, also known as the Society, wanted to meet with me. For what, I'm not entirely sure, but what I know is, when they call, you answer.

It could be for something simple they wanted to discuss with me. I'm this year's chosen host for the Society's annual ball, so all in all, it could be to discuss the role.

Hosting is out of my realm, and I have no idea why they asked me instead of someone more devoted to the Society—someone like Mother—but I don't question the Society.

Mother is pissed about the Society choosing me to host instead of her, and I bathe in that anger every fucking day.

Though, we've connected over the ball details electronically, so I'm not confident that's why they called an in-person meeting with me.

Looking down at my book, I flip through the pages as I wait. The moments I get while drinking my coffee is the one time I get to truly relax.

The killer in me disappears while I'm here.

Here, I can be the bird guy. The lonely guy. The guy who's drinking his coffee and enjoying the weather.

I can be normal.

I flip to the current bird I'm reading about. My current obsession is the crane. A crane is a white bird, with a long neck and long legs. Strong and beautiful. They represent good fortune and peace. Something I've never had. Not when I was in the foster system and damn sure not since I met Mother.

I need some good fortune. I need some fucking peace. Maybe that's why this creature piqued my interest. A bird not so known, a bird impossible to hide. A bird I wish I was more like.

"Elliot Jay," a man says as he sits at the same table as I. His features are unrecognizable, but the ring on his left hand is distinct—a simple silver band with a skull on it. Only members of the Society have them. It's how we track and recognize ourselves in the wild. I wear mine on my right hand. "I'm glad we could meet."

"Of course," I say, nodding in respect. The man doesn't waste time with a name or identity, just jumps straight to the point.

"We want you to kill Maria Jay." What?

I don't let my face show what I'm thinking. I enter a staring contest with the man across from me, a man who I do not know, but a man I have to trust. All I have to go off of is a ring on his finger and I'm supposed to listen to every word he gives me. Raising an eyebrow, I watch the man's face with unmovable force.

"You want me to kill Maria Jay," I repeat to make sure I heard the man correctly. He wants me to kill Mother. Mother, as in Mrs. Jay. Mother, as in the one person I've refrained from killing for the past three years?

"Yes." I stare at the man, who nods one time and promptly leaves my table. I peer around to find not a soul around us, and my heart races as his words filter into my mind.

He didn't even let me ask why they want me to kill her. Though I have an idea, and maybe that's why they asked me to kill her instead of one of their guards. Why me?

I sit with my book in my lap as I blankly stare at the spot where the man once sat.

I can't kill Mother. Surely they know that. Surely they know that, if I could kill her, I would've already?

But how would they know that? Fuck. I run a hand through my hair as I try to appear normal, but too many possibilities run through my head.

I can't kill Mother.

But I also can't tell the Society... no.

Hmm. Well. I'm fucked.

Chapter 4

Diora

That single text I sent three months ago has brought an onslaught of messages from Mrs. Jay. She has no boundaries, texting at any moment, and she texts like she is writing letters. I stare down at the one she sent me at five in the morning.

> *Dear Diora,*

> *meet me for afternoon tea and shopping. I'll pick you up half past eleven*

I push the cart behind Mrs. Jay as we walk around the home decor store. She's still putting all sorts of things in the cart, and I have no idea what for.

First, it was a light green dining set, then it was a pink one... then a purple. Now she's grabbing placemats and centerpieces.

"I think the greens complement the purples excellently," she murmurs to herself as she floats down another aisle. I try to match her pace, but these are the skinniest rows possible, and this cart is full as hell.

"Diora, darling, part of your training is to keep up with me." Her words make my skin roll with annoyance as I attempt to follow.

The way she speaks messes with my senses a bit. It's so posh and formal, it sounds unnatural. It raises my hackles. Even after three months of training under her, I'm no further into figuring out why she wanted me to be part of her corporation, Haven Corp, or how I am supposed to spice up her life.

On the surface, Haven Corp is a world's market trading company, and underneath, it is an organization of trained hitmen, ready to kill for the highest price tag.

Besides that, I haven't heard a peep about Haven the whole time we've spent together. I've had to quit my previous job as a grocery store florist to accommodate all the training Mrs. Jay and I have been doing. She's replaced my salary, plus some, so I can keep paying my and Juliet's living expenses.

Juliet can't work like I can. She'll do well for a few weeks, but crashes eventually into the world of mental pain she's constantly in, and during that time, she'll lose her job. Then it's up to me and our parents to keep us afloat.

"Darling, if you're not serious about this training, then we'll have to part ways," she says. Her voice is light, and any bystander wouldn't hear the threat in them, but I do.

She thinks I'm not serious about being a serial killer because I can't maneuver an overfilled cart in a skinny home decor store aisle?

"Does Paula Montry mean nothing to you, Mrs. Jay?" I ask. My fifth kill ever, last month, was with Mrs. Jay, and I killed someone of her choosing. I killed a woman named Paula Montry, and she was one hard woman to kill.

"That's old news," she says, waving the comment away. It was only a month ago. I scoff as I catch up to her with her obnoxious cart.

My poisons weren't enough for that one. I hadn't had time to drug her up properly and had to suffocate her by the end of the transgression. One thing I've learned is, Mrs. Jay always rushes things, and that pisses me off.

I woke one morning and Mrs. Jay said, "We're killing Paula Montry. Let's get moving," and that was that. She had dropped me off at an abandoned bar with only what I had on me, which was a tiny bit of foxglove in my pocket.

So, to say I haven't figured out Mrs. Jay is an understatement.

"And that is only one person, dear. You'll need to do a lot more than that to not only solidify your place with me at Haven, but also with the Society," she explains, waving her hands about.

I had six months to train and prepare for my first four kills, and honestly, I think they were successful because of pure luck.

Mrs. Jay isn't the only person who knows about those kills. There is that name she mentioned—Mortes Ostium. Someone there was watching, too, unbeknownst to me and Mrs. Jay.

She didn't know until a man, who I later found to be the society's courier, dropped off a ring. It's a simple gold ring with a skull on it. I've attached it to the pearl necklace Juliet gave me for my sixteenth birthday.

The cool metal chills my skin with every move of my neck. Twisting the heart pendant next to the ring, I reflect on the first kill I made for Mrs. Jay.

Checking out, I let Mrs. Jay ramble on for the rest of our shopping trip. Acting as her personal assistant instead of a killer in training allows me time to think.

"Diora, darling, can you get the trunk for me?" Mrs. Jay says in her honey slick voice. Of course, I stop pushing the cart and run around it to open the trunk. Why she couldn't do it, I'm not sure. This feels like a test of my compliance, if anything, but she has my hands tied with evidence I killed four officers, so what else am I going to do?

I hear her hum, as I load her car with stuff for our next... project?

She told me we are hosting a tea party, but I'm not sure what for or if this is a regular tea party or a... massacre.

"Hurry, darling. I remembered I have a meeting in about fifteen minutes," she says as she continues not to lift a single finger to help load the car with only about one hundred little fragile plates and teacups and platters into her trunk. I huff, and my hair that's fallen in my face blows off my sweaty skin, only to stick back onto my cheek.

My bright yellow sundress does nothing to help keep me cool from Michigan's summer heat. With it being freezing yesterday, I thought I dressed appropriately for today's outing, but Michigan's weather is about as wishy-washy as my hair wash days, and while I love Litchfort, consistent weather would be nice.

I hardly finish loading Mrs. Jay's car before I hear her turn the engine on and see the brake lights pop on. Is she leaving me? She is supposed to take me home. Slouching my shoulders, I quickly back away from the back end of the car and shut her trunk door. I step out of the way and grab the cart, too. Litchfort is a small town, but that's still a forty-five-minute walk back to my house after a long morning of following Mrs. Jay around.

"Diora, get in the car," she snaps.

"But the cart—"

"Someone else will get it. Now, let's go." I don't question her, but the thought that Juliet would be pissed that I left the cart in a parking spot grates my senses.

Though, the cool air conditioning blasting out of the vents distracts me enough to be grateful Mrs. Jay didn't leave me. I'm surprised she hasn't told me to run beside the car as she drives to build up my stamina.

"I have a client who has paid for Haven to kill off his competitors, namely their cousin's family, and I was thinking, why not hit all our targets at once at a tea party?! They'll never see it coming. It'll be so fun Diora, dear. What do you think?" Whenever Mrs. Jay asks me what I think, she's not really trying to hear my opinion. She wants a yes man.

I glare at the world outside the car window as she goes on talking about the tea party. She goes on and on about how she wants to rent a ballroom, needing to hold one hundred people, and that fact makes me scrunch my eyebrow. I don't get how the clean up works on a hit like that, as much fun as it sounds. But it's not like I have the power to question her.

She's now got five murders to hold over me.

"Speak up, I can't hear you," she says, her tone turning me away from the window as the sunshine disappears behind rain clouds.

"Yes, Mrs. Jay," I say, making sure not to mumble, since that also irritates her. It's like she's my—

"Mother," she says, her annoyance snapping to a smile, as if that will convince me to call her the name she tries so hard to get me to use for her. I don't get it.

She's not my mom. I have one. One who tried to kill me when I was six, but still, I have one. Not that I would tell her that, 'cause she would probably go kill her to take her place.

The last person I'd want to be my mother figure is Mrs. Jay. She's nosy, controlling, and most of all, she's blackmailing me. At least my real mom is truthful with how she feels about me.

"Are you taking me home?" I ask, trying to gauge what is happening next.

"I think it's time you meet the Strays," she says as she turns the wheel with her white gloved hand.

I turn my head to look out the window. She says things grandiosely, and it grates my skin. I just wanna go home. "Strays?" I ask, trying not to let my annoyance come through. I don't want to meet anyone, let alone trained killers.

"Haven Corp is made of my Strays—the killers I've given a home and a job to. I want you to get to know the other Strays, get comfortable with them and them with you. You will be part of my special team. They go by Top Dogs," she explains as she pulls up to a considerably blank, large building.

"I don't think it's a good idea—" I try to fight meeting these "Strays", but by the smile that drops from Mrs. Jay's face, I don't know if I really have a way out of this.

"I don't want you to *think*; I want you to *do*. I am the thinker, you are the doer. Don't forget that," she explains, like it's a simple math formula that doesn't make my brain break into a frenzy. As much as I would like to wait to meet these highly trained killers, it doesn't seem I have room to argue.

The best I can do is make the most of this meeting and figure out what Mrs. Jay really wants me for, I guess. That thought doesn't settle the butterflies in my stomach like I hoped it would.

A small hotel-type building comes into view as we drive. It's pretty tall for a building in a small town such as Litchfort. It has a round driveway, where we pull in and a valet takes Mrs. Jay's car keys.

I quickly follow suit, getting out of the car, seeing she's already walking up the red carpeted path to the main door, where a man is pulling the door open for her. My yellow dress flows behind me as I catch up to her. I try smoothing my hair down and re-doing my updo.

If I knew I would be meeting, well, my co-workers, I would've put more effort into my appearance this morning.

Not that I know what to wear when meeting a bunch of trained killers. I probably reek of newbie energy, but I can't do anything about it. Oh well.

I follow her to the elevator, where another man stands and nods politely to Mrs. Jay and proceeds to press a button to the top floor.

Am I really walking into a room of trained serial killers? Looking over to the beaming smile Mrs. Jay has, yes, it seems I am. But Mrs. Jay isn't a dumb woman; she wouldn't introduce me if I wasn't ready... Right? Trust is such a fickle thing, isn't it?

I have a tiny baggy of foxglove petals in my pocket, but that's all I have in terms of weapons. What kinds of weapons will they have?

I've made five kills so far, so going up against these "Strays", let alone a group she calls "Top Dogs", is like a yorkie attacking a pit bull. Who knows how many kills each of these people will have? Probably more than five.

Hopefully, they'll think it's funny and not an annoying threat, 'cause that's all I have working for me.

She stops before she gets to the door that must be containing all these Strays, and I take this moment to breathe and settle my dress.

"They eat fear, darling. Don't be nervous," she demands as she opens the door—the first door she's opened herself since we got here—and strides into the room. I follow quickly behind her so as not to show fear, but I think regardless of how I walked into the room, the shocked faces of the people here would have been the same.

"Everyone, this is Diora. She's a new Stray who will be working with you on our next assignment," Mrs. Jay announces.

The room has large windows that span three of the walls and dark grey carpeting. One long table covers the middle of the room, where everyone besides me and Mrs. Jay is sitting.

Chills cover my arms as we walk into the room, and I can hear the air coming through the vents in this brightly lit room.

I hear whispers, but for the most part, everyone keeps their composure. Straight backs and squared shoulders and heads held high as Mrs. Jay walks to the head of the room. My eyes instantly track to the head of the table where a man is sitting. His eyes glitter with trouble, yet he isn't the one my eyes are drawn to.

"I'm Enyo, and this is my brother Elliot," the one at the head of the table says.

Elliot is to the man on his left side. He remains relaxed in his seat, dressed in a plain white t-shirt with a crew neck over with Litchfort embroidered on it and golden colored hair and skin. His brown eyes melt with sunlight shining in them. It makes him all the more beautiful. He is truly a handsome boy.

Despite knowing everyone here is a killer of some sort, almost everyone here looks... normal. We're dressed in regular clothes and have features we'd see people have out in the town.

I'd probably seen these people at a grocery store, or the movies, and didn't even know they were serial killers.

I guess the same could be said about me.

I can't figure out if I find that comforting or worrisome.

Dragging my eyes away from the two men, I survey the rest of the room and count seven men in total. Including me and Mrs. Jay, that makes nine people, and depending on what kind of operation she has in mind, I can't tell if there are enough people or not.

Even knowing nothing about Mrs. Jay's plans, nine people isn't a lot for a massacre of the size she was rambling about. Even if the seven men here are muscled enough to take on a small army each.

"There's only nine of us?" I mutter.

"These are the highest ranking Strays in Haven. Each Stray works hard to become a Top Dog, but as you see, few make it," Mrs. Jay explains. She smiles like a proud parent, and I nod.

"So, how many Strays work here?" I slowly ask, wondering why Mrs. Jay hasn't snapped at me for talking out of turn.

"Including you, two-hundred-three," a man rattles off the top of his head. He's got scars of cuts across his face and body, a snare on his lip, and one on his eyebrow. I nod once in his direction before turning my attention back to the head of the table.

Two-hundred and three other people like me. That's... That's a lot of bad people in Litchfort.

Chapter 5

Elliot

The woman in the room doesn't belong here. She appears to be in her early twenties, with straight posture and dead eyes. The whites of her eyes are dull. Her full lips are down-turned at the corners, creating a permanent frown. A natural pout.

She shouldn't be here, but not because she isn't a killer. That I can tell from her eyes alone, but because she's a woman.

Mother doesn't recruit female Strays. She says she finds women to be too emotional, but I knew the truth. Mother doesn't like competition. Another female presence, another woman to grow feelings for, would throw her real mission off. It fucks with her desire to be loved, admired—the object of our obsession.

Fighting for boys' attention is all part of her game.

Female Strays are never real Strays. They are her possessions to sell in the trafficking ring.

Still, here she is with a young woman. A woman with the eyes of a soulless killer. Why now?

This woman can't be a Stray.

My gaze moves from Mother to the woman as they converse about how many Strays there are at the corporation.

Mother loves her Strays. In this industry, Strays are the best victims to turn into cold-blooded killers. I had started out as one of her Strays. Now, I've moved up to a status only one other person has reached: Son.

Haven corporation has three ranks: Strays, Top Dogs, and Sons.

Mother loved me so much as a Stray, she kept me close. Though the title is Son, my place in her eyes is more like a dog. That may bother others, to be seen as a dog for a powerful woman, but it hasn't bothered me.

Not until now. Not until I realized I deserve better; that the Strays here deserve better. Not until I realized there is no way out. Even though it bothers me, I can't leave her. Not without one of us dying.

I've known Mother for a long time. My parents died, or didn't want me—fuck knows—and I was in the foster system until I was fifteen and made my first kill. My first kill was an accident, but it doesn't change it being my first.

An accidental loss of control changed everything. The foster father was a drunk, sexually touching the girls in our foster group, and I couldn't stand around for that shit. I may have low morals, but child molestation is one thing I can't fucking stand. It's one of the few things that makes my skin crawl to the point of setting a lighter to it to get the itching to stop.

As much as I had tried to protect us, it wasn't enough. Nothing was ever enough. One day, I snapped and killed both the foster father and the mother. James and Lea Hartford were found dead by strangulation in their bedroom. Lea wasn't fucking innocent like she pretended to be. She let it happen, and that offense was as great as the act itself to me.

So, they both died that night. With the help of handcuffs, pillows, and a young boy's anger.

Maybe it wasn't so accidental. Still doesn't change anything.

Since I killed them so obviously, I was on the run at fifteen years old. None of the other kids said anything—not that there was anything for them to tell. They didn't see or hear a thing, apparently. Just woke up to our tormentors dead. The authorities went searching for me, of course, but by that point, Oliver Longstead was dead and Elliot Jay was born. Mother had found me, stalked me, and trapped me.

She somehow knew I had killed my foster parents. She said she wouldn't go to the authorities, that all I had to do was to come home with her and my life would be different from then on.

Little did I know, I escaped one monster only to be ensnared by a bigger one.

My eyes drag away from hers and move across the boardroom meeting. The highest ranks had been called in to discuss the latest hit on the Mayor of who actually gives a fuck, and even though I only took part behind a computer screen, watching the team execute the plan through video footage, I have to be here.

I think we've all figured out the real reason we were called here: her.

"Elliot. Elliot," Mother calls, snapping her fingers in my face as she strolls past. I can hear her and she knows it, yet she makes such a show. She makes everyone take a seat so she can pace behind us, like a warlord, or a drill sergeant. The action doesn't make me uncomfortable anymore, but it sure as shit does some of the other guys. I loll my head to the side, swiveling my chair so I am facing the table.

My eyes jerk back to the woman who stands a few feet away from Mother, her eyes racing around the room. She has tawny brown skin, dark brown eyes, and her long dark hair pulled up off her shoulders. Those damn pouty lips call to me. She has on a long yellow dress, and she's wearing a pearl necklace on her neck and the Mortes Ostium ring next to the heart pendant on her necklace.

She's a member of Mortes Ostium?

Well, that means Mother can't kill her, then. But that still doesn't explain why she's here.

She looks like a regular civilian. I wouldn't guess this woman had killed four officers and a rando on Mother's shit list, but she has, according to Mother's rambling about—my eyes dart to the digital clock on the wall—fifteen minutes ago.

I guess others may say the same about Brother and me, but it's… unusual when it's a woman. Her body doesn't carry heavy muscles like the mens' in this corp do. Her muscles are lean, and

I can see them, but it doesn't make her masculine. They make her more feminine, if anything, and it doesn't quite make sense.

I glare at her as her eyes meet mine for the third time. Of course, her eyes don't dart away like a normal girl's would have. She continues to stare at me, this time openly and unwavering. Who does she think she is? Does she even know who she's standing behind?

"Nevermind the boring stuff. I've gathered you here for our next assignment. This one is going to need all of our best hands on deck," Mother explains as she makes her way past her chair to the right of Enyo and to the whiteboard behind the table.

"We are putting together a tea party," she says excitedly, clasping her hands together.

"Do you really need us to have a tea party, Mrs. Jay?" Tom, one of our newest teammates, asks. His brows furrow as some of the others snicker. They should know better than that, but maybe the new Stray has made them relax. Fatal mistake. That's why they will forever be Top Dogs and never Sons.

I remain silent, watching for any signs from Mother and the new girl. Her eyes haven't left me, and yet I'm not completely annoyed by it. She better hope Mother doesn't catch her. Mother doesn't do well when others are interested in her Sons. Ask my first and last girlfriend, Clair Letover. She's dead because of it.

Diora. I watch her chest rise with an inhale and her smooth skin entices me to touch her. She already gets on my nerves.

Mother's eyes narrow before she picks up a pen, clicks it open, and throws it hard enough to land in Tom's arm. From across the room.

"Not that I ever need to explain myself, but I need as many hands as possible on deck for cleaning up. These deaths won't be bloody, thanks to Diora's extensive knowledge in herbs and teas, but we will absolutely not be doing the clean up of ten bodies by our two selves. Will we, Diora?" Mother says as Tom does his damndest to hold back his flinch and not reach to the pen sticking out of his forearm, which was lax on the table moments before.

I sigh, tearing my eyes from Tom and catching Brother's scoff as he leans back in his chair shaking his head.

"Details Mother, time, place..." Enyo asks.

"Yes, well, we will plan those as we get well acquainted with one another," Mother says, eyeing Diora who raises her eyebrows as she tears her eyes away from mine.

"Is the girl necessary?" I ask, finally giving Mother the recognition she craves so much.

This comment earns me a glare and if I was close enough a smack up-side my head but I am across the table and way out her reach. She's also out of pens.

"Yes, if you were listening Elliot, she will make our jobs much easier,"

"And less fun it seems," I quip.

"This isn't about fun, it's about money." Mother rolls her eyes. "Our first meeting will be tomorrow morning, seven am sharp. If you're late you better hope you're dead."

With that, she floats out the room without her new Stray, and the rest of us remain seated. She wants us to get to know the new Stray, and we can't leave until we do.

"Dear, please have a seat across from Elliot," Enyo orders in his silky smooth voice as he stands to take control of the meeting. He always followed Mother's orders to a T, and I wonder if that is what made him the first Son and future owner of her company.

"Have you ever killed anyone, sweetheart?" Hank, one of the other Strays, says, a laugh hanging off his words. It pisses me off how dismissive he is of the girl, but I can't pretend I hadn't been wondering the same thing. The one thing I've learned over the years is to never doubt Mother, but she brings in the most innocent looking girl, who barely reaches my chin and is maybe 130 pounds soaking wet, and she's supposedly as dangerous as a room full of highly trained and desperate men?

"Five," she mutters as she smoothes her dress down as she takes a seat. She doesn't blush, she doesn't smile, she just stares. Directly at me.

Diora doesn't flush under the gaze of seven men, known hitmen on top of that.

I narrow my eyes as I meet her gaze once again, and she puts me in a trance. Somehow, it's just me and her.

"Who?" I ask, even though I already know the answer.

"Josh Panko, Kyle Montery, Lewis Karplie, Orlando Jones, and Paula Montry."

"That sounds like four men and one woman. How did you take down four men?" Tom groans as he speaks the words, pulling the pen out of his hand and laying it in front of Hank, who is a trained medic. He's already grabbed the safety kit we keep stored in every room Mother could be in. He isn't the first to be stabbed by her in a meeting, and he won't be the last.

"The men were the easiest—maybe a stroke of luck or maybe a stroke of passion. The woman was the hardest thus far," she says, as if she's explaining a historical passage from a textbook at the collegiate level.

"Doesn't answer how, sweetheart," I voice, trying to understand the girl. She hardly moves, barely blinks, like a statue, but it's not fear making her still. The plywood table between us seems miles long, yet I am still too close to her.

"How can I trust you?" she asks.

"You're here, aren't you?" I say.

"Not by choice."

"Yet, you're still here, aren't you?" She doesn't answer, and instead scans the room, removing her eyes from me, which doesn't fill me with the relief I expected to feel. Instead, my eye twitches. My eye fucking twitches.

She raises her eyebrows as she takes in each of the men at this table, and she makes the slightest nod of her head as she finally meets my eyes again. "I guess I am."

"Diora, let me see the phone Mother gave you," Enyo voice breaks my concentration on the girl as he reaches out a hand toward Diora.

She slides the phone into his hands, and I hear the ding from everyone's phone moments later when he adds her to the group chat he insisted we all join.

"There. Now when anything happens, we can reach you, and vice versa. I've got better things to do than interrogate a little girl," Enyo says, leaving the room, and the rest of the group follows suit. I remain seated, as does Diora, who continues to watch me, so much so, my sixth sense of her gaze fades away.

"Why did Mother really involve you?" I wasn't letting her go. I couldn't. Not when I trust every Top Dog here with my life. Not when the newbie here is brought to a Top Dog meeting on her first day here. I'm not as fucking mindless as the rest of the Strays.

I can feel the pressure of the other guys' stares on the side of my head. But that doesn't deter me. This could save their fucking lives. It could save hers.

"That's something I would like to know," she says, swiping a stray hair off her shoulder. She matches my movements, down to the rate of my breathing, and as I stand, she gracefully moves, too, as if it is the most natural thing for her to do. To copy. To imitate. Why?

I take a single step back from my chair, and so does she. I watch as she uses her left hand, instead of the dominant right hand she used to hand Enyo the phone, to push in her chair as I do. Moving around the room, purposely switching my own natural movements to catch her mess up, she keeps pace.

We end up at opposite ends of the table again, and I chuckle. Surprise colors my insides, but doesn't dare show outside. This little piece of shit. Testing me on her first day.

"If you wanna fucking dance, then I've got better things to do," I hear Jones mumble. I wait until the others have followed Enyo out the door, leaving me and Little Crane alone.

A crane's beauty is soothing. It makes you forget about the predators that they are. That's the woman Mother has brought here. Cranes carry an elegance, an aurora of calm and danger all mixed into one, and Diora exudes that unconsciously, as if she can't help it.

"Stop," I command. I freeze, and so does she. The room now feels impossibly small and hot. With each step I take, she gets farther away.

"What?" she asks, innocently. So innocently, someone could forget she killed five human beings in less than six months by herself.

I'm on her in the next second. Crossing the room and grabbing her wrist. She may be fast, but I've been playing this game my whole damn life. Pulling her in close and abruptly invading her space, she gasps. The first fucking sign of humanity in her.

Her body meets mine, one hand still on her wrist as another wraps around her waist. I don't know why I'm doing this, or trusting her being so close to me. I almost want to save her.

The Top Dogs don't know her fate. Not like I do. Not like the Society does. I wonder if they care. If they're pissed and led her straight to me. I wonder if they planted Mother to find her.

Everyone's yet to realize we haven't had a new Stray stay for more than six months. But I do. I do, and I found out what has been happening to the Strays who were going to be recruited.

Mother sells them, and instead of selling Diora, she brought her here. Why?

"Keep your eyes on me. There are two cameras with audio in this room," I say, with my nose in the crook of her neck. She smells of raspberries and jasmine, and I don't register the sharp intake through my nose as I sniff the girl.

Soft skin welcomes the heat of my calloused hands. "Mother finds up to three Strays a month, but she has never brought one to join her highest ranked team in under six months. Why do you think that is? Better yet, as of late, I've yet to see a new Stray after three months of training. Where do you think they go?" I say this to knock her cocky confidence, but I also wonder what she knows.

People throw away things they render useless, but not Mother. She finds different uses, different jobs for Strays who can't kill, yet, as of a year ago, these Strays have been disappearing.

A few months ago, I discovered Mother's best kept secret, and it's a lot worse than running an organization of hitmen.

And now, after years of having a male only organization, she brings in Diora Moss.

Why? Does the profit of little boys not fill her greedy bank account enough? Do the deaths of her buyers piss her off?

Does she think I'll stop if she switches her demographic?

"So, I ask again, why does she have an interest in you?" Her breath hitches, and I feel the loss on my cheek. I lean back slightly and watch her eyes darken. Her lips part with no hint of a word coming out. She only looks at me in question, as if I have the answer.

"I'd tell you to run," I say as my fingers brush the soft skin of her wrist for probably the last time, "but it's already too late."

She's not only stuck in Mother's trap, she's also stuck in mine.

I let her go, and she stumbles back, her eyebrows scrunching. I watch her face for one moment, one single moment, before I turn toward the door.

"Wait," she calls, and I stop. I turn and meet her eyes, then tilt my head toward one of the cameras and raise my own brows.

She gulps, the first sign of her nerves, before she licks her thick strawberry red lips and takes a deep breath. "Why?"

Careful with my words, not knowing which Stray is watching the constant surveillance of this room, I shrug.

"Mother deals in more than good little hitmen." She deals in skin too.

CHAPTER 6
Diora

"Okay, so we're throwing a killing spree disguised as a tea party. Who are the targets, and how are we going to get them there?" the tall medic who was stitching up Tom's hand yesterday asks.

We have been pulled into an immediate meeting for the Top Dogs to create the plan for Mrs. Jay's tea party. She has a careful, intricate plan here. I wonder if putting this party off on us was always part of the plan or something she's doing to piss the guys off.

"It'll combine all our current targets, all from differing backgrounds and purposes, so the deaths don't look connected," Enyo answers. He stands at the head of the table, a presentation being shown on the projector, and the golden dream of a man sits at the first spot to the right of Enyo, typing away on the presentation.

I've learned some of the team members' names by now. There is Enyo—the leader when Mrs. Jay isn't around. He's also her favorite and most trusted. He is a Son. Son is the highest level of Strays, and there are only two in this entire organization. He seems to love smiling, as he always has one on his face. He has light brown skin like mine and knows what colors work on him, based on the muted green cable-knit sweater he wears. He has a light amount of facial hair and black hair in a buzz cut style.

The second Son, my handsome boy, is Elliot. The man with the questions and adorably soft hair. He also knows computers and databases like a wizard. The rest each have some sort of specialized skill. Hank is a medic, Tom is a gun enthusiast, and the rest, I'm slowly figuring out. But what I can't quite figure out is how I fit into all this. I know my herbs, but is that enough to be within the ranks of these professionals?

"Who are our targets?" Tom asks, raising his eyebrows. This is quite the unusual setup, but I'm not at a point of outwardly questioning Mrs. Jay. Not yet; probably not ever. I don't even know why she wants me here.

But Elliot does. He says new recruits go missing after three months, and yet, here I am, clearly not missing. So, what's different about me? Is it because I'm a girl? Am I a distraction? To whom? Elliot?

Elliot seems to be the one with information. Enyo's a Son, so he should know more than the rest of us, but he either doesn't know, or he doesn't care about the missing Strays. Isn't he the owner? Why wouldn't he care?

"We have two main groups set as our targets: the blabber mouths and the dirty politicians. Here are the listed names of our targets. The names listed under your name are your responsibility. Your job is to get them to the event," Enyo informs us. My eyes instantly find my name and my list of targets.

<u>Diora Moss</u>

Daniel Kallous

Matthew Oppin

Jules Hartford

Mayor Jack Kilthmore

She knew exactly who was on my list. How? I haven't told her jack shit. She knows of Juliet, of that night. She probably knows more about me than I can imagine. My eyes met Elliot's, and he's watching me. Does he know, too? Are they conspiring together? That sneaky little bitch.

"Newbie gets the Mayor of Litchfort? Already? Damn," Parker says, twiddling with a knife, marking up the table.

"I don't make the assignments, I just relay them," Enyo says. "We'll need someone to do the boring shit: find tables, chairs, rentals, etc. Mother has the decorations down already." He's incredibly bored with this meeting, if not the whole event, yet he stands here, putting everything together. Everyone here truly follows every word Mrs. Jay says?

"Normally, the newbie does that, don't they?" Tom asks with excitement coating his tone. He smiles at me, and it takes everything in me not to raise a challenging brow. He wanna bet?

"Well, our newbie here is busy with something else, so Tom, find ten round tables big enough to fit five people at each—"

"Wait, that makes fifty targets when there're not fifty names up there..." Hank says, pointing at the projected lists. Hank is a man in his forties, with graying blond hair and a lean, crooked nose. He was mid-process into creating a splint for the huge man sitting next to him, cradling his hand. I think his name is Roan.

"Strays will be placeholders throughout the tables to ensure that this event goes smoothly," Enyo says, rolling his eyes. Gosh, he's a lively one.

"Diora, we will need a drink strong enough to kill. Do you know what you'll be preparing?" Enyo asks, raising an eyebrow. I watch each of their facial expressions.

"There are a few options, but one that is tasteless, pretty much undetectable, that I can grow enough by the time we put this event on: Oleander. We're using oleander," I say, thinking back to the corner of my greenhouse I have cleared for this special event. Oleander is a flowering shrub, a beautiful pink and red shrub that affects its victim's heart. "The plant contains toxic cardiac glycosides which leads to death. It'll be the most convenient to use, little to no mess. The problem is getting our hands on it."

"Just another thing on our fucking to do list, then, huh?" Elliot says, adding it to the slides.

"Don't rush into the negative—" Enyo defends, but Elliot quickly interrupts.

His hot and cold game is running lukewarm and confusing me. He gets all in my personal space, telling me things I shouldn't know, then acts like he hadn't had his nose in my hair the day previous. I can't decipher if he wants to be close or not.

"How do we know she can actually do it? Grow this plant and make enough to take out our targets undetected? Three months under Mother's wing doesn't make her some sort of super killer." Elliot doesn't bother glancing at Enyo, but directly at me. Like he's arguing with me, when all I'm here is to do my job, as far as he knows. As far as he knows, I'm another one of the damaged souls Mrs. Jay is recruited to be a hitman. What has he found out in the last twenty-four hours that's made him wary of me?

"Well, now that you brought her training up, Brother, Mother has assigned her under your wing." Enyo sighs as he delivers the message, but the curses under Elliot's breath don't go unnoticed.

"I don't know shit about plants."

"But you know shit about murder. More importantly, how to get out of any situation, and she needs that kind of training."

"Why doesn't she run drills like everyone else?"

"Because she's not everyone else. Mother explicitly said she wants you to take over her training," Enyo says. That gets Elliot to stop. For some reason, he's compliant when it comes to Mrs. Jay—a woman he seems to hate. He resorts to glaring at me, as if I told Mrs. Jay to assign my training to him.

As if I'd be stupid enough to ask Mrs. Jay anything and think he wouldn't use said request against me. I bet, if I asked the woman for a cookie, she would give me a brownie, if she'd even give me anything in the first place.

"Everyone is dismissed," Enyo says, waving his hands. I stand, collecting my purse before slinking out of the room. That is, until a hand grip my shoulder. I see Roan, the brute strength of the group with the broken hand. I bet he could toss me through a wall if he wanted to, with his broken hand even, but his warm smile tells me he won't. Not right now. I can't trust anyone yet.

"Welcome to the team, dirt digger," he says. His green eyes shine bright against his tanned skin as he chuckles.

I only nod my head, watching the room to see if they picked up on the nickname he tried to give me.

"It's Diora," I say. Nicknames have never been my thing. I have a name, a full name, and I don't like to be addressed by anything other than my name. Juliet calls me Dee, but Juliet is, and will always be, my exception.

"Blossom?" Tom calls as he passes us and heads into the hallway.

"Absolutely not!" Roan says. He shakes his head and scrunches his face, displeased with the nickname. My face breaks into a grin at the distaste of such a girly name. It would be the one name I'd probably like out of all the names they'd come up with.

"How about sprout?" another says. His name is Jones. He has dark hair and moody eyes and smooth brown skin, deeper than mine. I'm not sure what his special skill is, but if I had to guess, by his top heavy body and lean legs, nimble fingers and sharp gaze, maybe... a shooter.

"None of you twats have a nickname. Her name is Diora to you," Elliot murmurs, but it's enough to get the group to settle down.

"Why don't we go by nicknames? Nicknames would be so cool," Tom asks.

"Because we're not superheroes. We're killers," Enyo answers, his back facing the group.

"Diora, you're coming with me," Elliot commands. He surges toward me with a hand out to reach for my arm. I let him take it, liking the feel of his large hand wrapping around me. I grin, watching as his eyes narrow.

"Why?" I ask. I don't see his motive. I don't know if he's working with Mrs. Jay or against her, but I've come to appreciate his truly pretty face. Elliot is a work of art. His strong brows and light brown eyes almost hurt to look at. His jaw is sharp and his cheekbones high.

"I've got to train you, don't I?" This time, his brows rise, and I see the tiniest peak of his lip on the left side turning upward. He's happy. His eyes spark a bit in challenge, and the thrill of excitement runs up my spine.

What kind of trouble are we getting into?

CHAPTER 7

Elliot

Little Crane was put here as a distraction. A decoy. A chance to either prove my loyalty to Mother or a chance to get me off Mother's case.

Either way, it won't work.

I can see Mother's plan a mile away. Over a decade together and she tries to pull a fast one using the same tricks she's used on her targets. Using the same tricks she's taught me.

Distraction is a fine weapon, a method to make even the strongest opponents weak, and she's trying to use it on me.

Even though none of this changes anything. I still have my assignment from the Society higher-up to kill her.

"Let's see what you know, Little Crane," I say, walking toward the mat. If she's gonna be my fucking trainee, then I get to give her a nickname, and *I'm* the only one who gets to call the cocky little shit by said nickname.

No one else.

Her arm is soft in my hand. The second my words leave my lips, she doesn't let the softness linger in my hands. The moment her feet hit the mat, she yanks her arm free of mine and creates distance between us.

A chase?

Oh, a chase. I smile. A thrill runs through my limbs as I watch her. The crane should know better than to run from a predator.

"Mistake number one, Little Crane: your safest bet was to get so close I couldn't get a proper swing on you. Anything's fixable, though," I say and approach the bird. She jumps back, circling me like I'm the one who's trapped. I let her.

As an herbalist, I would imagine she doesn't have much experience in combat. It's not her strongest suit I'd say, based on her tactic here, but she doesn't seem completely clueless.

I use my height to my advantage, taking one large step to cut the distance between us. She's in my hands and I'm lifting her over my head. She curls her body in on herself, getting ready for impact. She rolls as I drop her on the mat behind me.

The spring mat rumbles under me as she jumps back into a standing position and advances on me. Whipping around, I catch her foot mid air before it can strike my back. I deliver an elbow jab to the area above her ankle. I'm not dumb enough to hit bone. She tries to yank her foot back, but I jerk her forward, crashing her body to mine.

"You seriously need more combat training, Little Crane."

"My name is Diora," she grunts and tries to break free but can only get as far as her leg is long, since I still have her foot in my grasp. She jumps and uses her other foot to deliver a sharp kick across my face, which forces me to let her go.

My head snaps as I stumble, and she's on me in a second. She jumps on my back and wraps her arms around my head, leaning back to pull my head with her. Damn, she has some tricks up her sleeve. I smile as she yanks my head by wrapping her hands around my jaw.

Too bad for her, I weigh more than she thinks and I slam down on the ground. I don't let my full weight land on her, just enough to knock the wind from her. I hear her mutter a curse.

I flip over and trap her beneath me. Grabbing my wire saw from my back pocket, I pull it over her delicate neck. Holding it tight enough to barely cut her, a beautiful thin line of ruby red blood bubbling from the front of her neck. Now that's fucking precious.

"I won," I say breathlessly. She crunches her brows, and that's when I feel the tiny stab at my side.

"Did you?" she asks with that same smirk she wore on the way to the damn training room. She digs the knife a little deeper, drawing blood I'll have to clean from this shirt. She's cutting deeper than I am and that shit fucking stings.

"Tie," I say, moving my wire back, her blood coating it, making me more aroused than I fucking should be. I yank her back up, forcing her knife out of my side. "There are no ties outside of this room. You plunge that knife into my side and then you yank it out and keep stabbing me till I don't move. You got it?"

Not that she'd be able to do that to me if we were in a real fight. Her head would be a bloody mess on the ground before she could stab me again. But everyone's not me.

"Got it," she says and even salutes me. The little shit.

I don't let her other arm go, dragging her to the clean up counters. I don't think Mother would appreciate a mark on her prodigy, and the least I can do is wipe it clean and make sure it doesn't get infected.

"Why do you kill?" she asks. The randomness of the question makes me freeze.

"That's personal," I say, glaring at the audacious crane. She is quite the proud thing.

"I kill for me."

"You kill for Mother. You kill for your sister. But not for you," I say, rolling my eyes at her. Her curls are frizzy, about an inch halo over her head, and sweat drips off her skin. I've yet to break a sweat, but I wouldn't be a Son or a Top Dog if I did while training a newbie.

"No, they give me a reason to justify being a murderer," she says, gazing off into space. "But the urge. The itch. The craving. That's always been there."

I watch her as she answers. The same urge found in all of us Strays. It's something we were born with. It's not an instinct that can be created or learned. She has it. I have it. Enyo, Mother—we all have that itch. She pushes me back against the counter, and I let her. She swipes a cloth off the stack we keep and lifts my shirt.

"What the hell are you doing?"

"Cleaning your wound," she says. "I got excited and stabbed too deep."

"It's fine," I say as her hands skim my skin. I don't let my breath hitch as she gets closer.

"Why do you work with Mrs. Jay?" she asks. Moving away, she looks through the line of cabinets, searching for a saline solution, probably.

"Why do you? Why are *you* so close to her?" I snarl. What the hell is up with the twenty-one questions? Is she trying to open me up? Learn what I know to report back to Mother?

"Does she seem like the kind of person to let someone in? To let someone help her?" she asks me, as she presses a cloth to my side. The knife barely made it in, not enough to call Hank, but enough to draw blood. "Do *I* seem like a team player? A person who wants help? *Her* help, of all? You think I don't see the monster she is?"

"You know about it?" How much does Diora know? Does she know about the molestation, or the trafficking ring, or more?

"It's not about knowing. It's about aura, a gut instinct." She says this so simply. As if trusting your gut is as easy as taking your next breath. It pisses me off. I tense as her little hands press against my skin. An unnecessary action, since she has her own wound to tend to. Though I barely touched her, the thrill of holding her between me and the wire of life and death was ecstasy.

"And you trust yours? What if you're wrong?" I mumble. It's not a question I'd ask anyone—least of all what I should be asking her—but it slipped. I slip around her, and I never slip. I can't afford to slip.

"I'm not." She gazes up at me this time, and I let her stare into my eyes as she tells me she truly believes in herself.

"Then why are you working for such a monster, as you called her?"

"Probably the same reason you are."

"Which is?" I ask. I don't deserve to ask, but I do. I can't help the hope that blooms in my chest that she'll answer.

I suddenly wanna know everything about Diora. Down to her soulless core. I need to know how she can trust herself so well.

She blinks before smiling and moving away from me. The loss makes me regret asking, but my curiosity fills the loss as she plays with the gauze we keep in the training room in front of the silver framed mirror that hangs on the wall.

I take some alcohol and a clean cloth, coming up behind her and clutching her fragile neck. The cloth between my hand and her neck holds all the restraint I have not to squeeze. Not to steal her breath. Not to turn her around and press my lips to her alluring pout.

She huffs, tilting her head in my grasp. "She caught me. I never even knew she was there. Following me. Watching me as I planned and executed my first four kills. She actually came in and introduced herself. It was the strangest encounter."

"You got caught in her web," I murmur, watching her disbelief at being caught by a much bigger monster than herself. It's a humbling experience, but I can't pretend it hasn't made me a better killer.

"I can't imagine anyone willingly walking into her crew of deception and destruction."

"I did," I whisper, watching her neck instead of meeting her eyes.

"Did you? Or were you stuck with no other options but to walk into her open arms?" she asks. I can hear the genuineness of her question. I can hear the rush of air in my ears, but all I can smell is jasmine and raspberries. Her scent consumes me as my lips linger over the top of her head. I can't help but want her skin over my lips. But I refrain.

Diora Moss is an observant person. She seems to not trust anyone but herself and that I can respect.

"I was twelve. Most Strays are recruited at a young age. They're more bendable. Teachable. Mother loves young boys." Her body stiffens under me. I can feel her eyes beating at me through the mirror, but I can't look at her. Keeping my eyes closed, I breathe in her scent again.

It's not every day these words are spoken out loud. A running secret amongst the unlucky few. But Diora is my crane in the mess of fog. She could be my shining light. My luck is clearing this fog of the same fate to the next lost boy with an uncontrollable rage. A loss of moral compass and a need to fill.

Their need for loss won't be filled with anything but the strength to fight their demons.

"I was six when my mother snapped," she whispers. "It was the day I knew the only person who'd ever loved me was Juliet."

I watch her deadpan face as her words process into my mind. "What do you mean?" I ask, even though it's none of my business.

"My mom tried to kill me when I was six," she murmurs, like she's talking about the weather. As if the words hold no shock or value to her. I scrunch my eyebrows as I wait for something, anything, related to an emotion from her.

I don't get anything but her dead eyes.

"She couldn't love me like she loved Juliet."

"You don't resent Juliet at all?" I ask, turning to lay my cheek on her head.

"Do you resent Enyo for being the favorite?" she retorts. There is a sharpness to her voice, as if my question offended her, and it makes my eyes open. I watch her in the mirror as she stares at me. She raises a brow, the most expression I've seen from her face since meeting her.

"That's not quite the same." It's not the same, 'cause Mother isn't my mother, not like she is to Enyo.

"No, I don't resent her. I love her."

"Love?" I ask. Love is a word used freely, and yet I don't sense Diora uses the word often. It's interesting to hear people like us use the word Love. What does it really mean? What does it mean to her?

"My soul is bound to her. I owe her her happiness, not because she loves me, but because I want to. I want to see her every day. Talk to her. See her happy. It's a desire to see another fulfilled," she explains, holding a hand to her heart. I see the devotion she has to Juliet. Something I've felt one time and from only one person ever.

"It takes a special person to hook themselves to us, doesn't it?" I say, watching as she silently nods a single time and looks away. I couldn't imagine having my person be someone like Juliet. Someone weak. Someone I'd have to defend. Worry about their safety. There's a strength in Diora that I don't have. At least my person is like me. A killer.

I know about what happened to Juliet Moss. There is no written report of it, but it's not hard to connect the dots. Juliet isn't the only victim of the political game of Litchfort, but with Diora on her side, she may be the last.

If Diora can survive being a Stray. If Diora can survive Mother's plan. Juliet will get her justice. I sigh as I release her throat and lift my head off of hers.

"We're done today, Little Crane."

"Again tomorrow?" she asks, and I see that damn glitter of her smile. The slight upward turn of her lips reveals her eagerness to play again.

"We'll see," I say, leaving the training room. I spot Enyo leaning against the wall and raise my brows at his overly smiley face.

"That wasn't so bad, was it, baby bro?" Enyo says, laughing, and it takes everything not to knock him on his ass.

"Shut the fuck up," I say, rolling my eyes as I stride straight past him.

"Hey, wait." Enyo sobers, pulling my arm to slow me down as he matches my pace. "You saw the ring?"

He's talking about the Society ring dangling around her delicate little neck. I sigh and run a hand through my hair.

"Yeah, I saw it."

"How is she already a member? It's been three months since she met Mother. According to Mother, how much can someone learn in three months?" he asks, rambling, as if I have the answer.

"Wait." I hear a soft voice from down the hall and stop. Taking a deep breath, I slowly turn to meet the eyes of Diora, who runs to catch up to us. I swallow the spit pooling in my mouth as she gets closer.

I almost lost my cool back there and didn't want to face her so soon afterward but I can't seem to ignore her.

"You know about the rings," she says, and both Enyo and I show our rings on our hands. "Tell me about it."

I scoff and turn back around. What does she mean by that? As if she doesn't know what society she's joined, but wears the damn ring.

She pulls my arm with a glare set on her face. What is up with people pulling on me today? Damn.

"I know it's a society of serial killers, but Mrs. Jay won't tell me much else. As you probably know, she's not one for answering questions."

"And what makes you think I am?" I scoff.

"You're right," she says, turning to my brother. He smiles at her—the annoying ass.

You're right. Her words, her honesty, rings in my ears, and one thing Diora isn't… is hiding. Even when she was talking about her sister. The damn girl bleeds honesty, and it's in a way to make you like her. She's blunt. It's an odd trait in a killer.

"Well, the Society is completely separate from Mortes Ostium. The kills done for the Society aren't for money," the damn traitor says. As Enyo's talking, I watch as her attention fully moves to him, and it pisses me off.

I don't know why because I met the girl fucking yesterday, but I don't like her attention on him. I want it on me. Only me.

"Members of Mortes Ostium kill for fun, for release. The name is Latin for Death's Door. We were founded by Jack the Ripper and have been running for over a century."

"Okay, so what are the rules?"

"You don't know the fucking rules?" I ask, trying to keep my shock to myself. I catch Enyo's eyes, and I can see the surprise in them.

This girl joined a society without knowing the rules? What the hell kind of game is Mother playing here?

"If you're that hopeless—"

"Stop with the lame insults and answer the damn question," she cuts me off, and I get in her face for the second time and smile as she takes a step back.

She smells so fucking good.

"Or what?" I cruelly smile, wondering what the Little Crane will do.

She smiles, too, which turns me on more than I care to admit.

"Or I'll go ask someone else and they can answer all my questions. I'm sure they will."

"Who?" I snip, not liking that fucking idea at all.

She turns back to Enyo, who's been watching us with his arms crossed and an eyebrow raised.

"Enyo?" His name comes off sickly sweet, and it makes my jaw tick.

"Yes, darlin'?" His tone is heavy with the Michigan accent as he loops his arm with hers, and I damn near rip his arm away when I yank him back.

"Oh, are you actually gonna answer, Brother?" he asks, and I shove him backward as I fill his spot next to Diora as we walk down this long ass hallway.

"You get to call on to the Society for big shit three times, and three times only, so use that cautiously. Now that you are a member, the only rule is in regards to the ball."

"The ball?"

"The annual ball, where your boy, Elliot, is hosting," Enyo says, laughing as he catches up to us.

"How do you get to the ball?" she asks.

"You have to submit eight kills."

"That's it?" she asks.

"Yeah, that's it," Enyo confirms. Diora nods her head as she turns back around and walks down the hall.

I snap my head toward Enyo, who shrugs his shoulders. "If the Society lets her into the ball, then I trust her."

But what he fails to realize is that they let Mother in, too, and I damn sure don't trust her. I need to know more about Diora, beyond what she tells me.

I shouldn't let her in as easily as I am, yet I can't figure out a way to stop it.

CHAPTER 8
Diora

It's humid in my little old greenhouse. The moisture in the room is high today, since the air outside is particularly dry. My hair gets as big as my tallest plants and sweat covers my forehead and fingers.

I smile as I twist a stem of my first angel trumpet between my gloved hands. I picked the plant this morning when the flower bloomed. White delicate petals imitate a trumpet's bell, skinny then wide. When I hold the flower upside down, I can see a ballroom of beautiful women twirling around in swishing ball gowns.

This is my happy place. This is the one place where no one can hurt me. Tending to my plants here is the only way I stay sane.

My plants are protected here. My plants can grow and bloom within these white glass walls found off the abandoned forest trail. It's supposed to be just my plants and me here, yet uninvited guests keep appearing within these four walls.

"Diora Moss." His voice is instantly recognizable to my ears. Chills cover my arms as a blush covers my cheeks. I can't begin to understand why or how I can be hot and cold at the same time. Why it only happens when Elliot Jay comes into the room. How I've never felt the reddening of my cheeks before. I turn to face the stranger on my territory.

He stands under the metal door frame as his eyes meet mine. Hot boiling eyes travel over my frame, and the wish to have worn a better outfit fills my coming thoughts. His golden hair is dull yet alluring, nonetheless, in the midmorning light and pushed back, as if he ran his hands through it before he walked in here.

I hold the smile that tries to break free at seeing Elliot Jay again so soon. As beautiful as this man is, I still make note of where my foxglove is. It's not enough to save me, but if I can get him to consume enough, it'll take him out eventually.

I'm not stupid enough to think I can outdo Elliot Jay. He's got years of experience, training under the monster that he calls Mother, and a chip on his shoulder because of it.

It doesn't take a genius to imagine the kind of training she put him through, even at the young age of twelve. She's been hard on me, sure, making me run for an impossible length of time to improve my stamina and recall facts off the top of my head, where the wrong answer earns me a slap across the face with her jewelry still on. But I saw the training rooms. The brass knuckles, whips, and blood-stained mats. I've seen the kids in the halls, devoid of smiles and that fucking *light*.

A creak snaps my attention back to the real world. Elliot comes inside. His predator-like stride inside my space is enough to let me know this would be a flight situation and not a fight one. I know he was going easy on me during our spar yesterday.

Even if I could stuff an intense amount of foxglove poison into his mouth, Elliot would probably find a cure within minutes and get ahold of it within an hour, but those sixty minutes would be torturous. In those sixty minutes, he would think of me.

I like that.

"Elliot, how may I help you?" He's the Son of Mrs. Jay, and for that, he is my superior. I respect him enough to know my limits with him. Even after our conversation yesterday, he never answered my questions; even after I offered my own answers. That's always worked with Juliet, but maybe she's a special case.

"I need something," he says, coming closer. In the light, I see he's dressed in the same casual attire. This time, a simple black t-shirt and plain slacks. He doesn't waste time and is direct, without so much of a knock or hello as he approaches my work bench where I'm sitting.

"What could you possibly need from a newbie like me?" I ask, turning around to fully face the predator in front of me. Yesterday solidified the point that Elliot Jay is not someone I should let my guard down around. Even if he makes my face hot and fingers shaky.

The careful steps of his leather dress shoes are calculated and avoid any loose vines and leaves of my plants. I can't tell if he is being careful not to leave traces of his presence here or care that these are... mine. *My* plants.

I'm supposed to keep my distance from the man in front of me. I shouldn't crave his presence the way I do. He's not part of my plan. The kind of change Elliot Jay brings isn't one I think I can handle.

Too many people in my circle could cause it to disrupt.

But here he is. In my space, deeply hidden in the trees, I wonder, if one of us screamed, would anyone hear?

"Can you build a resistance to poison?" he asks, as he gazes over the single room that is my greenhouse. I've filled it with many colors, mainly greens, pinks, and purples, as my plants grow into full bloom weapons.

"Mithridatism?" I ask as my brows scrunch. Why would he want to know about that?

"Yes, is it possible?"

"It depends on the poison. You can't be immune to all kinds of poison. You'd have to pick and choose which you'd like to build on," I say absentmindedly. It's not a practice I partake in, but many scientists do. It's tricky and hard to tell if it's real. I've never had an issue with someone trying to poison me, let alone poison me enough to kill me. Most poisonous plants are used to weaken the body, and if someone had actually gotten to me, I've thought it would be cruel to rob them of the win.

"Okay, so it's not possible?"

"No one can say for sure. You have a better chance at weakening your body over time than building a resistance,"

I say. It's hard to tell with the human body. We get sick on a whim. We die so easily, it would be hard to determine if it was really our time to die or if the buildup of whatever poison became too much.

"What would you use to weaken someone over time? What do you and Mother use?" Something clicks in his eyes, and he nods a single time before continuing his line of questioning.

"Mrs. Jay and I talk about a range of plants. We use fast-acting poisons; she likes a more immediate win..."

"Which is her favorite?" he quips, raising his eyebrows. As if I owe the man an answer.

To ask why is on the tip of my tongue. My eyes search his. Not that I can read them, but so maybe I'll pick up on something he's not saying. The man could have figured this all out on his own without asking me. His skill in information is part of why he is a Son in the corp, so why is he involving me?

"Are you trying to get me in trouble?" I ask, stepping closer to my foxglove plant. Mrs. Jay's shit list isn't a list I plan on being on. Not this soon. I can't afford to be. I can't determine his motive, his larger objective.

Is this for his personal agenda, or is he secretly working for Mrs. Jay? He acts like he can't stand the woman, yet still calls her Mother. They could be conspiring against me; his hatred of her may be an act. Is she using Elliot to test me?

"Diora, if I wanted to get you in trouble with Mother, I'd simply kiss you." He sighs, sitting on the stool I'd previously sat on. This makes me taller than him, and his golden hair and deep brown eyes shine in the sunlight. I want to run my hand through it. It's smooth and airy. I breathe heavier when he's this close, but the air I breathe is cleaner. More enticing with notes of his smell in it. "Mother is an extremely jealous woman, remember?"

My mind jumps back to the conversation we had yesterday when he mentioned Mrs. Jay's adherence to female Strays. How she feared they would turn into competition. What did he even mean by that?

"I need the name of the poison you give Mother. The one that she works with alone."

"Without me?"

"Without you. The one she takes home."

My mouth is dry, and I swallow as he towers over me. Once again, the question why is fighting against my lips, but I hardly think he'll tell me. Are he and Mother working on something else? Why doesn't he ask her?

"She doesn't remember the name?" She should know. This simple question will tell me if they are working together or not.

"No."

"Oh." A lie. Why lie? "What's going on?"

"Darling, you could barely scrape the surface." He chuckles darkly, and his eyes narrow at the question. I watch his face as hints of emotion dance across his cheekbones and eyebrows. I enjoy looking at Elliot Jay's face.

"Then tell me," I whisper as now he's leaning forward.

"Why?" The word falls off his lips in a seductive tone. Not *can I trust you*, not *it's not your business*. This man asked me *why*. Why would he tell me? I... I don't know.

I hold his gaze as his honey brown eyes peer into me. I slightly shake my head. No answer I could give him would persuade him to tell me.

"What poison are you giving Mother?" he asks again. This time, he's leaned up so close, he's whispering and his words hit against my cheek.

I remain stock still. Hoping the predator doesn't attack. I don't have time to go back and forth. I have a choice to make and it's not one to take lightly. I can take the risk and betray Mrs. Jay by telling him, or I can protect Mrs. Jay.

I should choose Mrs. Jay. I know her more than I know him. She's been helping me since she discovered my itch. Even with her less than ideal ways and blackmailing, she's still helped me in her own way.

The good thing would be to stick by her.

But I'm not good, now am I?

And Elliot's a way hotter alliance.

"What do I get in return?" Our faces are mere inches apart, and I like the intoxicating smell of his cologne wrapping around head. I could close my eyes and be whisked away to a world where only I exist. More so his scent and me. A dreamland where we were free. Where *I* was free.

"Ahh, I knew the bird would come to play," he says with a wild smile and a chuckle. He leans back, completely relaxed on my stool. "Mercy, my darling Little Crane. You'd get mercy."

I wet my lips as I turn away from him.

"I feel I may already have that, Elliot," I say as I push away from the overcrowded workbench. I pull my white t-shirt, trying to cool down from the intensity that is Elliot Jay.

"I guess you're right," he says as he shakes his head, his hair becoming sticky with sweat. "I did come to ask you, instead of the million other ways I could have gotten what I needed." He shrugs.

"I want the truth," I say, staring at the pink foxglove patch, growing taller than the normal three to four feet that it usually does. These are as tall as me and will need bigger stakes soon.

How would they have grown so fast independently?

Am I responsible for my growth or does that come from the support of... outsiders?

Wordlessly, I stalk toward the plant he's asking for.

"Now tell me, Diora, what plant would you want to use to kill someone over a few months' time?" The answer pops into my brain before I can process his question.

It's the same plant I've been harvesting for Mrs. Jay.

"If she's trying to poison you slowly, she'll use elephant ear. It's hard to kill someone with this, but it's effective in weakening the body. It takes five to ten leaves to kill, and as you can see, they are huge. What are your symptoms?" It's the most unsuspecting plant. Making it easy to dose someone over a length of time.

I hover my hand over a leaf, not letting it touch my skin. I'm so sweaty from the temperature and Elliot's presence I would probably sweat out the effects of touching this poisonous plant, but I don't give it the chance to hurt me.

Not like I've given the chance to Elliot.

"Burning and itching."

"She's rubbing it on your skin?"

"Tsk tsk, Little Crane. I don't think that's a story you want to hear," he says, and the light in eyes dim as the corner of his smile shakes. He stalks behind me as I stare at the elephant ear millimeters from the skin of my face. I don't dare make contact. It takes rubbing and constant contact to do anything, and I'm breathing in enough fumes and toxins circulating in this room to make a grown man weak. "This looks more like a botanical garden than a greenhouse."

"A greenhouse is to shelter plants while keeping the temperature and humidity desired for the plants to grow. That lies in the structure of the building. What I do inside of it, how I make it appear, is up to me."

He hums as the pads of his fingers trail up my exposed arms and back down. "It's nice."

I sense complaints don't come often from Elliot. Something about being the most dangerous man in the room leads to a man who can't show weakness, which equates to kindness in this case. I turn around, bumping into his body directly behind me.

"Why do you let her hurt you?" I ask. Is she poisoning his drinks? Body lotion? How is she using the elephant ear against him?

"Probably the same reason you haven't told Mother all about your plans to kill Yara Holdings. My dominos will fall when they're supposed to," he says with a shrug. My head snaps to him at the name he drops.

How does he know about Yara Holdings? I raise an eyebrow in question.

"You think I didn't do my research on you?"

"That information isn't public."

"That doesn't mean it isn't findable, Little Crane."

I see his chest rise with a deep inhale, and I notice his nose impossibly close to me. Does he like the smell of sweat and dirt?

I sidestep away from him, and even as I slide underneath his hold, he follows me. Shaking my head as I step back to my safe zone—what's supposed to be my safe zone, my work bench—but he follows me. It's like having a doberman follow you. His being dressed in black, and his haunting shadow over my shoulder, make me shiver.

"Elliot."

"Yes, Little Crane?" he answers, still standing over me. I take a deep breath, preparing for another unanswered question.

I lean against my workstation, and he traps me in again by leaning both his arms on the table behind me. Breathing in his woodsy dark chocolate cologne swarming my senses.

I tilt my head slightly. The smile I've been holding back since he got here breaks through my defense and I see a glint in his eyes.

"Why are you still here?" It's a bold question, as Juliet would call it, but I sense Elliot could've figured out this information without me. He could've left, should have left by now, but hasn't.

I answered his questions.

Why else is he here?

"Little Crane–"

"Just tell me whatever it is. I don't understand this game we're playing," I cut him off. He has something to say but isn't saying, and I'm nowhere close to figuring out what he wants exactly.

He smiles and shakes his head like I told a joke. The act ticks me off, but I let him continue, anyway. He peers down at me. His gaze hurtling down on me... it makes it hard to process anything beyond Elliot.

"Do you think you can handle a monster like Mother?" It isn't the answer I was expecting. My lips drop their smile, and I watch as the seriousness in his answer bleeds over the room. "Because I do."

Kill Mrs. Jay? He thinks I could kill Mrs. Jay? A woman who runs a hitman organization and controls some of the most deadly killers in the United States. Who has been a killer herself for decades and has never been caught. Me, take her down?

"I think you overestimate my skill." I scoff and push at his strong chest. He doesn't budge. His presence looms over me as my thoughts run in circles in my head.

"I have more to lose—" I say my first thought running to Juliet. What if Mrs. Jay tries to hurt her, kill her, in retribution? I can't risk Juliet. I need her. She has to live.

"You have the same stake as I do, Diora. Juliet will be protected. I promise."

"You can't promise; you can't guarantee anything," I say, trying to push at his chest again. All I can see is him. All my brain can interpret is him. It's hard to think.

"I'll have Enyo on her twenty-four-seven." He speaks so surely. He's thought this through, but I can't say yes on a whim. I have a person in my life I can't lose.

"Why not ask Enyo to kill Mother? He's far more qualified," I ask, scrunching my brows. Why isn't he a part of this little vengeance squad?

"He can't be involved. It's too personal for him." Elliot waves that off, like it's obvious, and it makes me more confused.

"What does that mean?"

"We're too close to her. She'll see it coming if either of us do it. It has to be you. I need you." His words land like blows to my chest. Elliot needs something. Elliot needs *me*? This doesn't make sense.

"Can we even go after other Society members?" I shouldn't even be considering this. There is no way I could kill Mrs. Jay. As much as I'd want to be on Elliot's good side, this ask is too much. It's selfish. As a member of the Mortes Ostium, are we even allowed to kill each other? If I couldn't kill Mrs. Jay, there's no way I could go up against the Society. Breaking their rules is the last thing on my to do list.

"Yeah, you can. Especially when *the Society* is the one who tipped you on it," he says, and it makes me more confused. The Society told him to kill Mrs. Jay? Why?

"Why?" I whisper. I don't know much about the Society, but I don't think they'd ask him that.

"I can't tell you until you commit to the task, Little Crane," he says and takes a step away from me. It's like all the oxygen in the room comes rushing toward me and I can breathe normally.

I swallow my nerves and watch as Elliot walks out of my little greenhouse.

What changed in the last twenty-four hours for him to... trust me?

Chapter 9

Diora

"Please get through this dinner for me, Dee," Juliet pleads as we stand in front of our childhood home. The tan-colored house is bland compared to the new black and white builds around it, but Juliet loves it. This house represents a time for her I will never understand.

I know, deep down, that her childhood wasn't perfect. That no one's childhood is ever perfect. But I also can't help the urge to burn this house down. I can't help the mask that slips when I'm in these four walls. I can't help the memories stuck in my brain that took place in this house.

Her memories are different. She rarely knew what was actually happening here. In the shadows of the Moss' family home. She's the good one. She's their good one. She can't help that, and I don't want her to change that. She doesn't remember. Not like I do. She doesn't remember. I do.

I remember the sharp pains, the blood, the cry, the tears. The resentment, the fear that laced each parent's eyes. I'll remember the day she gave up on me. I'll always remember that my mother tried to kill me. I'll remember the way my dad rushed to her instead of me.

I also remember the way Juliet ran to me. Hugged me. Cried over me. Despite getting dirty, her arms and dress soaked in my blood. She still hugged me. She didn't care that I was different. Evil. She didn't think I was a monster. She loved me. *She ran to me.* Not our sobbing mother. Not behind Dad's strong legs. But to me.

After calming my mother down, all those years ago, my dad took me to the hospital. It was written off as a suicide attempt. It was the only way to explain how the kitchen knife got into my room and so deep into my hand.

Elliot's offer earlier today floats through my mind, and a sudden realization jet-lines through my limbs. Elliot didn't have a Juliet. He has an Enyo, whatever that may mean for him, but not a Juliet. Not when he needed one.

I turn to watch my beautiful sister. She's an inch shorter than me and far curvier than my rectangle frame. Her long curly hair is twisted up in a clip, her cream, soft sweater and warm brown skin. Elliot could've used the love I get from Juliet. The safety and warmth she provides to even monsters like me.

Those missing Strays don't have a Juliet. They don't have someone to save them through the deepest, darkest moments of their lives. Instead, they meet someone like Mrs. Jay. Someone who takes that darkness and makes it darker. Twists it up and forms it to create her own army of monsters.

I don't know why Elliot cares about the missing Strays, or what Mrs. Jay has to do with the missing Strays specifically, but if killing her will save them from whatever dark, twisted fate Mrs. Jay has planned for them, then... I should do it.

I plaster a forced smile on my face as I nod encouragingly to Juliet. It's not like I haven't done this song and dance before. We do this dinner once a month. I can handle three hours with my parents if it'll make Juliet happy.

More like, all *they* can handle with me is three hours.

Our dad, a tall Black man, with weathered skin and tired brown eyes, opens the door with a smile so wide his forehead wrinkles deepen as his gaze lands on Juliet. He welcomes her in by wrapping an arm around her shoulders. He asks about her day as they walk inside, leaving me on the porch. I watch their relaxed posture and their closeness from behind, wondering for a moment what it would be like to have this kind of attention. Would I even like it?

That is, until Juliet's hand reaches out behind her to mine as she smiles at Dad and answers his question. It's a deep reminder that, while I'm on the outskirts of this family, Juliet hasn't forgotten me. Or ignored me. Or wanted me gone.

Whatever. I don't need their attention. I need her. I have her.

"Your mom made pasta tonight. I hope you are hungry," Dad says excitedly, ushering Juliet to the dining room, as if she hadn't lived in this house for twenty years.

"Gosh, I'm starving. Are you, Dee?" Juliet asks with a light laugh, as I follow slightly behind them. Questioning if my presence is really needed.

"Yeah, starved," I say as I slide off my jacket, though the only person to hear me is Juliet, based on how my dad hasn't even glanced at me since I've gotten here.

The shine on the brown table glares at me as we sit and my mother comes in. The air always thickens when I see her. It's as if I'm frozen in time, analyzing every movement she makes. It's always been like this.

She carries the food she made on gingham potholders, and a small smile appears on her face as her eyes set on Juliet. My mother is a beautiful woman. She has dark hair and deep brown eyes, and yet all the warmth that radiates from her turns cold at the sight of me. She can't hide the dip in her smile or the squint of her eyes as they fall on me. If I wasn't so used to this, it'd upset me.

If she hadn't stabbed that knife into my wrist, this'd upset me.

"Diora, dear, how nice of you to come," she murmurs as she sets the food pan down in the middle of the table. She comes around the table toward me, and my body involuntarily tenses with each step she takes. She does this every time, and yet I can't get myself to relax around her.

We pretend that night never happened. We pretend the nights that follow didn't contain my dad having to lock my door every night in case the urge, the itch, overcame my mother again.

She wraps my head in her arms as she kisses the top of my head. Her cheek rests against the top of my head, and I can almost pretend I didn't see the disappointment in her gaze moments ago. I can almost pretend there is a world in which my mother loves me.

I can almost pretend we are normal.

"Dee got a new job!" Juliet announces. Her excitement tingles my cheeks as I smile slightly. The lie I told Juliet about my strange hours and increase in income stings, but the satisfaction her happiness brings me soothes it. "Don't be shy. Tell 'em, Dee." My mother lets me go, and I can breathe normally. She sits down in her spot across from Juliet, my dad next to her.

My parents stare at me with questioning gazes. They don't smile or nod in encouragement. They only stare. As if they are waiting for me to speak, not to listen, but so they can get back to worrying over Juliet.

"I'm an assistant florist down at, um, Sadie's Flowers," I say. Sadie's Flowers also happens to be a front for the Society. It's one of many they have almost everywhere, it seems like.

Sadie's is a real flower shop in Detroit, the closest major city in Michigan. The Society works out of the basement. Any time a member nearby needs supplies, the Society drops it off at Sadie's.

"Dee's always been good with plants, and she's moving up in life. Maybe she'll open her own shop one day," Juliet rambles as my parents switch their attention off of me and back to her. I can breathe normally as the attention drifts away and they ask about her and how her job hunt is going.

Juliet hasn't had a job since her incident.

Supporting the both of us on my cashier's job was more than tough, but I'd do it if it meant the one person who ever cared for me was safe.

"Juliet doesn't need a job," I murmur as I take a sip of water from the glasses already set up before we got here. I hate this argument. I hate the attention it draws, but it doesn't matter. "I make enough for the both of us." Even more so now, since Mrs. Jay pays a salary twice what I'd made before. I've yet to go on a kill for Haven Corporation, but we also get a commission based on the part played in a kill.

"Yeah, but Juliet, honey, you shouldn't rely on someone like Diora. You should be independent," Dad says, scooping some pasta into his mouth.

"That comment wasn't necessary," Juliet innocently says as her eyes shoot to me, then back to our parents.

"It's not safe—" Dad says.

"I've kept her safe for the last six months. We are fine," I snap, setting my fork down. They anger me to the point I can't eat. Every. Single. Dinner.

"No, I should be the one taking care of you, Dee," Juliet says as her smile dies. It pisses me off that they've had to ruin good news with this shit. I have it under control. If I, the one taking care of all the bills, doesn't mind, then neither should they. She's *my* sister.

"You both should be independent, living and taking care of yourselves on your own. How much does a florist assistant even make, Diora? How can you possibly be housing and feeding the both of you?" my dad argues.

"It makes enough," I say, keeping my gaze on the noodles, sauce, and cheese plopped on my plate by my mother, who hasn't said a word about this yet.

It didn't always make enough, though. Not when I was a cashier. They are right to a point, and that pisses me off more. I barely ate, Juliet barely ate. Hell, after rent and utilities, and phones, and everything else, we are in more credit card debt than I am comfortable with.

Not that they need to know that. No. Not when it'll be all my fault because I couldn't get a better job, or more education, because I creep everyone out with my silence and stares. As if it doesn't take everything in my power to keep my urges at bay. To make sure all blood stays inside of people's bodies instead of under my nails.

I failed her once, six months ago, but that will never happen again. And it damn sure won't go unpunished.

"Juliet—" my dad tries again, but Juliet cuts him off.

"Can we talk about something else? How was work, mom?" Juliet tries to be the peace in the midst of this storm, and as the golden child, it works. It works on all of us, as Mom smiles and lays her head on her hands as she goes on about whatever it is that she does. She works in corporate for a toy company. It keeps her young, she says. She loves the fun nature of the office, but also the stability that comes with working in a corporation.

I can't blame her. I get it, having a family and all, but her kids just can't seem to make the same decision. And I know it kills her inside.

"Honey, it's been good. We've got this new toy and—" Her words go in one ear and out the other as Dad's hard pressed stare drills in the side of my head.

"Diora," he says in a low voice, a voice meant for just me, and I let my head snap to face him. He thinks I baby Juliet. That she babies me. What he doesn't understand is the babying he devalues is what I call loyalty. I'm loyal to her, and she's loyal to me. "Don't hold her back. She's made for more."

Mom and Juliet's conversation goes on. It's only him and me in this conversation. I respect my dad far more than my mother. Though he gave up on me, it wasn't in the same way mother did. It's a strange kind of acceptance that my dad has over me that made sense to a point. He accepted I am what I am, but he also accepts that doesn't mean he has to love me.

Which I don't understand, either, because he loves mother and she's a monster like me. It wasn't until I failed Juliet that I could understand my father's anger toward me.

He failed to change me, and I failed to keep Juliet safe. We're just a bunch of angry failures waiting for a chance to right our wrongs.

I hum as his glare sets deeper. It brings a smile to my face. "I can do what I want."

"Diora," he growls, as if they ever affected me. "You'll corrupt her, Diora" And here this bit goes again. I roll my eyes. Juliet can't be corrupted. Not if she doesn't know.

I nearly giggle from the accusation. "Only, then, she would come crawling back home."

"Diora Rose Moss, you will take this seriously. Let your sister go," Dad nearly shouts as his shoulders rise in tension. It's the same song and dance every month.

I refrain from entertaining him any further, which makes his face turn about three shades redder. I give him a half-assed shrug, picking up another forkful of my pasta. I am getting a free meal out of this, that's for sure. I hear Dad grumble my name again, and that's when Juliet's had enough.

She's pretty sensitive to energy, to the atmosphere. The more tense or uncomfortable an energy is, the antsier she gets. Yet another reason I don't understand why she forces these family dinners.

"I think it's time for us to leave. Mom, Dad, thank you for dinner," Juliet says, shooting up from her chair.

"Yeah, we'll see you soon, yeah?" Mom says as we walk toward the door. The cherry red door does nothing to soothe our tension, and I can practically see Juliet's stress creeping up my back as she stares me down.

The car door slams, and Juliet turns to face me, huffing as the keys jingle in her hands. Her eyes bore, and I wish I had a sliver of guilt at my behavior at tonight's dinner, but there isn't. Dad starts the same argument every time. It's not just my fault we can't argue like normal people.

My eyes gaze over the stitching on the dashboard. I really didn't want Juliet to be mad. I can't get myself to say sorry and mean it. She hates that even more.

"I have work tonight. Can we go?" I murmur, keeping my view on the outside world through the window and nowhere near Juliet. I didn't want to see the disappointment of another failed dinner. Another chance failed to bring this family closer. She doesn't even know what she is asking of us, and when she looks at me with that frown of disappointment, I almost tell her everything.

She sighs and turns on the car.

"I don't understand why we can't all get along for one night."

If it was up to me, she'd never figure that out, either.

Chapter 10

Elliot

A bluejay flies by as I sit at Mallory's coffee shop. I gaze away from my laptop, where notes upon notes lay, containing details for the Society's ball I'm hosting this year. The last weekend in June is sneaking up and the final details need to be set in motion.

I've reserved the Musée de la Chasse et de la Nature in Paris. The nature museum seemed like an interesting spot for worldwide serial killers to meet.

My mind races back to Diora again and again. It's fucking annoying how much space she takes in my head.

I can't draw people. But sometimes, when I'm looking at her, I wish I could. The intricate beauty of her face, the symmetry of it, itches my hands to touch, capture. It's as if I, Elliot Jay, am not my own person anymore. I can't move, I can't breathe without thinking about Diora Moss. It's entirely frustrating, since I've only known the woman for about a week.

Looking up from my computer, I scratch at my eyes, tired of staring at a screen. I gaze over the outside seating of Mallory's; it's much more packed than it was a few days ago. Wait. Is that

Diora, or am I hallucinating? I scratch my eyes again, and sure as shit, it's her. The Diora Moss, walking my way.

She sees me before I see her. She strides over in dirty white sneakers. Her black skirt flows with her strides, and she wears a long-sleeved black shirt, tight to her body, in eighty-degree weather. I resist raising an eyebrow at her questionable fashion as she gets closer. I resist watching her hair blow off her slender neck. That same pearl necklace, with the heart and skull pendants, hangs around her neck. I bet she never takes it off. I bet if she got close enough, the scab of my cut across her throat from our sparring session would still be there—

"I'm in," Diora says as she immediately approaches my table and sits across from me. I snap my attention to her face. I raise an eyebrow, trying to gauge if the Little Crane truly knows what she is truly getting into. Does she care?

The danger she'll put herself in?

By joining me, she basically signs her death warrant.

I don't know what came over me in that greenhouse yesterday. Why the hell would I ask a newbie like her to join me? Work with me, as if I can't get enough of her already.

"In what?" I ask, playing stupid. I lean back into the metal chair, wondering if the white shirt I'm wearing will have stains from the black metal of the chair.

The time I used to spend here, dedicated to my bird studies, has been replaced with planning this ball the Society has me hosting, and to be honest, I'm not the happiest about it.

It is the only time I could do either task in peace, and I'd much rather read my books than aid in the plans of this ball any further.

Though, my involvement in the ball planning is killing Mother's sanity. Her jealousy of me hosting this ball instead of her is ripping at her seams, and I get nothing done around her. I've had to resort to planning it when I am alone, and now, here, her little *distraction* is disrupting my planning hour. Did she send her here?

What made the Little Crane change her mind? I was sure she was going to say no yesterday. Her loyalty to Juliet seemed to go beyond good moral standing. Nothing mattered more to her than her sister. So, what changed? I watch as she scans our surroundings one time and flips her long, curly hair over her shoulder.

"Saving the missing Strays; all dogs deserve a chance to live," she mutters, her eyes trained on her hands in front of her.

"Even if it means that you could get hurt. Dogs bite, Little Crane," I say, trying to gauge her thoughts behind this decision. I carefully slide my own coffee mug in front of her. She wrinkles her nose as the smell hits her, and I raise my brows in amusement. The girl doesn't like coffee. Interesting.

Turning my head back, I make eye contact with the cashier at the front. Mallory's is an inside-outside coffee shop, where the walls of the front of the shop open and the whole space is connected. I nod toward my new coffee date, and the cashier comes over to me.

"Can I get a tea for my date?" I ask as the woman whips out a notepad. She smiles and turns to Diora, who looks to be glaring. Her eyebrows are furrowed as she concentrates. On what, I'm not quite sure.

"How much is a cup of tea here?"

"It's on me, Little Crane. Order," I say. I know she is terribly poor. At least she was before meeting Mother. Maybe that's why she fell into Mother's arms? Maybe it was truly a coincidence that she joined Mother.

"A rose tea, please, for here," Diora orders.

I still don't know whether to trust her. As much as my mind may call to her, I can't always trust my mind. It's led me down roads I can't recover from.

Diora Moss is gonna get me in trouble. I should stay away from the Crane, and yet, every turn I make, there she is.

I lay my leather-bound journal down on the metal table as the birds around us chirp a musical melody. This scene would be nice if the two people occupying this table were any sort of normal.

If we were strangers meeting casually for the first time.

Not serial killers with an agenda.

Her gaze settles on her hands as if she's nervous, but I doubt it's nerves wracking her body. Other outward signs of nerves are non-existent. She rarely shows what she's thinking. It calms me more than I'm used to. I don't have to try to read her so hard. Try to find the lie. She hides so well it turns everything I know about her back on to chance. A simple choice that I could make mindlessly. There are no signs, no signals, that I should've, could've, would've myself to death over.

Her chest rises and falls at a steady rate. Though her focus is on her hands. Her hands aren't sweaty or trembling; they are slim and delicate. I have the urge to touch them. Feel the weight of them on me.

I take one. Her fingers gently uncurl onto my palm, and I see what she is focusing on. Tiny white scars lace her fingers. My gaze shoots up to her face. She didn't get these from kills, did she?

"Thorns," she says without me having to ask. Not that I was going to. Or maybe I would've. I don't seem to have control when it comes to her. You don't ask about scars or wounds in this business.

"Thorns can leave scars?" I ask. I never knew plants to have a bite like that. Scars?

"Yes, if they reach tendons, they can leave scars," she says. Her eyes peer into mine. Two predators lounging at a coffee shop.

I hum in response, reluctant to let her soft, scarred hands go. Her dainty hand fits in mine, resting atop mine, and I don't have the desire to change it.

"Little Crane, why did Mother bring you in?"

"Do you have memory loss? I told you I don't know," she says, scrunching her eyebrows as if she is concerned I may actually have memory issues. It almost makes me laugh. Somewhere deep down, I wonder if she's genuinely concerned.

"You're not working for her to stop me from ruining her, are you, Little Crane?" I ask, her hand in mind as I trace my thumb over each little scar line. I watch her face, though. For any sign of a lie, an omission of truth that could ruin everything I've worked for.

Diora Moss has to pick a side now, mine or Mother's. One monster or another. Neither of us can be trusted. Neither of us are heroes in any light.

But I need to trust she's on my side for this one. I need to know she won't go running into the Jay's arms when shit hits the fan, because it always does.

"No, Elliot, I'm not. It's personal now." I raise my brows. A truth. A deep truth. It's become personal. I can't determine if that is a good thing or a bad thing.

"How is it personal?" I ask.

"It's probably the last chance I'll get to do the right thing."

Her brown eyes track the room, as if looking for a listening ear. She isn't completely trusting. That's good. That'll keep her safe. "These Strays are puppies, correct? Mrs. Jay finds her recruits as puppies, which is another tick against me, a disruption in her usual pattern," she concludes. Mother collects Strays as kids and grooms them for all her different ventures. Whether to be a killer or to be sold off, children are the easiest to manipulate. A score that hits deep in my chest.

"You're in, Diora."

I snap up, grabbing my journal and keeping her hand in mine. If she's in, then she's gotta know what all she's agreed to. "Let's go, then. We've got work to do."

"Where are we?" she asks. Her face gives nothing away as her eyes run over the studio apartment in bum fuck nowhere—also known as Downtown Litchfort.

"My lair," I chuckle. Her hand is soft in mine. I got to hold it in the silent car ride here, and I grabbed it again on our way in. I don't trust her, or know her, but I know I like her hand.

"Stop being funny," she quips. "What's this?"

"What do you think?" I ask as I sit in the desk chair in front of my four monitors. This little apartment was bought for one purpose, and that is to keep my findings on Mother's doings a secret. Once I started digging into her little side projects, I had to completely disconnect from everything she had access to.

"Okay." She bites the inside of her bottom lip as she stares at one computer screen at a time. She runs over the names, places, dates, trafficking rings I'd compiled over the last year. When I noticed I wasn't the only one Mother was abusing.

"You're new, I'll give you that, but you're not the first girl."

"No?" she asks.

"No, you're one of four. There was Sage Newman, Theresa Miken, and Cami Lovestand. Ordinary names for ordinary little girls. They've killed, but they weren't killers. Not like us."

"Little girls?" she asks as she glances over their pictures.

"Aged seven, twelve, and fourteen. All went missing three months into their training with Haven Corp. Directly under Mother's supervision."

"So, why did Mrs. Jay put me under your supervision, then?" she asks.

"You're a killer, and you're a distraction. She'll ask you what you know about my findings on her or what I'm going to do about it, eventually," I say.

"Do I tell her I know nothing? She'll see that lie coming a mile away."

"You'll give her a piece of the bone, but not the whole treat. Something to satisfy her, but not enough for her to do anything," I say.

"Where are these girls now?"

"Sold to their highest bidders," I clip, anger skimming off the skin of armor.

"What?" Her head whips toward me, and I like the attention she gives me. All mine.

"What does Mother love more than anything else?" I ask, even though Mother's desires are practically written across her forehead.

"Money? Fun?" Diora guesses. She's leaning against the desk, and seeing her in my space warms me from the inside out. I wonder if I looked in a mirror, if I would see a blush. She's so close to me. I can feel the pressure in my upper cheeks, but what does that actually look like?

"Power, Little Crane. She loves power," I say, turning toward the screens. "Alive bodies are more valuable than dead ones."

"She's trafficking kids," she says. I don't hear a note of disbelief in her voice. I don't see a drop of shock in her eyes or her posture. She lowers onto my desk chair, though. She stares at the girls' pictures and sighs. "Fuck, are we taking down a trafficking ring?"

"Yeah," I murmur. She scrunches her eyebrows, and I tilt my head toward the next screen, showing where each girl was sold and who they were sold to. I wondered if she knew. Had an inkling that something was off with Mother. By the lack of shock on her face, I questioned the strength of Mother's exterior and if her exterior only fooled me. Maybe her gut instincts are truly better than mine. Cause I didn't know. I didn't know I was walking into the arms of a disgusting beast.

"When did you figure this out?" Diora asks; she doesn't waste time. She pushes me aside to study the screens closer. Everything I've found out is spread across them, and I watch her eyes trail over each detail.

Her jasmine and raspberry scent wafts under my nose and over the skin of my cheeks as she leans forward in front of me. I'm compelled to get closer. To touch the innocent skin of her lower back mere inches from me.

I could trace my fingers over her skin. Get a taste she may never give me willingly.

I shake my head, stepping away from her. No. I can't touch. I shouldn't touch. I shouldn't have touched her in that damn meeting room or her hand at the coffee shop, and I damn sure shouldn't touch her now.

But the addiction has already started. I knew I'd get attached and yet I tried it, anyway.

Fuck.

"A year," I say. It's taken me a year to find out who these women were to Mother, where they went, and how they died.

I'm not a hero by any means, but even serial killers have their boundaries. My boundary is the skin trade. I'll take a life, but selling something I do not own is crossing a line. I hated how Mother used to touch me, and I know these people, the bidders, are doing much worse.

So much worse.

I'm not a hero. I never have been, never will be. But these trafficking rings—these rings end with me.

Diora snaps back, turning and facing me, as the questions I'm sure she has run marathons in head.

Clearing my throat, I back away from her, so she can have the space to look at whatever she wants. Stepping away from the computers, I stride to the kitchen.

It's hard not to go racing after these trafficking rings and start shooting people, but I can't rush this.

I can't risk the kids there by fucking this up.

I watch as Diora sits in my chair, deeply into the information on the screens. The more I watch her here, the more I'm sure it was the right call to bring her on.

CHAPTER 11

Elliot

Little Crane has turned into my little shadow. She didn't even complain when I called for a four a.m. training session this week.

And I've been loving it. It's only been a few days since I asked her to join me in taking down Mother's trafficking rings, and she's got a fight she hasn't shown me before.

I haven't worked on a kill with Diora yet, so today is not only a side mission with the Top Dogs, but a test to see if she can work with the strongest at Haven.

"Okay, boys and... lady... we have an assignment from Logan Lightmore. He wants his competitor Marcus Mikeson dead."

"Why?" Parker, our knives specialist, asks. But I don't know why, since Enyo is the absolute last person anyone should ever ask.

"Does it matter?" Enyo asks, shaking his head. "We are hired to kill."

I might be cold, but Enyo is heartless. My brother doesn't need a reason to take a life like the rest of us do.

His sunny personality balances his heartless nature. He was left at a fire station when he was a baby, then was in the foster system until Mother found him at sixteen.

He was here when I got here. He was the first Stray to talk to me, and we've been banded together ever since.

"Mikeson kidnapped Lightmore's daughter a few weeks ago and killed her. He wants retribution," I answer. The fire lights in the eyes of the Dogs and Diora.

I raise my eyebrows and cock my head at Enyo. "See, motivation matters, Big Bro."

"The location is a boat dock. Parker and Tom, I want you on the surrounding cliffs on watch. Roan, you're too fucking big to hide, so you're the front man today with me and Elliot. You act as our bodyguard." He runs through everyone's roles, and we all strap up with our gear, getting ready to go.

It doesn't normally take this many people to kill one fucking guy, but this is a test more than it is an assignment.

"Diora, you are playing our little lamb."

"Lamb?" she asks, scrunching her brows.

"Yes, lamb. It seems Mikeson likes his woman... unwilling. So, we'll be giving you to him in exchange for our meeting. Once the four of us are inside, the party is popping."

"Who's responsible for Mikeson's kill?" another Dog asks.

"Now, that is whoever gets the closest."

The boating dock is empty, of course. We had Parker, our knives specialist, and Tom, the gun lover, clear it out right before we arrived. Jones, Parker, and Tom all watch from various angles to ensure the targets don't leave this assignment alive.

Diora walks between Enyo and me as we near the boat where we were meeting with Marcus Mikeson. The wood beneath our feet creaks as we step across, the chilling lake air breezing past my skin.

My eyes slide to Diora, who is putting on an act, tripping over her feet and stumbling as I hold her arm captive. As our little lamb, she's supposed to be scared, trembling at the thought of what's to come.

I almost feel bad for Mikeson. After this week's training, she's no fucking lamb.

"Welcome, boys, please come in." Mikeson's voice booms, as he invites us in. He wears sunglasses indoors, and he's a balding man who is too afraid to let go of the little hair he still has.

In a tracksuit, of all things, I watch the man, hiding my disgust at the fucking sight.

This is our target?

Can he even throw a punch?

We step inside his yacht, and it's decorated as horrendously as his outfit. Red velvet covers nearly every inch of the room, and ... are those fucking Cheetah print couches?

"Thank you for meeting with us, Mr. Mikeson. Here's the girl, as promised," Enyo says, handing a "scared" Diora over to

Mikeson. I almost forget to let go of her, but I remember before Mikeson catches me.

Don't want him thinking I'm attached or something. That would sweeten the deal for him.

He'd probably try to hurt her in front of me just because I cared, by the history in his file we had collected. That thought makes my fucking blood boil. Shit. It hasn't even happened yet and I'm heated. I crack my neck, trying to relieve tension, but it doesn't help, even as I feel the pops loosing.

This is not the time to find out what I'd do if he hurt Diora.

Sighing, I take a stand across from Mikeson, keeping an eye on Diora from the corner of my eye. I trust she can handle her own. Roan enters, too, sunglasses and a suit on, as if he's a real bodyguard, standing behind Enyo and I.

"Okay, boys, so what did you want to meet for?" Mikeson asks, and I look over to Enyo, raising my eyebrows.

There are about five of Mikeson's men here, and four of us.

"We are here to deliver a message, actually," Enyo says, sliding a piece of paper from his blazer. It's all for show, of course. The paper is blank. Enyo just likes to be dramatic.

"This is for Logan Lightmore's daughter," Enyo says, grabbing his dagger from his jacket and swinging at Mikeson. He gets a snip of his arm, and Mikeson's guards are on him in the next second. Knives are always more fun than a gun.

Roan takes two guards to my right, and Enyo's on my left with two. That leaves one to me. Smiling, I take my wire saw out and whip it around flying body parts. I use one handle to swing the other end, leaving tiny but deep cuts on anyone who gets too close as I make my way toward Mikeson.

"Fucking do something, you idiot," Mikeson's voice yells out as we get closer and closer to him.

The one guard protecting Mikeson by standing in front of him finally comes close to me.

The guard lunges for me, and I dodge a few times before finally getting his hand trapped in my wire, sawing through it like fucking butter.

The clean is going to be a bitch, but the sharp slice I get is worth it. I can practically taste the clang of the metal as the swish of the wire going through his wrist sounds the room.

He screams as his hand flops on the floor, and I fly forward, not giving my opponent a moment to think before my wire is around his neck. I turn to face where Mikeson and Diora are.

I bring my handles together and back, slicing the guard's head off. As his body drops to the floor, I see Diora standing on the couch behind Mikeson. He's crying, and she looks toward me. Her hair falling in front of her face as she leans forward.

She grabs one of his shoulders and quickly brings her dagger to his neck, stabbing it clean through. She stabs until the skin of his neck meets the hilt of the knife, and this woman fucking smiles.

Her deep brown eyes shine bright as blood splatters over her face. Watching her eyes is like watching the rebirth of an angel realizing they're damned to hell ... and they're excited. Finally, feeling normal in one's skin. It's the satisfaction of finally doing what you're meant to do.

It's absolutely beautiful.

Mikeson drops dead, and so do the guards that Roan and Enyo were fighting. My Little Crane stands with a spray of Mikeson's blood on her clothes, standing like a fucking angel over his body.

That was the hottest fucking thing I've ever seen.

"Mission accomplished?" she asks, tilting her head with a victorious smile on her lips.

"Mission accomplished, Little Crane."

"Alright, we're done here, Dogs," Enyo says as he and Roan step off the yacht. I remain frozen as Diora slinks to me. Her blood-covered hands land on my chest, and I feel the heat radiating from her body.

"Good job, Crane." The words fall off my lips as if I'm in a trance, and I can't break free. Her eyes peer into mine and I'm stuck.

She pushes me to sit on the sticky couch, and I let her. She looms over me, breathing heavily as we come back down from the high of killing.

"Thank you, handsome."

"Handsome?"

"It's my nickname for you," she says, her dirty hands playing in my blond hair. "It's the first thing I thought of when I first saw you. *My* handsome boy."

Her round plump lips beg me to ruin them. To smear them with my touch and feel them under the prick of my teeth. Shit.

Her chest rises and falls faster now that she's looming over me. Maybe she's noticed how close we are. So close I could reach out and grasp her slender neck and feel her breaths in the palm of my hand.

She peers down at me through her lashes, and I feel my chest cramp with need. She could be my kiss of death and I would take the risk just to feel her lips just one time.

"Diora." Her name rumbles in my chest, and I watch as she raises an eyebrow.

"Are you gonna kiss me or not, Elliot?" Her words settle like clouds around my ears. I'm listening through the fog of my want, my desire to feel those annoyingly pouty lips on mine.

I smirk as my hand reaches for her neck, my palm lightly squeezing the side, as I pull her torturous lips to mine.

Soft. Delicate. Mine.

I lean forward, one hand caressing her neck and the other scooping her body to sit on mine. Get closer. She straddles me, my desk chair creaking at the weight of two people. Her lips never leave mine. Harsh exhales from her nose shower over my skin, and I press her lips harder. Rougher. I need more. Crave more.

Fuck.

I taste black tea and roses on her tongue. Her core grinds against mine. Her lifted skirt leaves her thin panties as a barrier between my pants and her sex, and fuck, that's not a lot of fabric. A hardening I'm all too familiar with builds in my pants. Shit. Like a damn schoolboy, I jerk as she moves.

"Calm down, cowboy," she mutters and giggles, before meeting my lips again. Her hands grip the front of my shirt, pulling me closer.

Since when does she take control? My face flushes as she curls into my body.

"Diora, please." The words slip past my lips. I can't think. I can hardly breathe with Diora this close.

I've never had urges like this. Not to this level. I've kissed other women, but this ... not this. Not this kind of desperation. An animalistic need to devour the crane in my hands.

She breaks away from me with a pop. Leaving me a heaving mess as she smiles. She presses a much more simple, quick kiss to my lips.

"Go to the Mortes Ostium ball with me," I ask. I run a hand over her hair. She doesn't move away from me, and I'm grateful.

I've never begged for a fucking thing in my life, and one taste of her lips has me desperate for more.

"The ball? As in *the* ball? Go with you? As your date?"

"Yes."

"I don't have anything to wear." She shakes her head as her eyes drift away, but I drag her gaze back to me with a hand on her jaw.

"I'll take care of it." I don't care if she wants a six million dollar dress with jewels the royals wear. I'll spend every dime I have if it means she'll make that night a little more bearable.

I'll spend everything to make her stay by my side.

Her eyes search mine. They bleed hesitation. Worry. I should be the kind of man that soothes all her worries. Encourage her, shower her with compliments, tell her how much fun it will be. How it'll be a once in a lifetime opportunity. A chance to see Paris, France. Convince her it's every woman's dream.

I don't want to do that with her. I wanted her to say yes because she truly wants to. I want her to choose me. To go to Paris *with me*. Not because I coerced her, persuaded her, convinced or manipulated her, but because she wants to.

I sit silently with her in my arms. Waiting like the patient man I never have been.

"What do I tell Juliet?" she says with a small smile. Her pretty little eyes fill with acceptance, and I chuckle.

"That there is a wedding job from Sadie's in Paris, France and she needs all hands on deck," I say, bringing her closer to me. She leans her forehead on mine, and I can't get rid of the fucking smile on my face.

"Then we're going to Paris together."

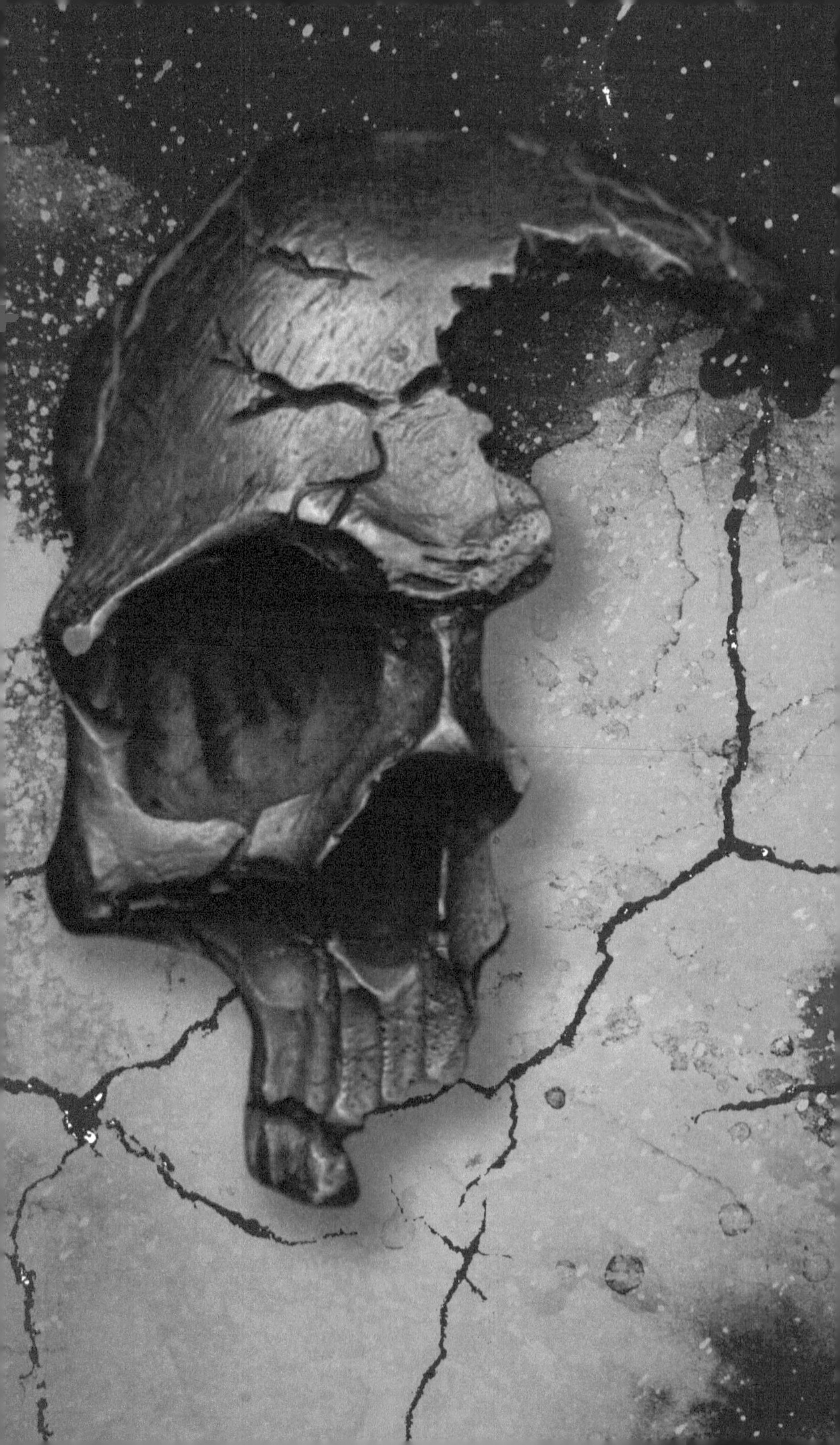

Chapter 12

Diora

He's off to Paris. He's off to Paris, leaving me with a scathing kiss. I wish it was my first kiss. Maybe then, I'd actually want to kiss people. Twisting my fingers, I walk beside Juliet. She wants to go to the city today. Something about following a new candle shop online and going to their grand opening. It will make her happy, so of course I asked if I could come, too. She lit up with joy as she twirled on her heel to go get ready.

I should've let her go on this journey alone. A chance for her to go somewhere alone for the first time since her accident, but I can't let go. A therapist would call me an enabler, because I don't let her grow apart from me, but I call it love.

We walk out of the store with three candles we would've never been able to afford before my itch started making us money.

"Thanks for coming with me, Dee." Juliet strides beside me with an undeniable smile gracing her face. "Hey, isn't that Sadie's Flower shop, where you work? We should go in."

My head whips to the little shop on the corner. The supposed place I work at. Sadie's doesn't have lights or a huge sign. A little shop, on a discreet corner, where the Society can run supplies to and from their members. I look over at Juliet's wide eyes and widening smile.

Sadie's huge front doors face the round sidewalk of the corner. Huge pink doors and white weathered brick with vines and all sorts of greenage growing on its walls. A small wooden sign above the doors lets you know you're at Sadie's, and how Juliet spotted that from here makes me question the girl's real motive for coming down here today?

Was it really the candle shop or did she want to see where I work? Thank goddess I came, if the latter is the real reason she wanted to visit the city.

"Not a good idea," I say. I grab her arm to steer her in a different direction. Any direction besides the one leading to a place where serial killers get their supplies.

"What, why?" she asks, dragging me toward Sadie's.

"No, really Juliet, they must be busy with that wedding coming up," I say, trying to use the excuse Elliot gave me to convince her to leave the idea alone. It doesn't work, of course, and I hear the bell ring above us as we step inside. Huge checkered, black-and-white flooring greets us, with green potted plants lining the way throughout the store. Rows and rows of potted plants make up the majority of Sadie's, moving through the space like a guided maze. A wooden checkout area, an area of wind chimes, yard decorations, and a stand for local handmade crafts makes up the rest of the flower shop.

Looking around, Juliet's smile softens. "So, this is where you spend most of your time now?" she questions, and I think the words are more for herself than for me, based on how low her voice is.

"Yeah, it's a nice gig and pays better than the grocery store," I say, following behind her and watching our surroundings. I don't feel fear often, but I don't know what kind of threats there could be here for us. A serial killer hub is the last place I'd want Juliet to be in.

Footsteps I don't recognize come closer, raising the hairs on my arms as I grasp Juliet's shoulder, ready to yank her behind me.

"Well, hello, ladies." Enyo appears from around the corner of this maze of plants. The moment he steps in front of us, Juliet is already behind me, and I have one hand around a potted plant to shove on the ground in case I need to buy time.

"Oh, do you know him, Dee?"

"Dee? Well, Diora, I don't recall you telling us you had any nicknames?" he says, like we're actually close. We've had like two conversations and assignments together, but that's it.

Not that what he does is any of my business, but the way his eyes don't leave my older sister most definitely makes it my business.

"No, I don't know him," I say, glaring at Enyo. The man has given me no reason to like him, to trust or know him, and yet here he is, talking like he knows me.

"Is that any way to speak to your boss?" he says, moving his hand to hold his "wounded" heart.

"Oh, this is your boss? I thought you said your boss was a woman?" Juliet says, side-eyeing me.

"More like my manager who is never here," I snip, watching his face drop as my smile grows. I turn around to lead Juliet out of the store, but I feel the asshole resting his heavy ass arm over my head, like I'm a pole he can rest against or something.

He moves to talk to my sister. I could jab him in the side and break for it, as I know I'm not strong enough to fight him, but Juliet would lag behind. She'd probably be trying to see if the bastard was okay instead of running.

"I'm here enough. So, who are you, little darling?" Oh, hell no. I glare harder into his side profile.

"I'm Juliet, Dee's older sister." She nods her head toward me and blushes. The girl blushes. Juliet Moss is blushing at a serial killer worse than the one she unknowingly lives with.

Is she serious? She never blushes. I've never seen her blush, not even before... Not even before. I watch her now. I watch her eyes. They stay trained on him. Her pupils look as if they are larger than normal, just by the slightest bit. Warmer. Inviting. Juliet, do you even know who you're making googly eyes at? Would she care?

"I'm sure you're busy. I mean, a wedding in Paris is a big deal," Juliet says with a shy giggle. A blush and a giggle? I should get her out of here. I want to yank her away, but I can't get myself to destroy this tiny, tiny moment of happiness for her. Juliet is flirting.

I never thought she'd ever feel safe enough to flirt again.

"If you're taking my sister away from me for our ritual Friday night sleepover, I'd hope it's for work?" And her yip is back. I smile as I look up at Enyo, trying to see past his armpit to his gaze at her little snapback. I shouldn't encourage her to provoke a serial killer, but by the look on Enyo's face, I doubt I have much to worry about.

"Oh, the wedding in Paris? How interesting, I wasn't informed... First years don't normally go to such jobs," Enyo says with an eyebrow raised and a smile too wide for my liking.

"Yeah, well, I am," I say, narrowing my eyes at him.

"Well, Juliet, I'm saddened to be taking your sister away from you on Friday night, but rest assured, you don't have to be alone. I'm not going to Paris."

Yes, yes, she does need to be alone.

"I didn't realize that the *wedding* was... optional?" I ask with scrunched eyebrows. He's a member of the Society. He has the ring, but he's not going to the ball?

"I have other things to look after."

Is the "other things" my sister? I scrunch my brows as I look between the two. Did Elliot put him up to this? He did say that Juliet would be protected. Is this what he meant?

"Ahh, well, thank you." Juliet can hardly get words out as her face turns a deep beet red. She attempts to fan herself as she turns away from Enyo.

"Too bad I'm sure you're working, Enyo. They'll need someone to work the store." My voice comes out monotone as the games are now over. I grab Juliet's arm, letting Enyo's heavy arm drop back to his side.

"Hmm, well, since I'm hardly here, I won't be working at the shop. Juliet, phone, please," he says.

I watch as she mindlessly gives the stranger her phone, who either takes her number or types his in. I step in front of Juliet, blocking her view of Enyo, before settling a small potted tulip in her hands.

"Could you pay for this while I speak to my manager?" I ask, gently push her away.

"Don't play games, Enyo. You may be first Son, but if you do anything—"

"Is it wise to threaten a Son, Diora?" He raises an eyebrow, and my skin starts to boil as frustration fills the void of my emotions.

"If you do anything to Juliet—" I say, but he cuts me off. "I won't. Elliot asked me to look after her. That's all I'm doing."

"She's not normal..." I sputter, trying to find the right words. Juliet's damage isn't permanent. It isn't like mine. She can get better. She will get better.

"Must run in the family," he quips, and I glare at the man three heads taller than me.

"Enyo, I'm serious. She doesn't... She hasn't healed yet, and if you do anything to make that worse—"

"I won't, Diora. I won't hurt her, ever. I'm going to have to ask you to do the same for my brother." I scrunch my face as he talks, and his smile drops as the conversation gets serious for him.

"Elliot is strong, but he's been hurt so many times, and trust I'll stop you before you have the chance to hurt him. Trust I'll risk ruining my relationship with Elliot for the sake of protecting him."

"Then we're on the same page," I say. I'm huffing like I've run a marathon and my brain is beyond scrambled, but for once, I can say I see Enyo Jay. I can see his little family of two *means something* to him, as mine does to me.

"Then we're on the same page," he confirms.

Chapter 13

Diora

I didn't think a kiss would get me invited to the most esteemed ball of the serial killer world. I never thought I'd be flying to Paris only a week later.

My lips tingle as I recall the way he pressed his lips against mine. Elliot is an intelligent man, a studier, a practicer. When he kisses me, it's like I'm one of his subjects he's memorizing. It's... it's lovely.

My gaze settles outside the window of the private plane. The white seats are pristine, and full, soft leather greets my skin. I am more than pleased with the accommodations and less pleased with the company I must share it with.

Elliot and I still have a part to play. Regardless of where my alliance stands, Mrs. Jay has to think everything is going according to her plan. Whatever that may be.

Paris is supposed to be hot in June, but this plane is at a temperature set below freezing. I pull the sleeves of my soft sweater over my hands as I slouch in my seat, turning my gaze from the clouds we're above to the book in my hands.

"Diora, darling, how is your first plane ride going?" My eyes shoot to Mrs. Jay, who wears a light pink tweed suit and a smile that disguises the devil within her nearly perfectly. I watch the woman who took me under her wing. Whether through blackmail or bluff, she got me. Honestly, she probably wouldn't have needed the blackmail to get me to follow her. A weak-minded little girl is all I am in her eyes. A truth I couldn't deny, not face on, not deep down. I left myself the perfect target.

"Good," I say shortly, keeping my eyes on her. I see the pocket knife peeking from her jacket and the white gloves slipping from her skirt pocket. There was no TSA to try to take that knife away from her. I guess that's a benefit of flying private.

I tilt my head in wonder, though. She normally has the two switched. She never puts her gloves in her skirt pocket, so why today?

One object requires easy access, one doesn't, so what makes this trip to Paris different?

"Nice, darling, since this is your first event with the society, we must clear up a few house rules," she says, smoothing her hands down her skirt before delicately crossing her legs. "The Society has a lot of rules regarding their events. This ball, in particular, is important. If you don't follow the rules, you are killed immediately. Do you understand?"

I remain silent as I stare at her. I nod my head a singular time which has her releasing a breath. I've never seen her this way. She goes on to talk about the absolute no killing each other rule for the ball and the mask requirement. Then the suggestion of making no kills while we're in Paris. She goes on and on as I stare at her, nodding when I'm supposed to.

"So, now that is out of the way, I'm glad you and I have a moment to discuss something that's been boggling my mind," she says, and my skin lights with nerves. The one woman who has truly been able to scare me is her. Hairs on my arms stand, but thankfully, she won't be able to tell, since I have a long-sleeve on. I raise a brow, and she takes that as her confirmation to keep going.

"How is the training with Elliot going?" I scrunch my brows and frown. I wasn't expecting her to ask that.

"I was not asking the air; I'm looking for an answer," she snips, and my head snaps back to her.

I set my book down in the plush seat next to me and sit up. Pressing my hands into my knees, I look at Mrs. Jay, tilting my head in thought.

"He hasn't taught me much, honestly. Not yet, anyway," I lie. We've been training every morning for about a week, and I'm surprised she doesn't know that.

"Ahh, well, we don't rush our teachings here anymore. It doesn't always produce the results we want," she says, picking up her tumbler of hot tea and sipping it.

"He's yet to take on a one-on-one trainee. Most people are the softest with their first."

"Soft?"

"Well, yes, failure is acceptable now. We don't want to push too much, go too far and such," she says, as if the information is obvious. "I need my Strays to snap—that's what makes a good killer—but I can't have my Strays snapping and killing themselves."

I hold my face perfectly still, but the training here is so hard people are killing themselves? I mean, I guess it makes sense that the only way out of a hitman organization is death.

"Who was the first Stray you trained?" I ask.

"Elliot."

"Were you soft on him?" I ask, even though I already know the answer.

"I'm not most people, darling. I was the hardest on him."

"Yet, he's not the first Son?"

"Having the hardest training doesn't make you the best." Nor the most loyal, I think, but keep that bit to myself. "I recruited Enyo first, but didn't start training him until after I got started with Elliot. I didn't want to break Enyo too quickly."

She talks about them like dogs, and it makes my skin crawl. I guess that's what the name Strays comes from, but... they aren't dogs.

"Tell me, why did he invite you as his date to the ball?" she asks. I should've known this question was coming. I sigh and lean back into my chair. Still, I keep my eye contact with her, not wanting to give any indication I'm lying.

"It's part of my training," I say as I watch the emotion change on her face. It moved so fast that, if I wasn't already staring at her, I would've missed it. The quick down-turn of her lip and narrowing of her eyes almost seem too obvious as I stare at her.

I wonder if she wants me to know she doesn't like my answer. Still, she fixes her face and smiles as she looks at me.

"What exactly are you supposed to learn from attending the ball?"

"What it's like being at the top. He said this will signify the start of my training. Once I see what it's like at the top, I will have to train like hell to make it here on my own." The words flow like they're mine. I watch as she eats up every word. He knows her more than she may like to know.

"And continue to train to stay at the top. Hmm. I did the same thing with him, you know. Maybe he takes after me more than I thought," she says.

"Maybe," I say, watching as she also leans back. I let a part of me slip. The me Mrs. Jay knew before I met Elliot. I watch as she takes another sip of her drink.

"Why are your gloves and pocket knife switched?"

"My observant little girl." She laughs, a genuine laugh. A laugh I would think a grandmother could have with their grandchild curled in their lap. A laugh I would have no idea existed if I hadn't watched cartoons growing up.

It startles me. I almost jump in my chair. Still, I wait for an answer.

"It's to show I'm not a threat to the Society. No inkling that I'm here to cause trouble. A simple technique to show I'm here for a fun weekend." She laughs some more, and I can't tell if she's telling the truth.

A stewardess comes into the main cabin—I think it's called—of the plane to let us know the plane will be landing in Paris. I slide my seatbelt on and watch the clouds go by us as we land in Paris, France. Alive and unscathed. Let's see if we'll leave that way.

Chapter 14

Diora

Sitting on a fourteen-hour flight isn't a comfortable experience, but sitting on a fourteen-hour flight across from a child trafficker is a hell I don't wish to experience again.

The itch, the craving, for the light to die in her eyes is strong. From the tips of my fingers to my forearms, I crave to satisfy the urge to attack. To plant, deceive, kill the woman in the tweed suit sitting across from me.

But I resist. I resist because I know when there is a fight I can't win. I resist, because Elliot still calls her Mother. Regardless of the relationship struggles between the two, there is still a motherly feeling there, and I can't risk Elliot.

I could slip some poison into her drink and call it a day. But she's too smart for that. She hasn't let me close to her drinks since I started training under her. Only if she's watching me does she let me near her drinks or food.

It kills me to know there is a chance I won't be able to kill Mrs. Jay.

Getting off the plane and to the hotel, I follow Mrs. Jay playing the dutiful puppy. If the hotel looks like this, I can only imagine what the venue is going to look like. Golden arches with gods painted into the moldings, ruby red rugs, and matching decor decorate the hotel's lobby. My eyes wander around, looking at all the people, the French language coming from all angles of the room. I've never experienced such a different life. I've never left Litchfort, couldn't afford to, so Paris is... Paris is completely different. I've yet to feel such awe toward anything quite like being in a different country.

Standing in the lobby, we wait for Elliot, who has already checked us in and needs to give us our key cards. At two p.m. sharp, he walks through the doors of the lobby. The wind pushing his loose shirt tight against his front and his hair blowing away from his face. All reminding me of the beauty I find in him. Where my attraction for him started and how I yearn for more. I hold back my smile at seeing him again as he approaches us, holding two keycards in his hands like playing cards.

"Hello, ladies," he says. He leans to give Mrs. Jay a kiss on her cheek, but his eyes stay on me. The serial killer winks at me, and I tilt my head, feeling a flush over my cheeks and neck. The decorations of the fancy hotel fade as my full attention is on him. He moves away from Mrs. Jay and waves toward someone behind me.

"Elliot, darling, how nice of you to show up," Mrs. Jays says, even though we've only been standing here for maybe three minutes. I watch as he raises his brows but leaves the comment unanswered as he turns to greet the bellhop, who is loading our luggage onto the gold rack on wheels. "Boys," Mrs. Jay mutters as she rolls her eyes.

"I'll take you to your rooms. We're on the eighth floor," Elliot informs us. The news instantly puts a frown on Mrs. Jay's face.

"Why not the tenth? Why did you book us for the eighth?" she asks, scrunching her brows.

"Air conditioning is best on the eighth floor," Elliot says as our little party walks toward the elevators. I can practically see Elliot's frustration, as if it were steam coming off of him. His body language remains neutral, too neutral, and that's his tell.

Silent as ever, I follow the pair and bellhop into the small elevator. The bellhop enters first with the rack, and I follow suit, with Mrs. Jay standing next to me. Elliot is last, and he tells the man who stays in the elevator the floor number. I'm not sure of the formal title of this position, since I've never been in a hotel this nice before.

Paris isn't known for air conditioning. That is one of the first things that any search on the city will tell you. This elevator must be one of the places they cut back on. I feel the sweat building around my hairline and neck. Swallowing my spit, I release a slow breath so as not to bring attention to myself. Mrs. Jay looks completely fine in her tweed jacket, and for a moment, I'm envious.

The sweat makes me feel dirty. Too dirty to be in a place like this, surrounded by people who apparently don't sweat. I'm out of place, and yet I see his hand out of the corner of my eye.

Elliot hasn't outwardly acknowledged me since seeing me, but I know that's part of the plan. We needed to hold off Mrs. Jay thinking we're getting too close for as long as possible. Elliot says, once that happens, either one of two things will happen: one is, she will assign me to someone else, probably under her, which could lead to me being sold into her trafficking ring.

This would only happen if I don't figure out how to overpower her. The second option is, she simply kills me, and that would be her favorable option, with my skill set right now. I wouldn't win that fight.

Still, I see his pinky finger move toward me. He sees me. I can't help the twitch in my lips. I cough, covering my lips with an elbow, moving as if the cough rocked my body forward. And I brush my opposite hand with his. His pinky hooks on to mine for the quickest moment. Enough for my smile to break through my face and the warmth I'm craving to spread throughout my body.

My lips tingle at the contact, the memory of me in his lap and our lips crashing together playing through my mind as we ride the elevator. Is this what a crush feels like? A craving for someone's presence? A carnal need to feel.

I haven't. I've never experienced an emotion quite like this. It's similar to the feeling of holding life and death in my hands, but not quite the same. I don't want this to end in death.

I want this to end after a lifetime together. A chance to experience sitting in rocking chairs on the porch when we get too old to worry about the small stuff, a dream where grandkids run ragged in the yards.

Juliet's always talked about this kind of emotion, but I've never thought I'd experience it. I didn't think I was hard-wired that way. Maybe I'm more like Juliet than I thought.

Too bad serial killers don't get happy endings.

The elevator dings, and we file out of the velvet red room and into a matching hallway, a single huge window, with a beautiful gold frame, at the opposing end.

Mother's room is directly in the middle, and she waits for Elliot to open her door. He does, and she quite literally dances into the room as if she was waltzing with a lover.

The white baby grand piano glistens under the afternoon daylight. The shiny floors, velvet couches, and crown moldings decorate the room that's bigger than my apartment back home.

Looking back at Elliot, who still stands by the open door as the bellhop unloads her bags, I raise both my eyebrows.

He shakes his head and smiles, walking past me to give Mrs. Jay her key. "I'm sure you need some rest, Mother." He walks out of the room, brushing my arm along the way.

I try not to react. I simply follow behind Elliot. Walking out of Mrs. Jay's room, the bellhop stands by the rack where my one suitcase is.

"I'll take it from here," Elliot says, and grabs my suitcase. The bellhop only smiles and nods before disappearing to one set of elevators. I look back to Elliot, who is already walking to a different set of elevators.

"What floor am I on?" I ask as we step back inside.

"We're on the sixth floor," he says and nods to the... elevator man? This time, Elliot doesn't settle for my pinky; he takes my whole hand.

"We?" I ask.

"Have separate rooms," he answers, stopping between two doors. He chuckles and looks down at me. Golden brown eyes meet mine, and they gleam. If I didn't know better, I'd say Elliot Jay is happy. He is either happy or hiding something. Maybe both? "Interconnected."

I can't help the giggle I let out. Sliding my hand from his, I snatch the keycard from his other hand and go into my room. I've never stayed in a hotel, let alone one as cool as to have interconnected rooms. What kids' movie did I just jump into?

A giddy feeling rises up inside and makes all my limbs feel light as I swing open the door between our rooms. He's already there, on the other side of the door, waiting for me. I scream in delight, a sound I haven't heard in years, and laugh as he swoops me up and drops me on my bed.

"Diora, Diora, Diora." He beams, turning away from me and grabbing something that is already on my dresser. That must have gotten here before I got here. I looked at him with a questionable brow. He turns around with a sleek black box. It almost looks like a sheet cake box. Except there is no plastic see through top, and the box is most definitely heavier than a sheet cake.

"What is this?" I ask, as I gingerly take the box from his hands. My hands shake, and I can't quite calm down as fast as I'd like. I watch his face more than I look at the box. His face turns red, a red even his golden skin can't hide. He bites his lip as he watches the box in my hands instead of my face. Is *the* Elliot Jay nervous?

"Open it, Little Crane."

I take another look at the box. It's not like I've never gotten a gift before. Juliet has given me plenty. She always gets me gifts for my birthday and Christmas. But this is weird. I feel ashamed of my excitement at what could be in the box. My cheeks flush and a smile so damn big my face hurts. With my head down, I try to hide my face, but his fingers on my jaw forces me to look at him.

"Elliot," I say, but I don't even know what to say. I can hardly hold the box in my shaking hands. I try to breathe, smile, breathe, stop smiling.

Come on, breath, Dee. Breathe, Dee.

I swallow hard, and he kneels in front of me. His smile dampens, and I hate myself even more. "I know, Little Crane. I know."

I breathe out as his words register in my ears. "We don't get to experience the act of receiving gifts like others do. I didn't get or give my first gift until I met Enyo. The nerves I had receiving my first gift nearly made me faint," he softly says with a chuckle. His hands weigh heavily over mine, grounding me.

"I get gifts from Juliet—" I try to excuse, but he shakes his head.

"Not the same," he says with a light smile on his face. It's odd, all the smiles he has. "Let's open it together."

His hands guide mine, moving over the top of the box and lifting the lid. A soft pop and the box is open in my lap, the lid released from the bottom, and Elliot takes it from my hands. Black matte fabric is folded in the box, and my mind brings me back to his apartment in Litchfort. When we kissed, he invited me to the ball.

"You bought me a dress?" I whisper as my hands lift the dress from the box. It slowly unfolds and the most beautiful thing I will probably ever wear unravels before me. It is a strapless dress, with a v-shaped neckline attached to a corset and a beautiful flowy skirt.

"I said I'd take care of everything if you came with me, Little Crane," Elliot says. I feel his eyes searching my face, and this is when my hands finally stop shaking. I put the dress down in my lap, and there he is.

My golden serial killer.

"Thank you," I say, reaching my hand to his cheek and drawing him closer.

"Thank God," he mumbles, bringing his lips to mine. I pull away and smile.

"Thank you." I kiss his nose. "Thank you." I kiss his cheek. "Thank you." I kiss his forehead and he swallows me up.

Launching toward me, lying on the bed, over me, kissing me furiously.

"I was so fucking nervous," he mumbles, and I chuckle. I like this side of Elliot. He isn't the big, bad, suave serial killer. He's the shy, nervous ball of energy that I want to consume.

"It's beautiful," I say, wanting to soothe his worries. Want is such a fickle feeling. A desire to do something outside of my selfish urges. Elliot is the only other person I've wanted to care for. It's odd to feel my circle growing, but I'm... I'm not mad at it.

"Elliot," I say, as he lays his head over my chest. My heart pounds and he wraps his arms tight around my body. The dress lies on the bed beside us, and I know I should hang it up so it'll be ready for tonight, but I don't want to move.

"My heart is racing, too, Little Crane."

I stare at him. His head is turned to the side as he cuddles me. Dangerous killers attending a ball in Paris, cuddling in their hotel room. I scoff at the thought. My hands lay over his shoulders, on his back, and we stay like this. I sigh, trying to breathe normally as if I'm not scared of this, of us, of everything with Mrs. Jay and Juliet.

It's just us here. Hiding from the big bad wolf two floors up.

She's gonna find out. She may even kill me for being with Elliot. As much as I'd hate to leave Juliet alone in this world, this moment, cuddling with Elliot Jay, is worth tempting the wolf.

"Do we still have to go to the ball?" I mutter, tracing mindless shapes on his back with my fingers.

"If we don't go, that would tip Mrs. Jay off, and we're not quite ready for that. Plus, I think the Society would be pissed if their host didn't show up."

I hum in response. He's right, of course. But it would be nice to say fuck it and stay here. This one time.

"Plus, this weekend will be fun, Little Crane. I promise."

Chapter 15

Diora

This isn't remotely what I thought I was getting into when Elliot asked me to the Mortes Ostium Annual Ball. The Society truly doesn't hold back. When they say they are putting on a ball, they truly mean a ball.

The natural history museum is drop dead gorgeous. We walk up the black carpet to the double doors, welcoming us to the event. I walk behind Mrs. Jay and Elliot as we grace the entryway. This ball's theme is black, so we dressed strictly following the theme color. My dress swings as I move, like a princess's would. I feel beautiful. My pointed heels click along the walkway, like my mom's did when I was a kid and she'd just come home from work.

I smile as I follow the two. Elliot slows his pace, sliding his hand in mine as we walk the black carpet. We flash our membership rings, mine still dangling off my pearl necklace, as we walk pass the security at the door.

"Remember, we're being watched at all times, so act accordingly," Mrs. Jay snips. I've never seen Mrs. Jay nervous. Not like this. She has a chilling excitement in her posture and the expression on her face. A forced smile with bright eyes. It's the strangest combination.

"Today is the dinner and dance, tomorrow starts the workshops and event, alongside another optional dinner, and Sunday has one last workshop with a brunch, closing the ball weekend. How exciting is this?" Mrs. Jay gushes over the itinerary as we glide through the doors. Sales booths line the hallways of the museum as we make our way to the ballroom, where this grand ball is held.

Stepping into the ballroom is like stepping into an enchanted world. My breath is stolen as my eyes gaze around the room.

The room is lit by candles absolutely everywhere. The antler chandeliers have candles on them. Black heavy tablecloths dress each table and centerpieces with matte black candlesticks and rust red and purple roses decorate the tables. It's a stunning sight and quite fitting for the kind of attendees this ball has tonight.

Everyone is dressed in black tie attire, and it makes me more thankful for the dress Elliot bought me. I wouldn't have been able to afford something of this caliber. Everyone has matching masks to their outfits that hide their faces.

So, even if I saw someone I knew, I wouldn't know that I knew them.

It's odd to look around the room and know that everyone here has killed someone. Even more so to know it wasn't accidentally, or because it was self defense, no, everyone here kills for the... thrill, maybe the joy, of killing and to see so many people here it makes my heart feel a little less, a little less lonely.

Elliot doesn't let go of my hand as he leads our little group to our assigned table. Old tan cobblestone walls and archways that a fair maiden would like to be kissed under make up the structure of this room. There are long tables in front of a stage, which our table is close to. I look over to Elliot, tonight's host, who pulls out my chair and pushes me in before doing the same for Mrs. Jay. He stands between our chairs, leaning against mine, and I can feel my flush. I hope my skin hides the coloring I feel taking over.

This is the first event I don't have Juliet to help me get ready, or be my social shield, taking over conversations and social normalities for me. Straightening my shoulders, the loose curls I left out of my updo fall over my shoulders.

But I have Elliot, who smiles and shakes hands with the members who come up to greet him. He laughs when he is supposed to, nods his head, interacts. He appears normal. It comes naturally to him.

I should feel the need to stand by his side, at least do the smiling and nodding with him, but he stops me with a glance and slight shake of his head that I barely notice. Keeping a hand on my shoulder to keep me sitting, he lightly traces the outline of something, animals, maybe birds. The touch is soothing, relaxing for me, and I am internally warm at the gesture. He doesn't look at me, though, almost like he's mindlessly doing it. It's cute.

As the guests flood in and take their seats, Elliot leans down and whispers, "It's time for my speech. Kiss my cheek for good luck."

"Mrs. Jay is right there," I whisper. She is sitting on the left side of Elliot. She's engrossed in a conversation with one of our tablemates.

"Quick, before she notices," he whispers. His eyes tell me he's not going to let me out of this one, even if Mrs. Jay was looking directly at us. I'm confused. Did he forget the precautions we have to take, or does he simply not care anymore? Is Paris a safe zone of some sort.

"Little Crane." He drags out the nickname, and I finally give in. I give him the fastest peck ever, my lips meeting the soft skin of his cheek and I catch the corner of his lips.

"Happy?" I ask, trying to calm my racing heartbeat.

"Very," he says as he walks toward the stage. I watch his back and I wonder if my lip gloss stained his cheek.

I scoff to myself as he walks on stage, looking like the dangerous socialite of the evening. His tight vest and button down add to his appeal, and gosh, it was a good call. I've always been drawn to the attractiveness of Elliot Jay, but the man dressed up, I could stare for hours and not get my fill.

He nods under the stage lights and taps the mic three times before starting his speech. "Welcome to Mortes Ostium's Annual Ball."

The audience claps, and he waits to continue his speech. He keeps his gaze moving over the crowd, and it's electric to watch him stand up there.

"Each of you has made eight kills this year, which has earned you an invitation to this weekend's festivities. With about one hundred of us here, that's at least eight hundred cold bodies, six feet underground, either literally or metaphorically. That means nearly one thousand successful kills made this night possible. How fucking fantastic."

That many people? I look around the room, at the various types of people here. I'm only here as a date and didn't complete my eight kills, but most people here did. Dead bodies made this night happen. Caving into our deepest darkest urges rewarded us with a beautiful weekend in Paris instead of a lifetime jail sentence. How ironic.

"While we may have killed for this night, keep in mind this isn't a free-for-all. This ball is for us special folk to have a night where we can enjoy our true, authentic selves. It is a time for our darkest desires to be celebrated, not acted on. No killing tonight.

"The Society has rented out the Musee de la Chasse et de la Nature, a beautiful natural museum with plenty of historic exhibits that are irreplaceable. That said, don't break jack shit. You will not be able to use your Society issued get-out-of-jail card this weekend, so, you break it, you buy it.

"Now, I wouldn't be walking off this stage alive tonight without giving a huge thank you to our society leaders, the lifeblood of Mortes Ostium, for this annual tradition.

"We have many events and workshops taking place this weekend, so please take advantage of every opportunity here, all provided for us by the Society.

"Have fun, but more importantly, behave. The Society is watching." Elliot smiles one last time as the audience claps before making his way off the stage and back to me. Waiters flood the room with trays of our appetizers, but my eyes are stuck on him.

His gaze darts to me. His sole focus is on me, and I almost crave the pressure. The attention is addicting. He aims straight for me before I watch hands of congratulations latch onto him. I smirk as his attention is drawn away and his smile drops. The ever-so-polite gentleman Elliot Jay can be.

I turn back to my chair as the waiter drops a plate of salad in front of me and I watch as Mrs. Jay picks up the tiniest fork for her salad. Mimicking her, I pick up the smallest fork I have laying in my place mat and take a slow bite of my salad.

"What a wonderful speech, dear," Mrs. Jay says as Elliot sits in his chair between us. The table congratulates him and he nods in thanks.

He turns to me, his entire body facing me and his back to Mrs. Jay, whose face is all but happy about it.

"Elliot," I mutter as he places a hand on my thigh.

"How'd I look?"

"I know nothing about speeches—"

"How did I look, Little Crane?" he asks again, leaning closer and taking up much of my personal space. It heightens my senses as he invades my space and I swallow down another bite.

He wants my approval. *My* approval. How adorable. I flush again under the attention he has put me at the table. Thankfully, no one is paying attention beside Mother, whose hard stare is pressing into his back.

"Incredibly... alluring, Mr. Jay," I say. 'Now, eat, please."

"Anything you say, Little Crane," he says. He quickly pecks my cheek before sitting correctly in his chair and digging into his salad.

I sigh in relief as Mrs. Jay wraps him up in a conversation about Haven Corp.

This was going to be a long weekend.

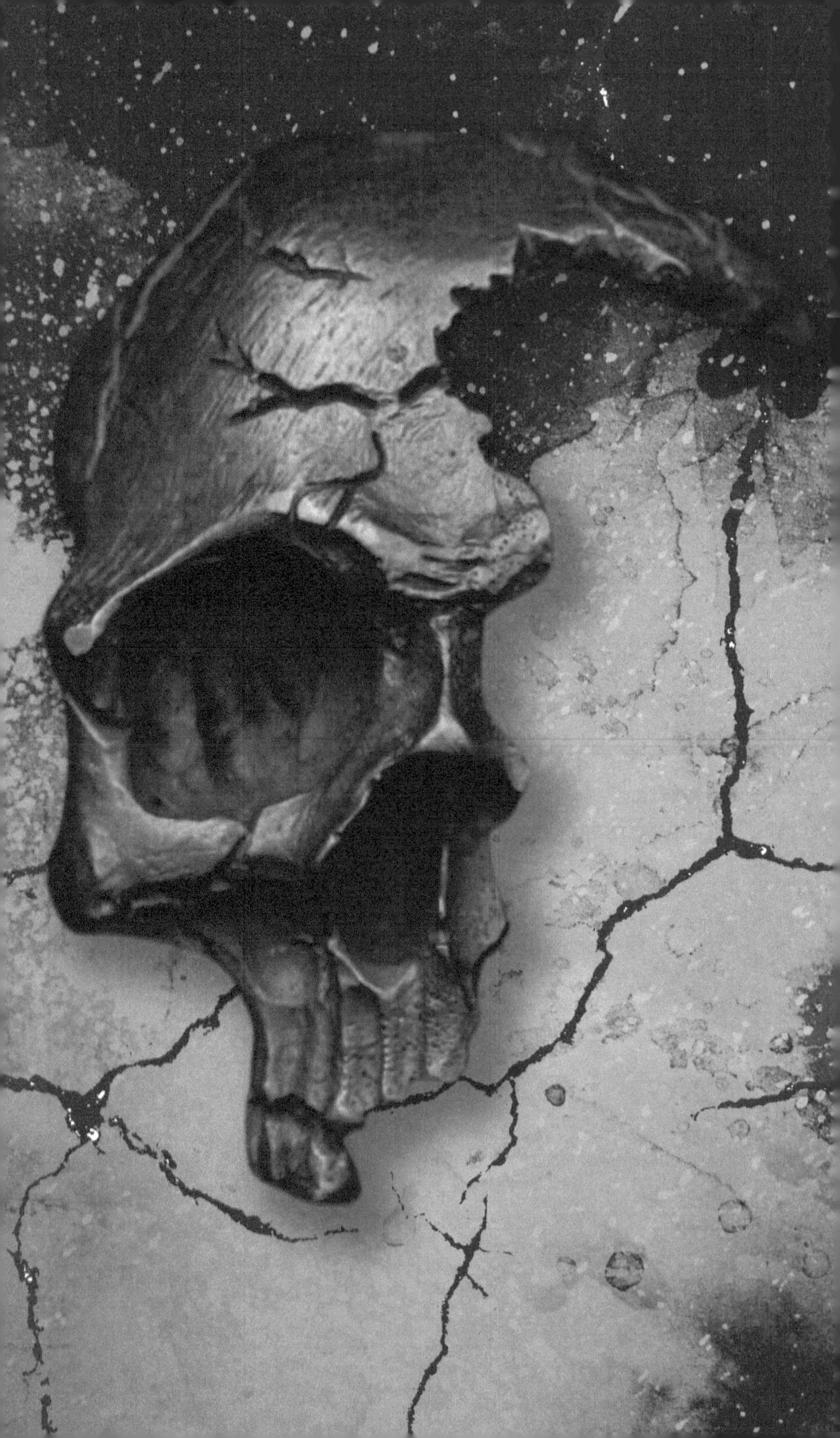

CHAPTER 16
Elliot

I love Litchfort, Michigan. It has become more than a base for me. It is home, but I never thought I'd see the day I would miss being in Litchfort. When I left a few days before to help prepare for the ball, I thought the uneasy gut reaction to my every step away was because I didn't want to leave my home.

Until the first day of the ball, when I noticed my gut reaction wasn't because I was leaving my home, but because I didn't want to leave Diora. Not just because I was leaving her with the devil incarnate, but because I missed her presence. I missed seeing her skin, the feel of her lips. I missed it. Craved it.

I got that same reaction dropping Diora off to her room last night. Walking steps away from the pull toward her was astonishing, and I couldn't wait for morning again, just so I could see her.

I had to wait all damn day to see my Little Crane again. My hosting duties for the ball only contained helping out in preparations and doing the introduction speech so the rest of the weekend is all mine.

Or so I thought. I mindlessly forgot about the third guest to our party, Mother, who would want to be up my ass the entire fucking time I'm here. Like I'm twelve again instead of twenty-six. I try not to set the damn woman off. I try to be peaceful, but the more I learn about the damn trafficking ring she runs and the more time I spend with Diora, the closer I get to saying fuck it.

We're in the Musee De La Nature again. Mother, Diora, and I dressed much more casually than last night. I'm back in my khakis and t-shirt, Diora is in a short pink dress that barely covers her ass, and Mother is in a dress suit, without her usual tweed jacket.

We spend time at each event that runs the length of the day. A few hours at the ax throwing event and a few hours at the gambling event. Watching the clock, I pull Diora to me as I lean down to whisper in her ear. "We're gonna leave her here."

"Won't she get pissed?" she asks, her deep brown eyes peering up at me as I slowly walk away from the gambling table where Mother sits.

"I've got something more exciting than watching her gamble all night," I say and lead Diora to the prehistoric human section of the museum. This is where the hunting and stalking event will take place today.

"Oh, hunting? I'm not much of a hunter, Elliot," she says, pulling on my arm to stop us, but I shake my head, a laugh escaping me.

"Good thing you're the prey then," I say, and a smile breaks along her face.

"Oh, is that so?" She laughs, too, and the sound strikes lightning in my heart. A sound I want to hear again and again from my Little Crane.

"Whether you decide to partner up amongst yourself or target one of our animals up here is up to you. We will release these animals, and whoever is decidedly prey, into the arena, and after fifteen minutes, the hunt will begin. Please keep in mind not to break any of the artwork within the museum and to stay in our arena," our instructor, a professional in our field, says as her eyes light up with excitement.

I'm sure my eyes are lit, too. As are Diora's. The hunt is an alluring mix of hot seduction for probably everyone here. It lights a fire under my skin. My Little Crane is going to be my little prey for the next hour and a half, and I can't wait to trap her wings in my hands.

My hand grips her thigh as the instructor goes on. I should be paying attention to the lesson, but all I can comprehend is the thrum of my heartbeat in my ears and Diora's jittery thigh under my hand.

Each workshop comes with a lesson in this classroom-looking room within the museum, and eventually, we'll get to the application part of the workshop. It's meant to be honing our skills, but all I think about is getting under her skin.

There are rows of desks fit for two people, like in science class, and my Little Crane sits with me.

She listens attentively, like the good little bird she is. She doesn't take notes, but I see her mind running.

Too bad she won't be using the knowledge she's learning in this lesson today.

Today, she is my prey. My chance to get a taste of that delicately soft brown skin. A chance to chase my prize in a place she'll feel safe. A place where I can test the waters and see how far she'll let me go.

Diora Moss is but a crane, and I am her golden eagle. One of the few predators of the crane, the eagle is one of the few large birds that a crane would have trouble escaping.

Leaning down, I get a whiff of her jasmine and raspberry scent, inhaling as much as I can before I have to breathe again.

"You can sniff me all you want, but you won't be able to track me by scent," Diora says with a smirk. She doesn't give me the pleasure of her eyes on me or her full attention, but I'll take the smile that I can get.

"I don't know, Little Crane, maybe I can, or maybe you wore this little pink number to help me find you."

"If I realized that I'd be running, I wouldn't have worn such a dress."

"So, why did you?" I ask, turning to face my bird. "I think you wanted to be chased, whether in this workshop or throughout this museum. I think you wanted me salivating after you, Little Crane."

"I guess you'll never find out," she says shortly.

"Oh, but I think I will," I say, tightening my hand over her thigh. My pinky meets the edge of her dress and I move so my finger can glide over the skin of her thigh. This time, she breaks, a shiver running through her body, which makes her face furrow in confusion.

Maybe she's as new to this as I am.

I've never gotten this close to another person. Not in this way. Not romantically. Which, yeah, means I'm a virgin, but I never needed, never craved a release like I do with Little Crane.

"Let's head down to the Prehistoric Humans room, ladies and gentlemen," the instructor says, as she moves to the back of the room where the rest of the museum is. We all follow suit, my hand finding Diora's. Finding her pulse, I can feel her heart racing. She's excited, my Little Crane. Good.

We walk to the Prehistoric Human room, which honestly looks like a forest encapsulated within four walls. Through the trees, we can see shadows of people that must be the statues of humans throughout time. The setup is perfect, with dim lights in the arena, even though it's mid afternoon outside.

"Okay, the prey will get a three-minute head start," the instructor says, and Diora lets go of my hand.

"Let's make a bet," she says, turning toward me. She is practically jumping in her sneakers, the smart Little Crane wearing walking shoes today.

"What do you want?"

"If I win, you take me on a kill with you."

"No," I say instantly. I know she can hold her own, but I don't want... I can't put her in any more danger than I already have. I shake my head as she jumps on her toes. "No."

"You better not lose, then, Elliot. 'Cause if you can't catch me..." She leaves her sentence hanging as the bell for the prey to start running rings. She dashes toward the trees before I can get in another word. I smile as I watch her go.

Shit. This is gonna be fun.

CHAPTER 17

Diora

I run. About fifteen or so more people take off, and some animals are let loose, too, when the bell signalling to start rings.

I run like my life depends on it. I run because I want to see the great Elliot Jay in action. Accompanying him on a kill would be like watching the big dogs from the sidelines. I've seen Mrs. Jay at work, and while she crosses lines, she's good at what she does. Her kills are near perfect, and there isn't a single detail that gets missed. Elliot probably only catches her due to growing up watching her. Watching Elliot kill would be pure fantasy.

All the training Elliot and I have been doing for the last week or so is definitely showing its perks now. Jumping over, breaching, and dodging the statues takes my full attention as I run in zigzags in the arena. I can hardly contain the laughter bubbling up in my throat. My hair falls from its updo style, and my sweat drips off my skin.

I hear a twig snap, and I have no idea if it's Elliot or not, but it gives me the boost I need to keep going. I think I saw this mock forest is about a mile or so in length, and I feel the strain in my calves already.

If it wasn't for all these obstacles, it wouldn't have been so tiring.

My breathing is the only sound I hear now, and I finally throw my back against a tree. I huff, trying to catch my breath when I hear it. I fucking hear it. A consistent thud of footsteps getting closer. Shit, a predator.

I take off like a deer crossing the road. I hold my smile back as I'm running again, not nearly as fast as before. It doesn't matter because I feel the grip of his hand wrapping around my waist and pulling me back. I look back, the single time I've looked back, and find a perfectly calm Elliot.

He's not breathless, or huffing, or even sweating. I scrunch my brows in confusion, but the thought quickly escapes my mind as he braces me against a different tree, his lips meeting mine.

"I got you now, Little Crane," he mumbles between our lips.

"Do you?" I ask and break his hold on me, sliding under his arm and taking off running again. It's only been probably fifteen minutes, and I highly doubt I can run against Elliot for the rest of the hour and fifteen minutes we have left, but I wouldn't be Diora Moss if I didn't try to give him a run for his money.

Dashing off, I hear his laugh fading away the farther I get. My pink silk dress is wrinkled and dirty, but that adds to the thrill of it all. I've never... I've never wanted to do things like this before. It's such a drastic difference from my life back home with Juliet. Such a difference from my life six months ago, before Juliet's incident, and yet, I'm happy? I'm not happy about Juliet's incident, but I'm happy with Elliot.

It doesn't have to be more complicated than that. I'm happy right in this moment. That's all that matters.

A giggle escapes me as I trip over a frickin' branch, but my hands are already launching me back up to continue running. Not that it even matters because my body is tackled back to the ground by a heavier force.

By the use of his weight, I know he won't be letting me go this time, and his scent lets me know it's him. Elliot Jay has me again, and my smile finally breaks through.

"You got me, handsome. Now what are you going to do?" I ask, tilting my head and getting all sorts of dirt in my hair. I hear the pounding feet of the other competitors, but I tune them out as Elliot locks in on me. He's the only predator I need to worry about.

He flushes at the question. "Oh, don't be shy now, honey," I say and lean up to meet his lips in a wild kiss. My hands find his golden, soft hair, and I tug him closer to me, my chest meeting his.

The way Elliot kisses me, he's shy yet demanding. His lips barely meet mine but then there's a switch, like a light ignites and he's smashing his lips to mine like there isn't a world in which he can't get enough. A man obsessed. His hands grip my waist like he's afraid I'll disappear.

"You taste good, handsome, I need more," I say, biting his lip, then his cheek and neck.

He moans my name, and the thrill of my name on his lips courses through my body. I feel like I got him more than he got me.

Hooking my leg over his, I switch us so I'm on top and leaning over him. My nails scrape over his t-shirt and bring the thin fabric up his torso.

I hate this feeling, but I crave it all the same. I've never needed someone's lips on mine like I need Elliot's. I've felt this need for skin in this way.

Throwing his shirt off, I wanted to see all of him. This forest floor isn't forgiving, even if it is fake, and still, I gaze at my handsome man below me.

I'm sticky with sweat and dirty from running, but his eyes darken as they gaze up at me. Like it doesn't matter.

I huff as he launches forward to capture me again, this time by my neck and chest. His soft lips bite my skin and my pussy throbs, and I can help the grind of my hips. A bubbling rush of warmth of urge surges to my throat, and I can't breathe properly.

"Elliot." His name comes off my tongue like a desperate plea. My hands move to grip his hair, and I feel his chuckle against my breast.

"I fucking know, Little Crane," he says, dragging the front of my dress down, snapping the straps. It slides down my body, and I raise a brow at my suddenly brazen partner. My nipples ache for pressure, for him, and my back arches to give it to him. "I just—I can't get enough."

The faint footsteps of the other contenders don't bring me to a halt like they should. Instead, my need makes me hasty. My breasts feel impossibly heavy as he presses the flat of his tongue on the underside of my boob and licks a straight line up to my nipple. He lashes me with quick bursts of his tongue on me and I moan.

His fingers roam over my body and land on my waist, holding me where he wants me. His touch is delicate, light, and I can't tell if he's teasing me or if he's... unsure. It's a desperate game of need and uncertainty wracking through his touch.

"Elliot," I mutter. He nips at my skin with teeth, and I arch into him as my head leans over his head. Holy shit. I can't think when he bites the round of my breast, and I rock into his lap, grinding over his cock.

His eyes peer up at mine, and I watch his eyes. The honey color darkens with lust as he stares at me with his mouth around my nipple. I try to commit this moment to memory. I want this moment to last forever.

He gently bites down, barely pinching me, but my body doesn't seem to notice as I feel the rush of heat toward my core.

He smiles against me before moving to my other breast with a pop. "Hmm, you like that?" he asks, more to himself, but I rock against him in response. I stare at my captor. My handsome boy. Another human being to call mine. I know Elliot Jay is stuck with me. There's no chance I'll ever let him go.

I wouldn't know how.

Lifting me up, he flips us over so he's on top. The forest ground and his shirt presses into my back, the pokes of pain and pleasure racking my body. Looking over myself, I see the light bites and nips over my reddening skin.

My chest goes cold as he moves down my body. I lay with my knees up, watching as his kisses slide down my body. Skin on skin on skin, I heat up as the anticipation builds.

"I've never wanted to eat someone as much as I want to devour you," Elliot murmurs against my skin.

"Please do, handsome." At my words, his tongue is thrust over my underwear, mixing my already wet underwear with his spit. "Oh."

Elliot has never been a man of many words, and I am more grateful for it at this moment as he rips my underwear and attacks my drenched pussy head on.

His nose dusts over me first, as if he's enjoying his findings, then his lips press against me in a kiss. He isn't shy, but he sure as hell takes his time. My hands find his hair, but I don't pull or tug like I want to.

I let him explore. I let him set the pace, and I give him the control. I'm trusting the man between my legs to satisfy me the way *he* wants to.

A choice I'm not sure he's been given before.

I moan and shiver under him as his fingers join in, his thumb on my clit as his tongue plays with my lips.

"Handsome, please," I beg. I fucking beg. I whimper and I moan, and I've never been this pleased before. Throwing my head back, I feel the gritty dirt mashing in my hair. Never has a promise so close to the finish line. I need him and, more than that, I want him. I want him so fucking bad.

His hands grip my thighs and yank me impossibly closer, ravishing me. He parts me with tongue before flicking at my clit. My legs shake as he continues torturing me with slow laps of his tongue.

His tan skin and shiny soft hair are all I see as my chest heaves up and down. Every time a moan slips past my lips, he doubles his effort, paying attention to me like he's learning something. Reading me like one of his bird books, as if I'll quiz him later.

I lose control. I'm lost to him, the sensations, his fingers. Everything down to his nose digs into all the right places. I grip his hair strands, blind to the fact I may be hurting him. I cry out as I come on his tongue.

"Thank you, Little Crane," Elliot says, as he licks up my cum between my thighs.

"We're done?" I ask incredulously as my head shoots up so I can look at him. He only smiles.

"We're only getting started."

I giggle, the ecstatic rush showering over my skin. I launch up to meet his lips as he crawls over my body. Grasping his head in my hands, I taste myself on his lips, and my body temperature spikes. I'm drenched in sweat, more so than the running caused, and completely filthy.

"I need you," I whisper. I try to hook my leg around him to flip him, but he slams me back down. My body hits the ground with a force he's yet to use on me, and I look at him with scrunched brows.

"What?"

"You do as I want, when I want you, baby," he says, unbuckling his belt. Oh, wow. That was hot. My breath catches as he lets his dick free. Hard and long, he runs a hand over himself, and I nearly come at the sight.

"Oh, God," I whimper while watching him. His eyes dart to me with an eyebrow raised.

"God? Baby, please, God isn't saving us." He leans down to capture my lips in a kiss, and I meet him halfway. We moan together as our skin meets in a sweaty blazing fire.

"I need to feel this pussy around me," he whispers as he lines himself up and slowly enters me. Our bodies join for the first time, and I know this like I know blood courses through my veins: this man is mine.

All I can comprehend is this man inside me. Not the beautiful forests around us, not the competition, not the fact someone could catch us. Nothing but the feeling of him thrusting inside me matters.

He focuses, picking up my hips in his hands and carrying me as he meets me thrust for thrust. I try to match him, try to meet him, but with my ass in the air and his complete focus on me, I can't move. I'm trapped and too wrapped up in his concentration. He watches me as he tries moving me, seeing what feels best and the attention to detail making me hotter.

He hits my sweet spot, and my eyes roll as he retreats, only so he can do it again. Slowly. I inhale through my mouth, trying to catch my breath, but it doesn't matter. "Elliot, please," I moan. "Faster."

He moves fast, then slow, and arousal chokes my throat. As if his hand was around my throat, choking me as he pounds into me. My nails dig into his back, covered in dirt and leaves, and I drag my hands down at the pleasure he is causing in my core. He'll have scratches to remember me by and that makes me flush all the more.

My back rams against the earth as his tip hits my g-spot over and over again. My body slides up, and I'm sure I'm causing a track mark in the dirt. His hands don't let me get too far, yanking my hips back to meet his.

The tension in my core expands and peaks, but the straw that breaks me is the feeling of his cum shooting into me. That and his muttered curse, and there goes my second orgasm of the day. He pumps into me throughout my orgasm, riding it out to the very end.

All I can hear is our tired moans echoing in the trees as he slides out of me. Specks of blood coating him and dripping onto my thighs. Leaving me fully satisfied, he tugs by my arm, pulling me to his chest and grabbing his shirt.

He wipes my face first, though it doesn't help much, and then he wipes between my legs and thighs. His face scrunches as I don't really get clean, and that bothers him.

"It's okay. We'll shower when we get home."

"I need to clean you, Diora." His voice comes out demanding, but there is a hint of desperation I wasn't expecting.

"It's okay." I try to smile and move his head, so he'll see my face, but he is focused on my body.

"I'm supposed to do aftercare. I need it. I need to take care of you," he mutters, still wiping at my legs. I cut him off by swallowing him into a hug, our naked chests pressed together, and I snuggle my head into his neck. This seems to be more about him than me, which is fine. I've never had aftercare before, not that I've been with very many people.

It's never felt this way before. Never this exciting. Never this satisfying, either.

He rocks us back and forth, kissing the top of my head every few seconds. We stay like that for minutes, maybe until the alarm of the hunt goes off.

"All remaining hunters and prey, please make your way north, back to the front of the arena." The instructor's voice comes through what sounds like speakers.

"Aww, man, I lost," I say, as we head back to the front of the area. Since my dress is ruined, Elliot holds it in one hand, and I wear his shirt, covered in cum, dirt, and sweat. It comes down to my thighs, so it's enough to be decent, but even then, it doesn't matter.

No one would touch me here. The Society has a strict "no drama" policy, and getting into a fight here is not worth the hell the Society would bring down. We are all on our best behaviors this weekend.

Elliot walks with a freedom I've yet to see and a genuine smile I can't get enough of. I'm sure my skin is flushed red, and that the state of my hair and the dirt on my face tells everyone what we were up to, but I don't care.

"I did catch you, Little Crane."

"That you did, handsome. How about you attend a kill with me, then?"

"Is that really a prize? Watching a newbie?" I slap his arm and glare as he laughs.

"You know you wanna watch me kill again," I say, swaying my hips as I walk in front of him.

"You'd be right, Little Crane. Who's next on your kill list?"

"Yara Holding." The tea party Mrs. Jay wants to throw will take care of the politicians that actually forced their dicks on Juliet, but it doesn't take care of Yara. I've left her for last. A dessert after a meal.

The name makes Elliot pause. Peering down at me, he raises both eyebrows.

"One of my mother's friends?" he says, scrunching his eyebrows. I'm sure he thinks I'm provoking the beast, but this doesn't have anything to do with Mrs. Jay and everything to do with justice for Juliet.

"The villain of Juliet's story," I correct, grabbing his chest and leaning up to peck his lips. "Are you in or not?"

"Consider it a date, Little Crane."

Chapter 18

Diora

Being back in Litchfort, Michigan is like walking through the door of your home after a long day at work. Whether it's a good or bad day, nothing beats getting home.

I walk through my apartment door with my luggage, passing by a deep cleaning Juliet as I head right back out the door. I don't bother unpacking anything more than the black dress Elliot bought me. We have a plan, Elliot and I, and we didn't have any time to waste.

All we needed was an opening, a chance to attack Mrs. Jay's ring, and we finally got one. Today. Right now.

We didn't know where Mrs. Jay was holding the Strays; she had them deeply hidden amongst systems that Elliot could break yet. What he did find, though, was tonight's exchange. An event for the rich and dirty to view the Strays they wish to purchase.

"Dee, uh, where are you going? You just got back. How was your trip?" I hear Juliet's voice meekly come out as she pauses, mid wipe over the coffee table. She has yellow gloves up to her elbows and a headband covering her hairline.

I stop in my tracks as our eyes meet. It's weird when you start having a life outside of your siblings. Juliet is still my world, but looking at her, seeing her manically clean while fighting demons I can't see, and I just... I just walked past her. Solely focused on the ring, when I should be focused on the politician and all those involved in her injustice.

I haven't forgotten, but I can't pretend I haven't been distracted.

An unsuspecting knock clears my mental fog, and I scrunch my face as I walk to open the door.

"What are you doing here?" Has Elliot been to my apartment before? How did he know I lived here? I look at the man in question, scrunching my eyebrows.

"Dee, don't be rude! Who is at the door?" Juliet comes to the door, ensuring her gloved hands don't touch anything, the door and me included.

I give the grinning man a pointed glare. I've worked hard to keep these two worlds separate and here he is stomping on all my efforts. What is he doing mixing what shouldn't be mixed? Good and bad shouldn't mix.

"We work together," Elliot says, sliding past me and following an all too welcoming Juliet inside.

"You work at Sadie's Flowers? Are you a florist, too?" Juliet asks, leading him to the kitchen, where he sits too comfortably on a barstool at the kitchen island.

"No, I do the books," Elliot answers, smiling.

"Oh, nice," she says, then offers the serial killer a glass of water. Juliet excuses herself to freshen up in the bathrooms, and I turn to Elliot with a glare.

"Do you even know accounting?" I snip.

"More than you, Little Crane," he scoffs, twirling in his chair to face me. His hands wrap around me, and next thing I know, I'm between his legs and his lips are right next to my ear. His hair grazes my cheek, and I flush as the reminder of the last time we were this close. I tilt my head up, my lips hovering over his ear, but not touching. I breathe in his scent. Dark chocolate and the freshness of oranges. I wanna take a bite.

"You can back out, you know," he mutters. I can barely see his eyes as the words drop from his lips. I try to move back, away from his alluring scent and skin, but he holds me tight against him. Back out? Do I look like a quitter to him?

"And why would I do that?"

"Going up against Mother isn't... We aren't fighting a fair fight, and you could get hurt." His voice is... pleading. Begging. But that's not... This is not what we do. How could he ask me that?

"So could you," I argue back. I'm not naïve to the fact that I'm new to the game. But he'd have to be stupid to think I wouldn't worry about him. He's at more risk than I am. Mrs. Jay hardly knows me. The betrayal wouldn't go as deep but she looks at Elliot like a Son, despite the outs they are on. She would feel scorned, and a woman scorned... is a whole lot more dangerous.

"It's not me I'm worried about," he says and finally pulls away far enough so I could see his face. I watch his brown eyes and I can see the fear. Elliot is scared... he's scared for me.

"That's fine. I'll worry about you," I say with a meaningless shrug. It was obvious to me; I guess it wasn't obvious to him. "You're mine, Elliot. We're a team. I worry about you, you worry about me. That's normal. Just like when working with the Strays at Haven or the Top Dogs—it's normal. "

"A team I don't want to put you at risk for." He rests his head on my forehead, and as much as I love this closeness, his words stab me.

"Elliot," I say in a breath, my lips trembling. "Are you asking me to back out?"

"Yes," he says simply. He doesn't look at me as he makes this request. He leans back against the counter, facing the living room. As if we are having a normal conversation, but it is anything but.

"You don't think I can do it? That I can't handle it?" I spit, trying to get these waves of emotions under control. My brows are scrunched and I'm... I'm frustrated. My skin is cold and he won't look at me. He won't fucking look at me.

"No, Little Crane."

"Then what is it?" I ask, my anger bleeding in my voice. I'm not, I don't do this. I don't have uncontrollable emotions. I don't spit, I don't yell. I'm turning into someone I don't know.

He sighs and turns on his barstool to face me. Fucking finally. He lifts a hand and traces my cheek as he sighs.

"I don't want a single mark on this skin," he says. "I don't want to see a cut, bruise, or tear on this soft skin or on your delicate soul, unless it's from me. Nothing matters more to me than your being, Diora. I need you."

"We're being good. We are saving those Strays." Convincing him seems impossible by the look on his face; he isn't backing down.

"That's the thing, Little Crane, I don't want you to. You don't have to be good, you don't need to be good. You are good as you are. And more importantly, I need you alive."

"I'm not good, Elliot. I need this. I'm not staying back."

"Please," he begs. I can hear the need in his voice, but I'm not backing out. This is my chance to be good, and I get to do it with him.

"No." He stares into my eyes. He doesn't get to do this.

"Diora Rose Moss, I didn't know you had a boyfriend?" Juliet's voice snaps me out of Elliot's bubble. The daze is so confusing and completely consuming. I turn in shock to Juliet, but Elliot only places his chin on my head and gasps.

"She didn't tell you?"

"No," Juliet says with wide eyes and a joyous smile. She sparkles, like she never thought she'd see the day I had a boyfriend.

Granted, I've never brought one home, before Elliot.

Wait, well, I didn't technically bring Elliot home. He ended up here uninvited.

"She's so secretive. I'm sorry, what was your name again?" Juliet asks, leaning against the counter opposite to us. Juliet does most of the talking as Elliot eggs her on. I stay frozen in his hold. Uneasy at the too easy atmosphere with a new addition.

I'm so close I can feel his body heat. I can almost feel his skin, and instead of an urge to see it turn gray and cold, I want to see him sweat.

I want to see his skin so alive that it creates beads of sweat and pants to the rhythm of his heart.

No, I'm supposed to be mad at him. I swallow and turn my head away from Elliot. Scrunching my brows, I try to erase my mind and get back to the present.

"I'm taking Diora out tonight," he tells Juliet, and it's my head snapping up to look at his face. I raise my brows, and I can see the resignation in his face.

"Is that why you were in such a rush to get out the door? I'm sorry to keep you up! Please," Juliet says, looking around like a madwoman and gesturing to the door.

"No, no, I was just dropping her dress off. It won't be for another few hours," he informs the both of us. A few hours?

I stare at this man in amazement. How many more tricks does he have? If I whack his head, will he disappear like a whack-a-mole, too?

"We're going dancing," he says.

"Dancing, huh?" I say, surprise coloring me.

"Dancing all night," he says with a smile I've gotten to see a lot lately. It's different to see him in this way, and I want to keep him here just to keep it this way.

"So, Juliet, may I have Diora tonight?"

"Hmmm," Juliet playfully says. Hand under her chin as she giggles. "I guess I can watch the news by myself."

I watch her deep brown eyes sparkle with amusement. Her hair is pulled tightly into a bun tonight and her light brown skin has a warmth to it that's been missing for a while. Not just in tone, but in... aliveness. The blood under her skin is warm and cozy and fuels her with happiness.

"I'll be back in two hours ladies, lock this door behind me," Elliot says, plopping a kiss on the top of my head as he strides back out the door.

"He came all the way to say that?" Juliet asks, tilting her head in question.

I wordlessly nod my head and grab the dress hanging over the couch.

Walking in the hall I shout his name and he stops. Turning around, I catch up to him, pulling his arm so he'll face me.

"Hours? Isn't it now?"

"That's what I came over to tell you: our timeline got pushed to tonight. Meet me at my place at nine," he says. He pulls me in, giving me a proper kiss this time, and I can't help but bite at his lip for pissing me off.

"You're not going without me," I mumble through our kiss. I consume his scent through my nose and fist his t-shirt.

He sighs into my mouth and pushes me backward with the force of his body, like he can't get enough.

"No, I can't do this by myself. I need you. But my need to keep safe will win every time, Diora. You say the words and I'll figure something else out. We don't have to do this tonight."

"We're doing this. First, we save those kids," I say breathlessly as he releases my lips. Then we'll deal with Mrs. Jay later.

I can't get the words to pass my lips, but we can only save so many Strays without killing the root of the problem. You have to kill the root to stop the plant from growing again.

Mrs. Jay has to die.

Chapter 19

Diora

"You ready?" Elliot asks as I walk through the door. The dress Elliot got me is a replica of the short dress that the servers are wearing. My costume is an extremely short black dress with semi sheer tights and black heels. Juliet straightened my hair and did my makeup, like a "big sister should"—her words.

I feel beautiful. Elliot looks away from his computers, his desk in the place a couch would be, and stares at me.

He rolls his chair away from the desk and has a glint in his eye I wish we had time for.

"Little Crane," he whispers.

"Hey, handsome," I whisper back, stepping into the distance of the man I'm finding myself head over heels for. "Don't mess me up. I have to look the part."

"You look so beautiful all messed up." He smirks.

"Thank you," I say, stepping into his legs and laying a hand on his head, bringing his chin up to meet mine. A light peck was all I was going to give him, but he wraps his arms around the backs of my legs and pulls me into his lap. He doesn't look too bad himself. He's dressed in a similar suit as he was for the ball, his waist adorned with the sexy as sin vest and tie.

Hmmm. This man.

He runs his thumb lightly over my matte lips. He tries to drag his lipstick-covered thumb down my chin, but I jerk away from him with a glare.

"Don't," I say, letting the word drop slowly off my lips. I want to let him mess me up. Make me sweat out my straight hair and make my makeup run, but I can't tell if he is trying to use sex as a distraction. A ploy to stop me from taking down this ring with him.

"Little Crane, when did you become so proper?" he rasps against my cheek, kissing my blush away, I'm sure. Trailing down my neck, I lean my head back, giving him more access. Shit. Elliot Fucking Jay. An impossible man to say no to.

This is bigger than us, though.

"We're not heroes, Little Crane—" he murmurs.

"Absolutely not. You don't get to talk us out of this."

"I'm not." He scoffs, but the slight upward turn of his lips tells me he is indeed trying to talk me out of this.

"Turn off the screens and go over the details with me," I say, slinking down his lap.

"I need the screens for that," he says, turning them off one by one as his face flushing red.

"Tell me from memory." My hands trace over his thighs, and I land on my knees in front of his desk chair. My nails trace the seams of his dress pants as I contemplate my makeup. Lipstick can be reapplied. My eye makeup cannot.

"You promise to be good and only come in my mouth?" I ask, peering at him through my lashes. His chest heaves, and I resist the urge to smile. Gripping the arms of his desk chair, he tilts his head as he stares at me.

"I promise," he mutters. His golden brown eyes blaze on me and my lips. I decide to leave the lipstick on and paint his cock with it, since he wants to mess my makeup up so much.

"Now, tell me, handsome, what time do we have to leave?" I unzip the zipper of his pants, his hips jerking up at the contact.

I hear his breath shudder as I pop the button of his pants, but I gaze back up at him before continuing. Raising a brow, I wait for an answer.

Gulping, his eyes track to the computer screen. He attempts to take a deep breath before answering, but his answer comes out on a shaky breath.

"Nine, baby. Nine p.m." I can hardly hear him as the anticipation of my lips on him kills him.

"Good boy. Now," I say, dragging his pants down. He lifts his hips for me and I bring them down enough to pull his cock out. He's hard and long, and my pussy tingles with the memory of him inside me. "Where is the auction happening tonight?"

Watching his eyes, how they dilate, his pulse racing under my touch. Elliot is a responsive man. I love how much he expresses when it is just us and the heat of need.

Elliot's my first for everything. I've never salivated over a man's cock before, let alone given a blow job. The drool pooling in my mouth practically drips from the corners as I lick my lips.

Gripping his cock at its base, I roll my hands over his shaft. A bead of moisture comes from his tip, and I use it to slide my hands over him, exploring the sensitive skin. His stomach tenses at my first contact, and he bites the corner of his lip. Holy shit, he's so fucking hot.

I start slow, more from not knowing what to do exactly, but he doesn't seem to complain. He keeps his eyes glued to my hands, and he attempts to control his breathing, though I like him out of control.

"Uh, oh, fuck." His words drop in the most attractive way. His breathlessness is heady, and my back arches from the sound of his voice.

I move my hand quickly, needing more noises. More moans and curses. I need Elliot to lose it. I need him to come in my mouth.

Leaning forward, I wrap my lips around his head, my tongue exploring the slit. My heart tries to beat through my ribcage as I take him down my throat.

With only the glow of daylight trying to peek through his blinds, I can hardly see what I'm doing, and the thought rings a sliver of embarrassment through my cheeks. Looking back to him from his cock, I watch as he throws his head back as I slide off his cock with a pop.

"Handsome, why haven't you answered me?" I ask, running my lips over his cock but not bringing him into my mouth. He jerks and his hips jump up, trying to enter my mouth again. His hands stay on his desk chair as if commanded by me to stay.

"It's in the, uh, shit, it's at Calix Smith's mansion in Ohio," he nearly spits in desperation. "Please, Little Crane, I need your lips back on me."

"My lips, huh? Only my lips, right?" I whisper against the head of his aching cock. He can't nod his head faster, and I smile, pleased with his answer. I can admit it makes me feel special. In control. I crave this.

I reward Elliot with my lips, bobbing up and down. Only skimming my teeth against him once by accident. Elliot doesn't seem to mind as his hands finally find their home in my hair. He tugs at my strands, messing my hair up. I'll have to comb my hair back out once we're done. I focus on him, his pleasure, as I taste him. Consume him in my throat.

I pull up off his cock. "Next question. Give me the address."

He thrusts forward, and I let my lips wrap around him again for a single stroke. Finding his voice again, he mutters curses.

"Um, fuck."

"Come on, Elliot, you know it," I encourage, letting my breath hit his tip as he shudders under me.

"Please," he begs. I smile, hovering over him, awaiting an answer. I breathe all over his cock, watching him throw his head back, trying to come up with the answer.

I give his cock a teasing lick and he nearly shouts. I giggle as I watch his stomach rapidly move back and forth as he loses control.

"Diora, fucking please. Wait. Wait. It's fucking, um, five six four Addline Street." And before he can finish his answer, my lips are back on him, sucking and bobbing. I have no idea if he made that answer up, but now, I don't really care.

He guides my head to meet his thrust. I let him take control, so long as he doesn't mess up the rest of my makeup.

I switch from licking and sucking him. Watching his face and hearing his groans of pleasure satisfy me, encourage me to keep going. With him setting the pace, I focus on the feel of him in my throat.

Elliot's big and hard, and I choke on him as I go down. My saliva makes a mess of my face and his cock, but by his face, I don't think he minds. Not at all. I can't help but want to smile, but I can't with my lips around his cock.

Each stroke of my tongue meets with the hollow of my cheeks brings him to come. His hot salty taste shoots down the back of my throat. I gag over him, which only makes his thrusts more erratic.

I suck him through his orgasm as he loosens his hold on my hair. He doesn't let me bring him again. Pulling me up in his lap, he smashes his lips to mine.

"Fucking hell, Little Crane," he murmurs against my lips as my hands twist in his soft hair.

At this moment, it's just the two of us. In a perfect world, it's only him and me. By the way I feel him stiffen under me, I have a deep gut feeling that is going to change.

We're not alone anymore.

"Is this where you've been hiding?" a deep voice yells, and it's at that moment, I'm thrown behind a now standing Elliot, who has a handgun pointed at the intruder.

Silence falls over us at the realization of the intruder being Enyo, first Son, and that Elliot's cock is still out. Sliding my hands to Elliot's front, I tuck him back in his pants, his cock hardening again in my hands. I shove my shock down, realizing Enyo is the one who found us. I don't know whether he's supposed to know about Elliot's hideout or not, and therefore, I don't know if I should be relieved it's Enyo or ready to fight.

"Aww, little bro finally lost his virginity," Enyo says, walking through the door and stopping right in front of Elliot's gun. "Are you gonna shoot me?"

Instead of a formal living room, with a couch and a TV, Elliot has his computers and a desk chair. With the chair long forgotten, since Elliot shot up to stand in front of me, Enyo's close to the computers where the screens are still off.

"I might. What the hell are you doing here?" Elliot doesn't let up. Clicking off the safety, he cocks his head to the side with raised brows.

He's more pissed than I thought.

"Looking for you!" Enyo quips. Has he ever been here? Was I the first guest that Elliot brought to his secret hideout?

I mean, Enyo was never part of the operation, so that means he's never had a reason to be here.

"What is this? What kind of secret operation are you doing here?" Enyo asks, as he casually leans over to turn the screens back on and looks over everything Elliot's been working on. Elliot lowers his gun, watching Enyo look over Elliot's work for the last year or so.

"Is this—?" Enyo starts to ask, but his words drift off.

"Yes," Elliot answers.

"Not only have you been hiding from me, Brother, but you're taking down a trafficking ring without me? I thought we were closer than that?" Enyo says, but there is a lightness to his voice that hints to him not being completely offended. He's slightly smiling as he lays a hand across his heart.

"Where, who, and how?" Enyo simply asks as he leans against the desk.

"This isn't for Haven, Enyo," Elliot informs his brother.

"Doesn't matter." Enyo shakes his head as if the assumption he only does things for the corp is obtuse. "It's with you, Brother. Anything with you is worthwhile."

"There's more on the table than you think. Are you sure you want to follow blindly?"

"When have you ever gone into anything blindly, Elliot?"

I watch the two brothers and their silent war. Enyo doesn't know who we are against, not truly. Would he still be here if he knew? Is Elliot going to tell him?

"If you must," Elliot says, gesturing toward the screens. "Calix Smith is the head. Take out the head and the body will follow."

"It would be fun to kill each motherfucker in there," Enyo says, danger lighting his eyes. Excitement, too. I wonder if it will always be odd to see this in someone else's eyes. I'm used to only seeing it in mine.

"It will take all night," I mutter, shaking my head.

"I'm in no rush," Enyo shrugs, and Elliot looks at me. It's up to me?

"As long as you focus on the security and I focus on the buyers, it could work." I know I'm not the strongest fighter and have no chance against someone completely sober, like the security I'm sure will be rampant in the mansion. But the buyers will be drugged and drunk, and that'll even out the fight.

"Let's do it," Enyo jumps up, energized, and clasps his hands together as he turns toward Elliot.

"It's quite the drive away, so we need to get going," Elliot says, turning his back to Elliot and facing me. He doesn't smile. My grump is back.

I let the broody men continue their little brotherly moment as I go off to what I assume is the bathroom in this apartment.

Opening the door, I look at myself in the mirror. My lipstick is smudged over my lips and even on my chin. My hair is starting to frizz and is in desperate need of a comb. But I look fucking sexy.

Too bad that's not quite the dress code tonight.

I pull my little black dress down as I leave the bathroom to stand beside his desk chair, which he sits back in. The dress is more something I would wear to a restaurant with candles, but I guess these traffickers are those of class?

These people have money. I can say that much for sure.

Finding a paper towel, I wash the matte lipstick off my face and reapply. Fixing my hair, I stare at the woman staring back at me in the mirror. Taking a deep breath, I straighten my shoulders back and smile.

I have some Strays to save. "Let's go," Enyo says, already heading toward the door.

"Is it safe to include him?" I ask, as Enyo walks out of earshot.

"He didn't give us a choice," Elliot answers, grabbing my hand. "Enyo's the only person I fully trust."

"If you trust him so much, why didn't you include him in the first place?" I am confused. "Does he know that it's Mrs. Jay behind this?"

"No, and I won't tell him. It would hold a different weight for him. Mother is everything to him." I fear Enyo isn't the only one who cares deeply for Mrs. Jay. Elliot's hand is firm in mine as he leads me down to his car.

Elliot may believe that he doesn't care for Mrs. Jay, but if that is the case, then why hasn't he killed her already?

Chapter 20
Diora

I split off from the guys once we arrive at the mansion. It took us an hour and a half to get here, and in the long car ride here, we went over the plan.

This is only one of the 'homes' that Calix Smith owns. Opening the door, I find myself surrounded by stained glass windows and high arches lit with dim candles. The walkways are lined with a velvety red carpet and hardwood floors with intricate moldings of angles and swirls, like a church.

A fucking church.

I could vomit from the idea they took design inspiration from a church for a trafficking ring event house.

I step in from the servants' quarters' door, dressed in an outfit far too sexy to be an average waiter. I straightened my naturally curly hair to fit the dress code. It was nice having Juliet help me get ready for tonight, for what she thinks is a date with Elliot. Is this a date? Our first date? Hmm, our first date.

No, the ball was definitely our first date.

I watch as everyone bustles around. Girls dressed like me running around with tremors in their fingers and a deep fear settled in their eyes. I figure now is the best time to lace all the drinks with dustings of crushed up hemlock.

The drinks tonight are liquor—old fashioneds, I think—in fancy, mug-like glasses that are supposed to be garnished with a fake white flower.

This plant I have is similar-looking to what is supposed to be garnishing the drinks white and is poisonous to the touch and more so when ingested. The amount I'll put in each drink will only weaken the buyers here tonight, not kill them.

Killing them will be done by my hands, well, knife. I'd use a gun, but my aim is shit.

All the trays are being filled with drinks and finger foods. As a man in a black buttoned shirt places the drinks on the trays, I follow behind with my beautiful plant that looks more like a garnish than a poison.

No one can tell this beauty is a poison.

It kills to be dumb.

I could almost laugh at what we were doing. Us being heroes? Being the good guys? Never thought any of us would see the day. But nothing is funny when I see little girls and boys being dragged into rooms in dirty robes and tears staining their cheeks.

Like this damned place is a church damning the innocent and serving the evil. I watch as the other frightened wait staff gather appetizers and drinks on silver trays, and I grab one, too, following their lead.

If anyone thinks I don't belong, no one says anything. The level of terror in the room is hard to swallow. Even as I venture down the halls to the room that Elliot and Enyo will be in, I still feel nerves tickling over my shoulders, but I also felt the itch to kill crawl its way up my spine and circle around my neck.

Having an excuse to be bad causes a thrill of joy to lace my limbs. We have two jobs here tonight: kill every single buyer in here and get the kids to a halfway house.

I dampen my smile, since no one else is smiling, and I finally make it to the room on the top floor. On this whole floor, there is only one door. One single girl with a tray like mine stands outside the door, probably waiting to be called in, but once she makes eye contact with me, she furrows her brows. I wordlessly tilt my head to signal her to move, which she doesn't.

Damn, I was hoping that would work.

"What are you doing?" she mutters, scared. Her brown eyes are glassed over, as if they're holding back tears, and her wrist shakes under her tray, spilling her drinks. She's outside the boss's room, and she's terrified, which means that if the girls mess up here, they're punished.

Maybe they're punished regardless of who they serve tonight.

"You're wanted." I speak lowly to her, getting way closer than I would like. Our noses nearly touch, and I smell her sweat and perfume mix.

"Why?" Her voice is shaky as she brings her tray down off her shoulder to hold with both hands. She's got the same dress on as I do, the same tights and four-inch heels clicking on the stone floors. While this dress may be sexy on me, it's a crime on her. She looks no older than fifteen and should be in big tulle dresses, not mini black dresses that almost show her ass.

She's got freckles lining her cheeks and curls straining under her heat pressed hair. She is a beautifully trapped girl.

"Do I look like I know why?" I snip, trying to keep my vocabulary short in case I mess up and use the wrong term.

"You've got quite the attitude for a newbie," she scoffs and storms off. I watch her swish her ponytail as she walks, and I could smile at the fire she still has, despite her situation. She doesn't know this will be her last night here.

Getting her to leave was much easier than I thought it was going to be. I replace her by the door. Wafting the drinks over my nose as I move the tray to balance on my hand and rest on my shoulder.

The flower floating on the top is pretty, but the extra leaves I had ground inside these drinks will do most of the work to weaken every drinker in this house.

Footsteps sound from down the hall, and my eyes snap toward the noise. According to Elliot, there is supposed to be no one here except for the one waiter outside the door. Who the hell is coming?

I wear my knife in a garter on my inner thigh, but if this is trained security coming up, I won't have the finesse to grab it in time. Rolling my lips, I wait and keep my gaze straight ahead of me as the thundering of boots gets closer. I hear male laughs and shit talking.

The men playing security guards must be here willingly if they are able to laugh. It's then I fantasize about my knife sliding clean through the sides of their necks. A quick movement. I wonder if my blade would poke through the other side.

"Hey, you're not the usual dime piece standing here." A voice snaps me out of my fantasy and my eyes jerk to them. Two of them. Smiles wide and hair buzzed. Muscle packed on muscle, and I know just by that alone I need something stronger than a knife. I need a gun.

I keep my eyes glued to the wall.

"What's your name?" one of the brooding men asks, as one of their fingers traces the line of my collarbone. It sets the skin ablaze, and I imagine a line of dirt following the path his finger makes.

Glaring at the one who put his nasty hand on me, I turn, ready to pounce, when I feel the cool metal of the one weapon I wished I had against the back of my head. The other security guy leans in, his hot breath hitting my ear.

"By the time a pretty girl gets to this level, the fight is gone and their lights are out, so tell me, what are you doing here?"

My lights are on? The lights in my eyes are on? My head snaps to the side, regardless of the gun pointed at my head. I meet the eyes of the guard, his face mostly covered by the ski masks they wear, but I can't help the hope that fills my gut.

"You can see my light?" I ask.

"Bitch, what the fuck kind of question is that?" the other one snaps, his spit landing on my face.

I watch their faces. I hope they can tell me just one more time. One more time, that's all I need. Maybe... if I could show Mom. Maybe if Mom saw the light in my eyes now—I shake my head as the scar on my forearm lights with awareness.

I don't know if it will change anything if she sees the light in my eyes now. I'm still her monster, and I probably always will be.

Clenching my jaw, I push back the weak girl who only wanted to be good. The girl who'd do anything to be told she had the light. I need to be sure the light is what these guys saw.

"My eyes have a light?" I ask again, looking at the guy with the dirty finger to see if he'll tell me. Why do I have the light now and not when I was six? Why now, when Mom can't see it?

She was so heartbroken over my eyes being dark, and the one time they have light is when... is when I'm on a mission. A mission to free the kids in the trade. A mission to kill everyone involved.

I guess they get tired of my questions, or maybe they don't feel the need to answer, because the guy behind me knocks my head forward with his gun, and that's when I see my chance to dip out.

The tray nearly drops from my hands, the drinks spilling on the carpet as I trip forward, but my hand grips the handle and is urged in the room before the guys could tussle with me anymore.

I sigh against the door, and I hear their sharp curses as they try for the door handle.

"Wait, the boss is in there. We can't go in," I hear one of them say. The pressure on the door handle stops, and I finally look up, only to meet unfamiliar eyes.

"Well, well, excuse the hell out of me, gentlemen. Normally, our girls are trained better than that," the unfamiliar man says with a light laugh, his smile wide over his naturally tanned skin.

Chapter 21

Elliot

This room on the highest floor is reserved for the special guests of Calix's. How unfortunate is it that his previously invited guest disappeared, decapitated somewhere in one of many of Michigan's lakes?

Enyo and I took their spots in the special show that Calix gives to the people who have the most money at these events. He asks for a deposit of five-hundred thousand dollars to be in this room. My wire burns in my pocket, itching to wrap around Calix's neck.

I smirk to myself as I watch my lovely bird freeze at the door. She keeps the tray balanced on her shoulder and hand. Her hair is roused in the back and not done by me, once again making the anger simmering under my skin spark to life.

Seeing her brings a sudden realization that she's not supposed to be in here. She snuck in. Which only means one thing: Diora was almost caught. She was threatened, and that makes my blood boil.

My eyes snap to her. Her hair swings over her shoulder as she straightens her posture. Diora lands right back into character, like a pro would. Her eyes land on Calix first, then move over to me. I don't move; I don't nod. I just watch.

"You like her, Kane?" Calix's voice grates against my ears. The name, though, reminds me of *her*. Of Diora and her constant battle between being good and bad. You know what can be both good and bad? A crane.

"I do," I murmur, a smirk slipping through the cracks of my persona.

"You can have her," Calix laughs as he puffs a cigar. "For a price, of course."

"Ain't that what we're here for?" Enyo boasts. He plays this role well. Only I would catch the fire burning under his skin or the sharpness of his eyes as he stares down Calix.

He doesn't know that Calix isn't the head of this snake, and I won't be the one to tell him.

"Yes, of course." Calix snaps his fingers, and Diora strides forward with the tray of poisoned goods. I swipe a cup from her tray before she can set it down. Giving her a reason to do something wrong before Calix notices. The girls here are trained rigorously, down to how they put the trays down, and Diora and I hadn't used our time earlier to go over such details.

Smiling down into my cup, I see the hemlock she's garnished each of the drinks with. Just knowing she did it makes me want to drink it.

"First one is twenty, for those who like them older, Kane?" Calix says as the first missing Stray is shoved onto the stage. The room is set up like a private showing would be. Two couches face each other, as the longest wall of the room is blocked with a clear plastic wall between us, the guest, and where the Strays must be.

Beyond the plastic wall is a stage and red curtains draped dramatically, as if this is a nineteenth century theater. Gold accents and trim line the entire room, and it's all grandiose and gaudy. The room gives me a fucking headache.

"I've got my eyes on something better," I snap, focusing my gaze on my little waitress. I should be focused on the Strays. The injustice here. The kids who needed protection and never got it.

But I was never a hero.

I was never the good guy.

If it came down to it, I know… I know I would choose Diora over the Strays. And that's why it's dangerous for her to be here.

I spent months looking for these Strays, for an opening, and now that I have it, I'm ready to throw it all away. It's dangerous. It's not an instinct I'm comfortable with.

"Aaron?" Calix's voice brings my attention back to him. He is looking at Enyo, who's going by Aaron.

Enyo wears a mask of indifference. Shrugging as he puffs on his cigar. He only smokes for show, as do I on occasion, but I feel the sudden need to be… healthier.

"Next," Calix snaps into the walkie. Out comes a younger girl, more terrified than the last, and my heart pounds behind my chest a little harder. My skin heats, and I actively keep my features blank as each girl and boy step on the stage behind the glass.

What the actual fuck.

I knew. I fucking knew they were taking children, but seeing it... seeing it is... Fuck.

Like an ice bucket, I'm reminded why I'm here. This isn't just about killing, it's about saving. Kids... Kids deserve so much more. These kids deserve so much better than me as their savior.

I see myself behind that plastic wall. A little boy mad at the world and an urge to make it right. I needed an Elliot Jay. I wonder if Oliver Longstead would still be alive if he'd never met a version of me back then.

I watch Calix bring his drink up to his lips, sniffing before taking a sip, and he leans back and smiles. Chuckling at something he's failed to let the rest of us in on.

We grab our cups, too, as if we are to take a sip. I don't watch if Enyo does, but I do. Keeping my gaze trained on Diora, whose eyes widen.

She tilts her head in confusion as I sip. I raise my brows, watching her shoulder straighten impossibly more as she moves her gaze to Calix. Does she think this will weaken me?

I've been consuming poison since Mother found me. When I asked Diora about poison resistance, I was wondering why the poison Mother's been rubbing on my skin recently switched.

Her touch burns. More so now than normal. After training, she'd call me to her room. She'd have me sit next to her on the couch and would rub my back. I thought... I wanted to think she was being motherly.

I don't tempt fate with another sip of this poisoned tea, but the worried look on Diora's face is worth the burn going down my throat.

"Boys, wait," Calix's smooth voice rumbles as his gaze whips to Diora, who freezes. "What's in this?"

Diora is quiet as she brings her hands behind her back, standing like the good little waitress she's supposed to be. I feel the weight of my gun in the back of my pants and the knives decorating my holsters over my body.

"Is this hemlock?" Calix asks, raising his brows and pointing to the garnish on the top of his drink. My jaw clenches at being found out so fast. How the hell would he know that?

At least that isn't the only plan we have in motion tonight.

Diora smiles, which throws Calix off by the dip of his smile. "You know your plants."

"I know my poisons." He chuckles, and it sets the hairs on my skin straight in excitement. It's about time to get this party started.

I can practically feel the taste of tangy blood on my teeth. I try to dampen my smile at the fight to come. My tongue licks over my teeth as Calix moves to stand with his gun in Diora's face. Nearly making contact with her skin.

And the band has snapped.

Both Enyo's and my guns are pointed, safety's off.

"I'm glad you fucking hesitated, Calix. If you'd have shot, we'd do worse than shoot you." My sense of urgency is fierce as the danger to Diora becomes real. My pulse thrums in my ears as my finger dances with the trigger. This is why I didn't want her here. I'd almost lost control.

It's not fair to hold her back just because my stupid soul needs her, but it is what it is.

"Who the hell are you?" Calix spits, panic slowly filling his brows. Is he not the head of operations?

"Better question is, who the hell are you?" Enyo asks back with a damning smirk on his face.

I answer for Calix. "Calix Smith, forty-two years old, never married, public stock market trader, undercover human trafficker and pedo." I ramble off the facts I'd pull from his profile, watching as his face drops.

"How-How?"

"You're not as private as you think, and when your staff is forced to work for you, for free, under the use of fear, well, money talks," I say with a shrug, as if it was easy to find this fucker.

It wouldn't be for the average killer, but I'm not average, am I? He's well-connected. His family is pretty powerful in the political scene, which means he has access to making evidence disappear. But unfortunately for him, I can access deleted records. Anything that has ever been documented on technology can never be completely erased.

With Calix's attention on me, Diora takes this chance to slip out of the path of his gun. She moves to duck behind the couches behind Enyo and me.

"Don't you fucking move—" Calix's words are cut off by my bullet entering his armed arm. He drops the gun and hugs his arm.

"You point that gun at what's mine again and you'll wish I put a bullet between your eyes."

"Are you fucking kidding?" Calix can hardly get his words out through the pain. I need my message to be painfully clear: Diora is off limits.

"Absolutely not," I murmur, moving to stand in front of Diora. Seeing that gun pointed at *her*, being in a real situation where she could get hurt, it all becomes more real.

If she got shot, *if* she got shot, I'd... I couldn't, fuck, I couldn't let the world go on if she wasn't here. Why the fuck did I let her come? I furrow my brow as I turn back to face her.

She raises her brows in amusement. I know she doesn't need my protection. She knows the risks of doing what we do, yet... I wanna keep her here, with me, in my sight. She has a mission, and I have mine. She's supposed to go off and attack the buyers now that we have Calix at our mercy.

She nods a single time before she turns to leave, and I can't help my traitorous voice.

"Wait," I selfishly ask. Calix's pleas to be let go drown out behind me as I stare at Diora in her sexy ass dress and tights. Her eyes peer into mine, and I love her attention. It lights my skin with a need to rush to her. To touch her skin and consume her entirely, but I don't. I just let my ask hang in the air as she contemplates.

She gives me a single nod as she gracefully sits on the couch. Patiently waiting for Enyo and me to wrap this up.

What a good fucking girl.

"Who are you working for?" Enyo asks, his gun itching to shoot, I'm sure. "'Cause ain't no way you running this operation."

"Help me, please help me."

A hit in the head keeps the dumb shit away. Calix's head snaps to the left as Enyo whips the butt of his gun across his face. Blood drips on the animal skin rug, and the fire lights brighter under the smell of fresh oozing blood.

"Don't make us ask again." His blood drips on the leather of my shoes, and I can smell the copper of blood filling the room. He's bleeding like crazy now. One deep inhale after the next, and a crazed smile covers my lips as I bend down to meet Calix's face.

"Boss?" I ask, despite knowing who the boss is. I know I'll have to kill him before he spills the truth to Enyo. I almost contemplate letting Calix be the one to break the news, but Enyo deserves better than that.

"She'll kill me," Calix whimpers.

"Hell yeah, she'll kill you. You're cracking and we've barely fucking started," Enyo laughs.

She.

She means Mrs. Jay, which also means she's not a distant player, which we knew, but hearing it makes it... real.

I glance toward Diora, and she's already staring at me. She doesn't give anything away. She doesn't tell me her opinion on whether I should let the beans spill or keep them between us. She doesn't tell me what to do.

"A name, Calix," Diora asks, though she, too, knows the answer. Her smooth voice fills the room, like a nice violin. I lean my head back, reminiscing in the sound of her voice. I am so fucked. She's following my lead, and that makes me hard as hell.

"It's Mrs—" Calix tries to spit out.

My gaze shoots to Diora, and before Calix can get the whole name out, I pull my trigger, putting a bullet between Calix's eyes.

Enyo can't know. Not yet. Not until I know how he'll react. Enyo is anything but weak, but I can't risk hurting him. Mother means everything to him, more than even he knows.

This kind of information marks a betrayal of their relationship. Finding out the person you hold closest to is capable of trafficking kids is a line we would never think that would be crossed.

"Elliot, what the fuck?" Enyo shouts, waving his hands about. "We could've—"

"Could've done nothing. He doesn't know shit. Let's save these kids," I say, heading for the door. I can hear the boots pounding down the hall; they must have heard the shots and come running.

"The guards," Diora says as the sound of heavy boots and cursing from down the hall gets louder.

"Crane, get the Strays and have them follow us as we make it out of this damned house," I say, pulling my knife out. I'm hoping to see some pain before death.

Death is far too easy for the nasty fuckers here.

Enyo doesn't argue, but his silence is worse than his questions. He's too emotionally connected for the truth, and I can't do that to him.

We're not here for the truth. We're here to save these Strays.

I'll tell him. I have to be the one to tell him, but I can't help but feel like, if I tell him… I'll lose him.

CHAPTER 22

Diora

My job wasn't to wait. The plan wasn't for me to stick around. I was supposed to go busting down doors and taking buyers out, yet Elliot asking me to stay changed everything.

I walk toward the plastic wall that separates the kids and the buyers. I need to get to the other side. Enyo and Elliot walk out the door, the shouts and sounds of bone breaking and fluids spraying the wall have the building in disarray. I hear the screams of fear from the staff and the sounds of crying kids. How the hell am I going to get them out?

I watch as girls in the same dress as mine run past the room, and I grab one of their arms, pulling her out of the crowd and into the room.

"This is our chance—" she cries and tries to pull my arm along with her, but I dig my heels in, yanking her to a stop. Her head whips back at me with confusion written all over face, but I don't give her the time to ask why I'm not running.

"How do I get the kids out?" I ask. The words can't come out fast enough. There is chaos, and I hear the boots of more security guards coming. Trying to stop people from running.

But none of it will matter. Not once they find out their boss is dead.

"Someone else will get them—" the girl sputters, trying to yank her arm from my grasp.

"Answer my question or this blade goes in your neck." It's shiny and clean of blood, but it won't be for long if she doesn't tell me how to get these kids out.

"The remote. There's a button on the remote that will lift the glass. Please let me go," she cries.

"Go." I push her away and turn back into the room with the trapped kids.

The black remote he had in his hands lays forgotten on the couch. I snatch it up and press a button, all the buttons, until the glass starts to move and the cries muted by the plastic become loud.

Oh my god.

Ohh my god.

These kids. Boys, girls, some as young as six, some almost as old as me.

I don't say anything as heads snap toward me. Tears and snot and sorrow cover the faces of every kid here, and I don't have the time, let alone the capability, to comfort them.

With the pressure of their gazes, I nod one single time and turn around, leaving the glass open and hoping these kids will take the chance and follow me.

"I'm here to... save you. Let's go." The words come out clunky and unnatural, but the kids nod, anyway. Like, even if they don't believe me, they already know there isn't anything better for them here.

I stay at the threshold as I guide the kids to leave the stage. They each step off the platform and through the opening, older ones guiding younger ones, and I am hit with an unfamiliar sensation.

My breath gets caught in my throat, and I whip my face away from the kids. Are there tears welling up behind my eyes right now? Of all times to be emotional. Saving these kids, kids like me, who aren't quite right, I just didn't think I'd feel this way. Watching them. Knowing they were recruits for Mrs. Jay, like me, but had a very different fate.

"Little Crane, let's go." Elliot stalks back into the room, covered in blood and heaving.

I nod and look back at the row of ten kids.

"How many more rooms do we have?" I ask as the kids huddle around me. I wonder if the buyers of each room heard all the commotion and left.

"Seven," he whispers as his eyes fall on the kids piling around me. One wet hand touches mine, and I want to recoil at the contact of tears, maybe snot, but I don't. I look down to the little boy with blond hair and blue eyes who grabbed my hand. His other hand is in his mouth, and tears fall from his eyes in a never-ending stream. I'm angry. I'm angry for him, for them.

I don't have the strength to pull my hand away from him. The little boy follows me like there's a string of glue holding us together.

Seven more rooms over the span of four floors, with probably just as many Strays in them.

Shit.

I follow the guys down to the next floor, the Strays following tight behind me. My knife is pulled and ready as we bust down the door to the next room.

Buyers are lounging on the couches, barely awake, as they laugh and wave their fingers, pointing to the little girl on the stage.

I let go of the boy's hand as I pounce, unable to control the hate running through my veins. How dare they treat their lives as if they are nothing. Objects.

I can't pretend I know what the Strays need or that I could give it to them, but Juliet would. She'd be the best mother, the best guardian, she'd know what to say. She'd be able to comfort them.

That's why she's good.

After the buyer on the couch closest to me dies, the other buyer jumps up from the couch, or tries to. He lands in a heap on the floor and I'm on him. My knife jabs into his neck, and his life withers away as he bleeds out.

Finding the remote for this room, the plastic lifts, freeing another set of kids and Strays, the same crying and fear permeating the air. I nod and they follow. What is telling these people to follow me? I'm not sure, but I'm glad it's working.

I wonder if Juliet saw this, saw me, if she'd be proud of me. I'm being good.

I'm being good. It feels... nice.

Seven rooms. Seventy kids. Endless amount of bullets, sweat, and tears. We are done. The wind from the car window blows my hair from my face, which is reverting to its curly state. As dirty as the three of us are, I feel amazing.

We dropped the kids off at a recovery shelter in Wisconsin, and we've been on the road back to Michigan since.

The little boy wouldn't let me go after we got back down to the lowest floor and we were getting ready to leave the mansion. He stuck tight to me until we got to the shelter and another woman gently pried him away from me.

Kids have never liked me before. Even as a kid, other kids stayed away. They knew I was different. I don't blame them for staying away; it may have been more survival instinct than dislike or hate.

I didn't need any other kids. I had Juliet. She is all I ever needed.

Though, holding his hand, even as I killed people, filled my hand with a warmth I miss. I want to hold his hand again. Protect him again. Keep him with me. But I can't. Not when his dealer is still hiding in plain sight.

Maybe I like kids more than I thought.

"We did it." Enyo's voice is a mix of a laugh and a yell, and his smile radiates in the car and even Elliot is smiling. "We fucking did it."

"They'll be free," I murmur. I know the guys may not have heard me, but it doesn't matter.

"We still don't know who was running it, though. I know damn well it wasn't Calix," Enyo says, furrowing his brows. Elliot meets my eyes through the rearview mirror for a split second.

He's not looking at me to make sure I don't spill. The question blares in his eyes of whether he should tell Enyo it's Mrs. Jay behind this. But I keep my face blank. I can't tell him what to do, Enyo isn't my brother.

"We saved the kids, and that's all that matters," Elliot says. His gaze moves out the window, and I get to see his side profile. Though this is a joyous moment, he works his jaw, his eyes hard.

Enyo's involvement puts a damper on things, but I'm not sure why. He doesn't know that it's Mrs. Jay behind the trafficking ring, but it seems as if there is... is more to it?

Loud ringing overpowers the sound of the wind, and Elliot curses before answering the phone.

"You're on speaker," he says, rolling the windows up.

"So, you thought you could go off on your own operation and I wouldn't find out?" Mrs. Jay's voice fills the car and covers my arms in chills. Shit.

"Hello, Mother," Enyo says with a roll of his eyes, which he makes obvious through the rearview mirror. I watch the Sons as their facial expressions change from annoyance to something worse: fear.

"Meet me at Office Three when you guys get back. All three of you." She doesn't yell, but her voice is hard, and it doesn't take a genius to tell she's mad.

The hairs on my arms rise, and the tension in my neck intensifies as the click of Mrs. Jay hanging up registers. The fresh, free air from moments before becomes suffocating as something close to impending doom covers my skin.

I lean my forehead on the headrest of Elliot's seat in front of me. He slides his hand between the door and his seat, and I take his hand in mine. His hand is warm, but in a different way than the little boy earlier. This kind of touch I crave.

I knew the risks coming into this, but now that it's time to face the consequences, my skin is itchy. The anticipation crawls like spiders over my skin, and I grip Elliot's hand like I might lose it.

What if I do?

What if Mrs. Jay takes him away from me? And even worse, what if he lets her?

Chapter 23
Elliot

We are fucked. She might kill us. Kill me. Kill *her*. Fuck. I should've never involved her. I should've never brought her on.

I got attached. I never get attached, and this is fucking why.

"Crane." Her name falls on my breath. She stares at me with wide doe eyes, waiting for my next word, like I'm the air she fucking breathes, and I don't deserve to be. I don't even know how to get her out of this, let alone be deserving of this gaze.

Enyo's stare drills a hole in the side of my head. He doesn't even know why Mother is pissed. Not really. I'm pretty sure Calix was going to say Mrs. Jay. I knew she was selling Strays into the ring. I knew and didn't tell him. Was that a mistake?

"You gonna clue me in as to why I'm getting my ass grilled when we get back, Brother?"

"The less you know—"

"Don't start that shit with me. Diora obviously knows." His gaze moves from the road to look back at her. "Tell me."

"Don't order her to do shit," I spit, getting pissed.

"I'm first Son—"

"And that's why you can't know," I say. The lie is dirty on my tongue, but he can't know. Not because he's first Son, but because the truth will hurt him.

"What's going to happen now?" Diora asks, not a hint of fear or doubt in her voice, and I could fucking smile at my Little Crane. She's brave, but has no idea the lion's den we'll be walking into.

Mrs. Jay doesn't take disrespect very well. We took down one of her rings and messed with her money, the highest form of disrespect in her eyes.

"We're in deep shit, aren't we?" Enyo mutters as we pull up to Corp's headquarters.

"Very," I mutter. I get out of the car and open Diora's door. I lean in and her sweat covered jasmine and raspberry scent fills my nose, and for a second, I want to whisk her away. It's a dangerous world we live in, yet she is the only person I want to shield from the horrors that come with being a killer for Mother.

Her soft hair grazes my cheek as my lips meet her ear. I press a light kiss against her ear and whisper, "Whatever you do, don't break. Don't let her find out you know she's behind the trafficking. She'll kill you on the spot."

I can feel her nod her head against me, and then I back away. Mother trained me; she knows me—how I move and how I kill. She'd kill Diora if it means hurting me, and I can't let her do that. I can't lose this fight.

Walking in first will tell Mother I was the ringleader for this one. I want her to give me the heat and let the other two go, but I know that won't happen.

The meeting room is eerily quiet as Mother stands at the head of the table, with eight men standing around the room.

"So nice of my top three troublemakers to meet with me. If we'd done this before your little mission, we could have avoided this, but," Mother pauses as she nods toward the men in the room, "you chose to be disobedient."

Her words crawl over my shoulders, memories of these words being said to me over and over again as she plastered my skin with welts or poisons or bruises. My hackles raise as my eyes catch Diora's. I didn't mean to look at her. I shouldn't have, but the urge for comfort has never been this strong before.

This need to protect, and to be protected, isn't an urge I'm used to. It's harder to fight than anything I've had to fight before.

The Strays under her command are on us the second she stops talking. I don't fight as two grab my arms and shove me to stand on one side of the table, and Enyo and Diora are on the other side. We're facing each other now, one hand pressed on the table. Three men hold me and Enyo down, but two are on Diora. Mother knows us well. She's noticeably weaker, obviously, because she's only had a few months of training, versus the years Enyo and I have been here.

"Sons, you know better, but Diora, my sweet Diora, you're new to this. So, I'll keep it light for you," Mother says as she cracks her gloves over her hands repeatedly. I can't help but stare at those fucking gloves. Those same fucking gloves, covered in whatever poison of her choosing. The same burns and rashes mark my back as if they are still there.

"Explain, Enyo. Go," Mother demands, staring at her eldest.

"Trafficking ring on Addline Street was our target."

"When did they become your target, Elliot? Go."

"This morning." It's a lie, of course, and she knows it.

"You randomly decided to take down a human trafficking ring at, what, nine a.m. this morning?" Mother asks with an incredulous smile.

"Yes," I confirm, giving her a half shrug, moving as much as henchmen one and two will allow me.

"If we're going to lie, then there is no point in talking," she says, and with a flip of her finger, one of the men holding down Diora pulls out a knife and slashes the back of her hand.

"What makes you think you can lie to me, my sweet boy?" she ticks as Diora yelps. I throw back my shoulders and trip the guy to my left. He lets go of me as he falls back, but the third man standing behind me lands a kick to the back of the knee, forcing me down, while the guy on my right slams my head down on the table.

My nose crunches with the impact and blood drops are left on the table. Yet it isn't my pain I'm worried about. I'm worried about Diora's.

"Don't make me hurt that darling face any more, Elliot," Mother demands. I see her mask slip. Those eyes that once loved too much. That craved the thrill of youth and wanted it in every sense of the word. The woman who broke children for pleasure.

I'm sure I'm the only one who caught it. That monster isn't for everyone, just her select few.

I sharply laugh, blood dripping from my nose and burning the skin on my lips. I feel the ripping of my skin as a knife is slashed through the back of my hand. I'm stuck watching the Strays holding Enyo down stab his hand, too. All because I couldn't tell him to fuck off. It's all my fault.

"I'm glad you find that funny, because the next time you three decide to venture off without permission, I'll kill you myself."

"Promise?" I ask, the sting in my hand getting worse as open air caresses my wound.

"Get out of my face, all of you." She dismisses the room and Diora looks at me. She always looks at me. She doesn't hide it, she doesn't shy away from it, even though she should. This is what following me will get her.

I can't protect her.

I can't save her.

I'm fucking useless.

I nod toward the door, and Diora leaves the room. I can't focus on anything besides that gaping wound on her fucking hand. I should follow her, apologize for involving her, and promise to never see her again. But I can't.

Coming to stand, I look at Mother. The wrinkles around her eyes are deeper. Her frown is more constant, and no amount of skin product can hide the aging of her skin. She looks tired.

"I said leave, Elliot," she snaps as she sits in one of the rolling chairs. She places her head in her hands, and though I see this moment of weakness, I can't, will never, forget the devil that lurks underneath that skin.

"I didn't blow your cover," I murmur, sitting in a desk chair across from her. I watch as her eyes close and listen to her heavy breathing. As if she did the stabbing herself.

"Yes, you did," she sighs. "I saw the way Diora looked at me. Don't play me for stupid."

"You created the ring, Mother?" I ask, even though I know the answer. It's about time to have this conversation. Admit to the fact that we both know what's going on here.

"Money is to be made."

"You thought we'd be okay with it?" I ask.

"That doesn't matter."

"You're strong, mother. You vile, disgusting, manipulative piece of shit," I say, rolling back in my chair. Standing, I put my unwounded hand in my pocket.

"Wow—" she starts to say, but I'm not done.

"But we loved you. You took that love and did what you always do."

"And what is that?" She raises her eyebrows. If we would've had this conversation years ago, I'd probably have a bullet in my shoulder, but everyone gets old. Everyone becomes tired and weak.

That's why she didn't administer the punishment herself. She has Strays to do it for her. She's not as strong as any of us believe anymore.

"Ruined it," I whisper.

"Like Mother, like Son, then, huh? Like you'll do to Diora." She lets out a sharp laugh. "Son, remember she's not your puppet. She's mine."

"Yeah, okay," I say, walking out of the room. Like hell Diora is her fucking puppet. She's mine. My Little Crane.

Fucking mine.

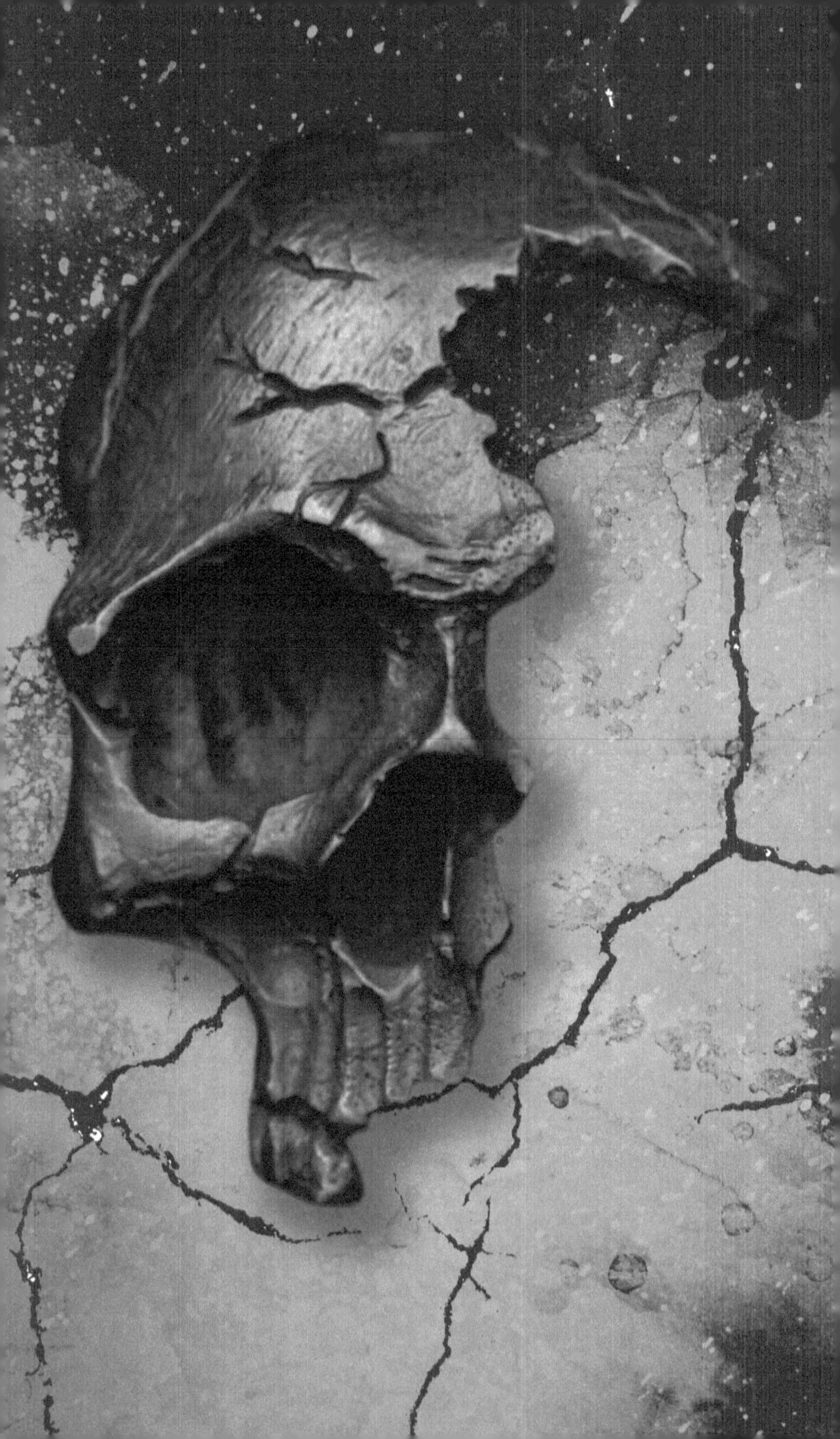

Chapter 24
Diora

It's the day of the party. I was summoned by Mrs. Jay, and there is no avoiding her or the event. It's not like I can tell her no or to rot in hell. I still have a role to play. One Elliot doesn't even know I'm playing.

The trafficking ring can't happen again. I can't sit on my fingers because the woman running them is his "Mother" or because she's my boss.

Mrs. Jay has to die and *I* have to be the one to kill her, because I don't think Elliot will.

Mrs. Jay must not see this coming, or must not view me as a threat, because since the day she stabbed the back of my hand for taking down one for her human trafficking rings, she's been blowing up my company phone. All she talks about is this dumb tea party she's throwing.

As if it's more important than her cover being blown.

None of us are good people, but Mrs. Jay... Mrs. Jay is on another level. It's ironic, really.

My wound has started to scab over; mine isn't nearly as deep as the Son's. I haven't seen them since the punishment. Elliot won't answer my texts, calls, emails, from either of my phones, and Enyo, well, I don't have his number.

I even went to Elliot's apartment in downtown Litchfort and demanded he talk to me, but he wasn't there or wouldn't open the door. I don't know. I should've broken the door down, but this distance is making my skin crawl. I'm doing things I would've never thought I would, like chase a boy down, and... this is not who I am. I think. I don't have these kinds of emotions. I don't chase men. I don't... I don't know why I'm so enraptured with him. I need him like I need my next breath. It's uncomfortable.

"Diora, show these men where the plants go," Mrs. Jay calls from the kitchen, pointing to the clueless group pulling little wagons filled with potted violas and pansies. She's turned this rundown building into a botanical garden. Pinks, purples, and greens light up the place with seven round white metal tables with enough pastel tablecloths and dainty trays to make royals feel flushed with pride.

I can admit it's gorgeous.

Pulling out the map that Mrs. Jay gave to me, I look for where these plants are labeled to go. "Set up these plants at each pillar between the main room and the hallways lining the room."

"It's like an old castle in here. How did we find this in Litchfort?" Enyo's voice comes from behind me, making me jump. I turn around to face him. He's dressed in his "casual" attire of a crisp white button-down and dress pants.

We are left standing around the pond in the middle of the room. It's honestly beautiful, with water that is tinged green, and natural plants and lily pads and stray stems floating in the water.

I wish I could enjoy the party. I wish I could enjoy the kill. But with Elliot going MIA on me and Mrs. Jay working every nerve I didn't know I had with all her demands and text messages, my brain is fried.

"Would you kill me if I pushed you in?" Enyo says with a light shove on my shoulder, and I whip around to face him. I can't tell if he is joking. He's always smiling and laughing. Always happy. Even with the wound with the wrapping still on his hand. He seems... normal?

He's really good at being happy or good at faking it.

Either way, I narrow my eyes slightly at the man, who holds both his hands up in what feels like a mocking surrender.

"I know you would. I'm just kidding." He laughs as he wraps a thick arm around my shoulders and pulls me under his arm. It's close, too close, and it hits me that he came over with a purpose.

"Have you seen Elliot?" he mumbles in my ear, keeping his lighthearted composure, but I can tell in his eyes and by the wrinkles by them, he's... upset.

I shake my head no, a quick movement that makes his shoulders slouch a bit before he finally lets me go. His eyes drop to my hand, where I've left the wound unbandaged to breathe, since it's already started to heal over. He blinks slowly and lets out a slowly counted breath as I move to cross my arms over my chest. It itches more when he's staring at it.

Like it does when Juliet stares at it.

Like it probably would if Elliot stared at it.

If he even bothered to come around.

I watch the room, looking for the man in question, knowing I haven't seen him for days and would be more than surprised if Mrs. Jay asked him to be here tonight. I wonder if she realized he was our ringleader in taking down one of her rings. I wonder what they talked about after Enyo and I left.

I almost miss his head of honey blond strands, but I spot them. I turn in the direction he's come from and so does Enyo.

I try to tame the smile I know I shouldn't reveal in this room of serial killers, but I can't. I smile as my heart settles as Elliot finally looks at me.

I take a freeing breath as he gets closer to Enyo and me. He's here.

"Where have you been?" I whisper, looking anywhere but directly at either of the men. I'm curious if he was at his apartment the other day when I came banging on his door. The asshole doesn't seem like he's done ignoring me yet.

I see Elliot shrug out of the corner of my eye, and I feel his hand fully grasp mine. In the sea of bustling workers and bodies, I'm sure we are concealed from Mrs. Jay's haunting eyes, but I almost feel the instinct to pull away. As much as relief washes over me, I can't forget that he royally pissed me off.

I don't pull away, though. Not even when his fingers brush over my wound. He brings my hand closer to his face, making a show of his interest, and I can't tell if it's purposeful or if he doesn't care what this could tell Mrs. Jay.

"It won't happen again," Enyo mutters, glaring at my hand now, too. He's pissed, too?

My eyes venture to Elliot's hand. His wound seems to be the worst. His white bandage is seeping with blood, and it's been five days already. It pisses me off more than it probably should. Is this what he's been dealing with in regard to my wound? This anger over it happening in the first place? The audacity of someone to mar what's mine and yet being helpless to stop it from happening.

I should be more pissed at Mrs. Jay for trafficking Strays than I am for stabbing Elliot. Rolling my eyes, I sigh. Having emotions is so fucking annoying.

I look up to Elliot, finally meeting his eyes. He raises a brow and I shrug, unsure of what we are communicating, but regardless, with Elliot, it doesn't matter.

"This isn't social hour. Get to work, Diora. I need you in the kitchen," Mrs. Jay snaps, and before we can break away, Elliot grabs the heart pendant on my pearl necklace and grasps it. When he lets go, I feel a newer cool metal bit underneath the heart pendant land on my chest, and I sigh at the contact.

"Don't take it off," he says as he and Enyo walk away, and as much as I would love to be left stumped, I have Mrs. Jay staring down from the kitchen door.

I nod once, more to myself, since he is well gone in the mix of people, but I know whatever it is, it got him to see me again.

I smile, even though there is not anything to really smile about, not in the grand scheme of things.

Mrs. Jay needs to be stopped.

Elliot, one of the few people I care about, might hate me for it.

Most of Juliet's offenders are still alive.

My smile drops as I reach Mrs. Jay, who gets more impatient as each second ticks past.

I try to move past her into the kitchen, but she grabs my arm with a force so fierce it makes me freeze. My eyes shoot to hers. She frowns, and for once in the seven months I have known Mrs. Jay, she looks worried.

"Diora, I want you to know, I'm not mad you guys took down the ring. It was a noble cause. I'm mad you did it behind my back, dear, that's all." Yeah, right.

I only nod my head, my lips pressed in a hard line, as I beeline past her to the stove. She has to know I don't believe her, but if she's scared enough to try to change my mind, she must have lost more than I thought.

The party is in full swing. The targets Mrs. Jay invited are all here mingling, including the political leaders and the mayor of Litchfort, all men involved in the politician's scheme in pimping out Juliet, an unconsenting member.

I watch as they huddle together, murmuring and laughing, as if they aren't dying tonight. It makes me smile. The tea they are all slurping has one to two doses of oleander in it. I needed something that could work in small doses, with a deadly punch, and I figured oleander was the perfect plant for this operation.

It only takes one leaf to kill.

Soon enough, they will get tired, they will take their seats, and that's when their heart rates will start to slow. They will drink more, hoping it will wake them up, and when that doesn't work, the shaking will begin. They are old, so they will think it's normal, something due to the tiredness and age, and soon after that, they will drop dead.

How fantastic.

I stand by the long buffet table, that's more here for show than anything. There is "clean" black tea served here and little pastries and sandwiches that the staff will eat. Everyone working here is on Mrs. Jay's payroll and knows not to drink from the teapots on the tables.

I grab a little Dixie cup and pour myself some tea. Holding it tight in my hand, I step off to the side as more staff grab food from the table. I watch as they smile, snickering to themselves.

"Don't drink that." Elliot's voice comes from the shadows, and I feel his grip on my elbow pulling me deeper in with him. His front is pressed to my back, and he slips the cup from my hand, placing it back on the table.

"We're not on good terms with Mother; we don't know what she'll do," he murmurs along my cheek. Pressing his face side by side against mine, he wraps his strong arms around my waist and pulls me deeper into the shadows.

"Where have you been?" I ask, leaning back into him. He has to know his disappearance hurt me. Hurt me in a way I haven't felt before, and it made the itch to feel blood seeping into my skin roar to life.

The same feeling I had the night Juliet came home covered in red hand marks and tears.

"You got hurt, Little Crane," he murmurs as he runs his fingers around my wound for the second time tonight. I turn my head to look at him, and he is solely focused on my hand.

Like it's his fault.

"It's not—" I start to speak, but he cuts me off with a short nod. His soft hair pressing against the skin of my face. I move my gaze down to the floor, the feeling of content swallowing me whole.

"I don't like it."

"Well, get used to it. I can't throw punches if I can't take them," I say, rolling my eyes. Men. Enough said.

He hums as if my statement was up for debate and he's "thinking" about it, but the first lesson you learn in fighting is don't give what you can't take. Of course, my trainers from before I met Mrs. Jay didn't think I'd use these skills to murder people, but the idea is the same.

I know I could die any minute; my chances of dying are so much higher since I entered this business.

"I have to do better," he says, and even then, I have no idea what he's talking about, and I have no time to figure it out because he's gone in the next second. My body feels cold and hollow as he disappears into the crowd. What the hell?

"Diora, why are you hiding? Come greet your guest," Mrs. Jay says, grabbing my wrist and pulling me out of hiding. "She's so shy sometimes; don't mind her, boys." She's pulling me into the crowd. I glare at Mrs. Jay as the men begin to eye me and smile.

But then I remember this is their last night alive.

And that simple little thought brings a smile to my lips. I stand up straighter and greet each man, shaking their greedy, grubby hands and looking into their eyes, snubbing them the confidence they had only moments before.

I'm not a meek little girl. I'm here for the thrill of a kill.

"I want to thank you for coming. We wanted a night to just enjoy ourselves away from the media and press. Thank you for coming," Mrs. Jay says with a smile so radiant it could make anyone doubt her ability to kill. "Where are the missuses?"

She's so innocent looking, yet her aura is so deadly. I almost forget the true monster standing beside me.

"Mine got sick this morning. Isn't that just a shame? She would've loved the frills of this event," Daniel Kallous says, and the other men in their little group pipe up about their sick or otherwise busy wives. Elliot was all about inviting them tonight to meet the same fate as their husbands, but they didn't do anything wrong. They weren't there that night.

Of course, the women, without plans, got sick, purposely, thanks to the team and I, who spent all night stopping by each other's homes and lacing their breakfasts with food poisoning. Cross contamination is a bitch, isn't it?

I sigh and my eyes trail around the beautiful room, looking for Elliot, of course, but he's nowhere to be found. I spot Enyo chatting up some of the female targets of tonight's event at the fifth table, and the rest of the team is spread out, making what looks like polite conversation.

Hmm. I wonder how long the cleanup will be.

"Oh dear, are you okay?" Mrs. Jay asks, reaching for the first man to be affected by the poison in their drinks. She guides him to sit in his chair as he places a hand over his heart to catch his breath.

The other men start to look deary and tired, and I can't help the smile brightening my face. "I think I need to take a seat, as well. Thank you for the invite, Mrs. Jay," Matthew Oppin says, taking his seat, and the four other men take a seat around the table. Mrs. Jay only winks at me before helping each man to his seat. Each one gets weaker with each minute that passes. I look at the watch on my wrist. It's been an hour since their first sip, but because they've ingested so much of it, it must be working faster. Just like I hoped.

"I'll see if these poor guys are okay," I say as I pull up a chair to sit at the men's table. They all look relieved to have a woman taking care of them, but I'm more excited to watch the lights die in their eyes. Especially as I reveal the real reason they've been invited to this special event.

"Would this count as six on my count for next year's ball?" I ask, more to myself than them, but they look at me in confusion, anyway.

"What?"

"I only need eight bodies a year for this new group I'm in. You wouldn't know about it, but I wonder if this would count toward my eight bodies minimum a year," I explain, joy lacing my tone and making my voice sound unfamiliar in my ears.

"Eight bodies?" Jules Hartford asks as his breathing becomes more and more labored. He must have had a lot more than the rest of the men here.

"Eight. Dead. Bodies," I clarify for them. This has got to be my favorite part. The part when they realize something is truly wrong. The fear makes my poisons seep in faster, so I have to move quicker, but hey, at least I'm one step closer to my goal.

"You're not killing us," Matthew Oppin attempts to laugh but can't.

"Your drinks are, though, and I made your drinks, so by extension, that means I am killing. That means I've killed everyone who has taken a drink from these lovely little teapots on these seven tables. But I don't care for anyone else—just you guys," I say, laying my head in my hands as my smile beams at the dying men, too tired to get up, let alone fight back.

"Why?" one chokes out.

"Does the name Juliet Moss ring any bells or jerk any cocks here?" I ask, tilting my head as if the question is real. Shoulders drop and stuttering words come rushing by, but I'm surprised her name rang any bells at all. They do this so often with the politician, I'm shocked any names ring familiar to them.

I watch dread fill their eyes, and some of their jaws even drop in surprise. They stare silently, as if I just revealed I knew one of their biggest secrets.

"Wow, you remembered. That's great for you. It's less explaining I have to do," I say.

"Those officers, Yara Holdings..."

"Yes, Mayor Kilthmore, those officers were first. They ignored the issue and got rid of the report, but you, you fine gentlemen who committed the act, are next, and Yara, the coordinator, is after that," I explain, tracing the lace patterns on the table as the men try to get up, try to reach for me but can't.

The one who gets closest is Matthew, who's roughly pulled down into his chair by none other than my white knight, Elliot. His hand grips Matthew's shoulder with a damning smile and wild eyes. Matthew tries to escape Elliot's grasp as his peers begin choking on their own breaths, but Elliot's strength is unparalleled, even when you're undrugged. Elliot's strength is hidden within his lean body, and it makes me smile, staring like a schoolgirl. Is this what I've been missing out on?

I love having a crush on Elliot.

Elliot chuckles when Matthew spits toward me. Of course, not having the power or strength to make it land on me. Elliot's fingers inch toward the butter knife on the table mat in front of them, gripping the knife as he stabs it directly in the middle of in the man's hand, pinning him to the table, drawing the attention of the rest of the dying souls in the room, who panic as the poison in their systems start to kick in. Elliot's eyes remain on the knife in the man's hand.

My eyes dart to Mrs. Jay, who sits on a throne on the one balcony in the room, like a queen, watching all the chaos take place. She meets my eye, and the truly crazed soul that lies beneath that skin comes to the surface.

There are Strays everywhere, inside and out, to ensure no one leaves and no one comes in. It's like a virus has suddenly taken over everyone and we are the select few who are immune. I watch as sweat, tears, and fear fill the bodies of the thirty-five people in this room.

A sharp sound draws my attention to the first kill of the night. I hear the life escape Mayor Kiltmore before I see it. As death takes him, his head hits the table, causing the room to go nearly silent. I watch with a sick sort of pleasure as his associates drop like flies.

I wonder if Juliet would be happy. If she would feel safe now that the majority of the people who hurt her that night are dying.

She'll find out about their deaths, as I'm sure it'll make the news, but she can't find out it was me. She wouldn't understand.

She wouldn't forgive me.

Chapter 25

Elliot

"Do it again," Mother snaps. Her cane pounds the floor as the Strays and we run this circuit again.

The day after the tea party, Mother calls the Top Dogs in for group training at five in the morning, and of course, like dogs, we're all here. Diora was called in, too. She's a pipsqueak next to us men, over six feet and packed with muscle that took years to develop.

None of us are as out of breath or sweating like her, but she's only been training for about nine months, and it's only been three months since she started training with Mother.

It's so hard to look at my Little Crane. It hurts to stare at her and see that fucking scar on the back of her hand.

It's my fault she has it. I should've fought her harder to stay home. Hell, I should've locked her up in my apartment bathroom and refused to let her go on that rescue mission.

"Diora, come in last again and I'm giving you another hour of running." I guess she's done being nice. Mother couldn't hide her anger if she was a four leaf clover in a forest of dense moss.

I know I've put a target on Diora's back now that Mother knows I like her. I hope she doesn't find out I actually love her.

As much as a serial killer *can* love someone, anyway.

I watch as she pants, resting her hands on her knees as she tries to catch her breath. It takes everything not to go scoop her up and just walk out of this training room.

I have a face to put on. I can't let Mother win.

Not over Diora, and not over Enyo.

"Put your hands behind your head, Dee," Roan, the brute strength of the team, mutters as he passes her. Her cute face scrunches as she slowly follows his suggestion.

It helps regulate breathing; a lot of athletes do it. So, it helps, but she doesn't know that.

Walking back up to the beginning of this overly done obstacle course that's recently been put in, we get ready to run it once more.

We're used to this kind of training. Stamina is the safest training in the whole damn corporation.

Diora seems ready to murder. Her eyes light as the thought must go through her brain. Her deep brown eyes appear lighter brown than normal.

I can practically feel the happiness it brings me to see her like that in my fucking gut.

"Go," Mother yells, and I watch Diora jet off toward the monkey bars. I go slow, jogging to the monkey bars instead of sprinting, and I see Enyo doing the same.

The mud pile is next, and I drop to the floor once, when Diora is already halfway through the mud. Crawling underneath the electrical net, we make it to the end with minimal shocks, but completely covered in mud.

Racing toward the end, Tom, the newest member besides Diora, makes it across the finish line first this time. Then Parker, Jones, and the others do, too, before Diora does. Last is Enyo, then me.

I stand in line with the rest of the team. I know I shouldn't have lagged behind, and I already know what's coming as Mother comes to stand in front of us. Everyone does.

Mother's voice is sharp in the stillness of the gym inside Haven Corp headquarters. "Leadership is a valued skill. My Sons have shown their ability in it year after year, and while that is admirable, life isn't fair. We leave soldiers unfit behind. I train you to let your comrades die. Though you did not come in last Diora, you earned not just yourself, but everyone, an hour. Go again."

Chapter 26

Diora

"Dee, we're going out to eat. Come on," I hear Roan's voice yell from outside the locker room. I sigh in relief hearing Roan's kind voice.

One thing I'm learning quickly with this group is that they don't complain, they don't blame, and they don't ask questions. They don't seem mad, based on their facial expressions and body language on our way to the showers, but I can't be sure.

See, if one of them earned me an hour of extra training, I would be close to biting one of their heads off.

I guess they are cooler than me.

My eyes search for Elliot's. Is he going? I watch as he stands farthest away from me, but I'm not sure why. His cold behavior makes the craving for blood under my nails intensify. At this point, I'd take anyone's blood, including his.

What the hell is his problem?

I turn to Roan, the friendliest of the group, and nod my head. If Elliot is going to ignore me, then I'm not giving him the pleasure of it irking me.

"Where?" I ask. I do my damnedest not to look at Elliot, but his voice perks my ears as he talks to Roan, not me, of course.

"She can't go." Elliot's voice comes fast as he glares at Roan.

"Why is that?"

"She's got other plans—"

"That isn't until later. Let's go," I say, interrupting the jackass, who suddenly found his voice. Wrapping my hand around Roan's arm, we walk to catch up with the other four members of the group. "Are you coming, too, Enyo?"

"Most definitely, Diora." Enyo laughs as he pats Elliot's shoulder as he walks past.

Oh, this is gonna be fun.

It doesn't take much to get Elliot to fall in line. He follows at the back of the group, while Roan and I walk ahead of everyone, since we wouldn't all fit on the sidewalk toward the restaurant. I do my damndest not to glance at Elliot. Two can play this game.

"What are these plans you have later tonight?" Roan asks, and I grab one of his arms with both my hands, playing the flirt.

"Ahh, I have a meeting. It's not related to anything here." I shrug as we sit at the high tables of a chicken wings based restaurant. Black on black, with splashes of orange, colors the restaurant. High windows and lots of TV screens everywhere. All sorts of sports play, and I watch as the Dogs fill up the space.

It's hard to miss this group. Seven tall, strong beasts of men enter a bar. Each of them surely meeting both men's and women's desires.

"Why so secretive, Dee?" Tom, the newest recruit besides me, pips, with a bolstering laugh and a contagious smile.

"Aren't we all?" I ask, sliding my wet curly hair behind my shoulder. The wet hair touching my skin and soaking my shirt bothers me, but I forgot a clip. A bubbly waitress comes up and takes our orders. Her pin-straight hair up in a neat bun and wide smile remind me of Juliet before the incident.

Would Juliet be as happy as this girl seems if things had been different? If I had protected her like I should have.

What the hell am I doing here? I should be getting ready to kill Yara Holding, not trying to make Elliot jealous.

"Tell us, Dee, how it's been going at Haven?" Hank, the oldest member and the medic specialist of the group, asks as his beer slides in front of him.

"Please ask something more interesting, Hank," Jones, the sharpest shooter ever, says, shoving Hank and turning the spotlight on me.

Juliet would flush prettily under the attention. I think about how it'd be nice to be like Juliet. Like a normal girl. I raise my brows in question, knowing I don't want to enter these dark waters of questioning.

"Where did that wound come from, Dee?" Jones asks. He points to the back of my hand, where Mrs. Jay's punishment is currently healing. It'll scar, but it was worth it.

A small price to pay in the grand scheme of things.

"None of your fucking business," Elliot snaps. He doesn't look at the group from his spot at the end of the table.

"Ohh, was it Elliot?"

"Wait, he has a matching one. Are you into some kinky shit?"

"Nah, Enyo has one, too, unless y'all are all together—"

"Shut the fuck up before I make you," Elliot barks, and it makes the guys laugh, Enyo included.

"Mother doesn't appreciate side missions is all I'ma say," Enyo laughs, sipping his drink with raised brows.

"Are your plans later concerning a side mission, Dee?" Tom asks, raising his eyebrows.

"An approved one, yes," I laugh. I can't help but to glance at Elliot. He's already staring at me, or more so, my hand. I purposely move my hand to the right and watch as his eyes follow.

He's not over that yet?

I roll my eyes as I focus back on the group. That's worse than him being mad at me. I have a guilty puppy to convince to love me instead of an angry viper.

"Okay, okay, well, let's talk about that damn tea party—"

"Let's not. We're in public, dumbasses," Enyo snaps.

Elliot remains silent throughout the lunch, and I feel... bad he's torturing himself.

But I also can't help but be attracted to the tortured man. That must be my type.

No, actually, I think Elliot is my type. That's it, no one else.

Elliot gets up to leave, and I follow him with a small, "I'm going to the bathroom," excuse. I follow him as he walks back to Haven's parking lot.

He must park his own car instead of letting the valet do it.

"Stop following me," he calls out, but I ignore him and keep a distance of five feet between us. He rolls his shoulders, as if he's getting pissed, and I smile. Good. Maybe he'll get a taste of what I've been going through.

He slips inside the blacked out car I don't care to know the model of. I slide into the passenger seat before he has the chance to lock it on me. His head snaps toward me with a glare.

"Are you dense, Diora?"

"Are you stupid, Elliot?"

"What the hell are you talking about?"

"You think giving me the cold shoulder will keep me away?" I say, drawing closer to the fuming man. I can practically touch the heat of anger coming off his skin, and yet I didn't care he might burn me. "You think you can ignore me? That it'd be easy to get rid of me?"

Reaching over, I click the lock on his door handle. I swing my leg over his seat, trapping him under me. The loud click of the lock rings through the car. I gaze at him through my lashes. "You can't get rid of me, Elliot Jay."

He glares at me, and I swear I melt a little under his stare.

"What if I want to?" he lies, but his eyes tell me he doesn't mean that. His light brown eyes burn, and his hands dig into the sides of my hips, holding me firmly in place.

I tilt my head as my hand cups the side of his face, his smooth, soft skin pouring warmth into my hand. I lean my face forward, just an inch, and his lips dart up to meet mine. But I lean away before his lips can meet mine.

"You clearly don't," I murmur against his lips as both my hands come up to reach his face. I lean into him, his dark chocolate smell fills my nose, and I grind against him, feeling him already hard for me.

"Fuck, Little Crane," he whispers, grinding his hips against mine. I jerk forward, filled with more than need—with desperation. Desperate for him, his scent, his cock.

I almost smash my teeth into his trying to get closer to him. Pressing my body completely against his, I lean further down, trying to find the lever to let the seat down. I need him, and I need him now.

He pushes my hand away, and his chair leans back as I climb over him properly. I straddle his hips as my hands press against his clothed chest. His clothed chest. Hmm.

"Let's take this off," I murmur, reaching for his shirt. He follows my lead as he eyes my top.

"Fuck that. I need one last taste," he says, and suddenly, my upper body is thrown forward, toward the back fucking seat. His hands grip my hips as he positions me right over his lips.

"My pants," I breathe, cursing that I put on sweatpants after my shower.

"Not a problem." He kisses my cunt over my pants. I hear a sharp click of metal against metal before a clean tear allows a harsh breeze of air against me. I shiver, sensitive as ever, as he continues ripping the seam of my pants.

"Elliot," I gasp. My hands land on the leather seat of the back as his tongue attacks my lips.

He licks me with long, savory strokes, taking his time as he riles me up. My arms burn from holding myself up, and it turns me on more. The frustration in my muscles from this and training settling into my core.

He doesn't answer me, solely focused on his task, as it is all self-serving for him. Yanking my hips forward to meet his mouth better, my knees rip against the leather of his headrest and practically dangle on the sides of his chair.

I can't move my lower half. I'm dependent on him. His hands grip my hips and grind me against his face. Shaking, I feel the pressure build.

"My favorite fucking meal." His words brush against me, and I don't think I can take much more. Fuck. My lack of core strength doesn't even allow me to run my fingers through his hair, and it irks the hell out of me.

His lips caress my skin as one of his hands moves away from my hips. I lift a bit, hoping he'll breathe, but the thought quickly disappears as he enters a finger into me.

Warmth crawls over my skin as Elliot relentlessly devours me like a starved man. And his starvation for me would be all his fucking fault.

He laps at me while his fingers curl, and I can't hold it any longer. I come against the flat of his tongue as he eats me to the very end.

He presses a light kiss against me before pulling me back down into his lap.

"Your turn?" I breathlessly mutter, trying to turn in his lap, but his hands on my hips stop me.

"Not today, Little Crane," he sighs as he kisses me. I can taste myself on his tongue. I try to take the kiss deeper, but he doesn't let me. He leans away from my kiss. I get a rush of disappointment but also something more.

Desperation? I feel him slipping through my fingers, and I don't know how to get him to stop.

"We have time," I mutter, wanting to crawl down his lap. It's not only the fact that I miss the taste of him, but that I know—I can feel—that once we leave this car, it's over. Something is over, and I can't—I don't want... This can't be over.

He doesn't let me move. My eyes shoot to his in a panic. I try to be seductive, warming, alluring. I don't know. I need something. I need him.

I touch the side of his face, trying to get him to look at me, and though he reaches my eyes, he's not looking at me, he's going through me.

His eyes fog over, and I can see him slipping back into his mind.

"Elliot," I say, trying to bring him back. "What's wrong? Tell me. I can't fix what I don't know."

"You can't fix this, Little Crane."

"I can."

"I have to do this myself." He sighs. He rests his hand on the back of my head and guides me to lie on his chest. I fall and rise with his breath, and my chest shatters. It constricts with a pain

I'm not familiar with, and I wanna meet Elliot's eyes, but now I can't.

I'm the one hiding.

"Do what, Elliot?" I ask. My voice comes out small, in a way I've never heard before, and it makes me want to stop talking.

He doesn't answer me again. Instead, he plays with my now dry hair, and I let him.

I let him, because this doesn't sound like a monster I can kill. This sounds like a monster he'll have to kill from the inside.

I sigh against his chest. My chest hurts as I lean to sit up.

"What are you gonna do about my pants?" I sigh. There is a hole along the seam that attaches the two legs together.

He sighs as he looks at me. Frustration brings his brows together as he leans forward in the car and searches through the consoles.

He gazes back at me like a wounded puppy. Like he's the one who failed. It's the same frustration from our time in the forest at the ball.

"I'll sit with my legs closed. It's not a big deal." He shakes his head, and I smile a bit, the sound warming the pain in my chest. He cares still, that much I know.

"Let's go eat, then. I really wanted some chicken wings," I say as I get out of the car from the driver's side. "You think the Top Dogs are still there?"

"Probably," Elliot shrugs, taking my hand in his as we walk back. "They practically live there."

I walk through the door of Juliet's and my apartment, setting my keys down, even though I'll be heading out soon. The secondary lights are on, meaning Juliet is home. She hates the overhead lights and prefers warm lamps and candles for lighting, which is fine with me. It's more visually pleasing, so I let her do whatever she wants.

"Dee! Hey," Juliet warmly says as she pops out of her room, seemingly listening for my arrival. She wears a long fuzzy cardigan, and I smile at seeing her so at ease. I watch as the sun set in the window and wonder how long I have before she falls into the darkest parts of her mind.

Yara Holding is Juliet's ex-girlfriend, lawyer turned politician, who will do anything to build connections and climb up the government ladder. She wanted to become the most powerful woman in government—the senate majority leader. While I could admire her ambition, I'll admire the light draining from her deep brown eyes as I kill her.

"Dee, why don't we have a girls' night? We could order in, watch a movie, paint our nails—"

"I can't tonight, Juliet. I have plans," is a sentence I never thought I'd say. She was always the one with plans. She was the popular girl, the kind girl, the one everyone liked and got along with, even if she was incredibly shy.

I never minded being her shadow, her darkness. I loved it. I still do. Killing Yara Holding is me being her darkness. She won't need to hold on to her darkness from that night after I'm done. Yara isn't the last on my list, but I crave her death more than the others.

"Plans? Again? With Elliot?" She's taken aback as her eyes stray from my face. She reaches for my hands to aid her pleading, and before I can yank them away from her, I feel her fingertips drag along the healing wound on my hand.

"Dee, what happened to your hand?" she asks in shock as she pulls me to the sink to wash an already washed and tended to wound.

Her eyes shoot up to meet mine before she sighs and gently lets go of my hand.

"It's nothing. I scraped it," I say, trying to put my hand with the wound in my pants pocket without flinching.

"Nothing? Are you okay? Did... did Elliot do this? Diora, you have to tell me if something is going on." Juliet's worry raises my hackles, and I try to dim her worry with a smile.

"No, he didn't. He scraped his hand, too. We were moving boxes at work and a sharp end got the backs of our hands. I promise."

"You promise?" She's watching every move of mine now, searching for the lie she'll never find.

"I promise," I confirm, walking away from her and toward my room. "I have to get ready for my date with Elliot."

"Can I help you?" she meekly asks, and I break. I wanna say no, since I'm not really getting ready for a date, but I can't say no to her. Not when she's like this.

Not when I can sense her night fritz is coming on.

I can see the tension in her shoulders build as her posture becomes impossibly straighter. Her eyes hold back tears that never drop. It's like her eyes glass over permanently, but I know it'll disappear by morning.

"Please," I say and wait for her to follow me to my room.

"Dee, are you hiding something from me?" Her voice is desperate, and it sends a thrill of fear down my spine. Few things scare me. I can list the things that scare me on one hand, and Juliet's voice right now is on it. Disappointment, fear, her desperation, are scary to me. I'm her sister; I never want to hear her voice in this tone. It sets my brain on alert.

I turn to face her. There's a tremble in her fingers and her lips shake, but I don't think she notices. I try to soften my smile, my eyes, as I grasp her hands in mine firmly. Grounding her the best way I can.

"No, Juliet," I lie, leading her into my room. I sit on the stool before my vanity. "Help me with my hair, please."

"I know you're hiding something. I don't know what, and I won't pry beyond this, but whatever it is, Dee, I'm your big sister. I can help you," she says as she picks up a spray bottle and a hairbrush.

"Not with this one," I mutter while picking up my phone. Now that Elliot and I made up, I hope he sticks to tonight's plan.

I pull up his contact and type out a quick message before Juliet can see over my shoulder.

R u still coming?

I wait for a response, a ring or vibration, something. I need something, a confirmation that he is going.

There is a chill I haven't been able to get rid of since I got home, and I watch Juliet from the mirror. She's fritzing as she brushes my hair, freezing and jerking the brush, and I let her. There is a lot of pressure for tonight to go right. Maybe that's why I am so... off. Why is Elliot acting so weird today? I don't know. I should stay here with Juliet tonight, but I don't know if I'll get another chance to kill Holdings. Am I rushing this? Too many questions and not enough answers. There is only one thing I'm sure of.

Elliot doesn't answer my text.

Something is wrong.

Chapter 27

Juliet

I shouldn't pry. I shouldn't pry. I shouldn't pry. But oh, do I have the need to dig. My skin prickles like it needs to be burned off my body, and my nails break under the pressure of my fingers digging into the island. Fuck. Another chipped manicure.

Diora's been gone for thirty minutes. She left. She went from never leaving the house to leaving almost every night. It's outside her pattern. It's not her normal.

People change, though? Yes. People change. Maybe Dee has some friends who actually understand her. Maybe she has found someone better than me. Not that it'd be hard, but she wouldn't leave me forever, right? She wouldn't. She loves me no matter what. No matter what.

I grab the kitchen rag from the sink and cleaning off the counters again. The counters could be considered clean, but I can't help but clean the entire counter again, even though my nail polish chips could've been cleaned by swiping them off the counter. But then, I'd have to sweep the floors again today, which doesn't sound like a bad idea, actually.

But what is she hiding from me? *Why* is she hiding something from me? After... everything, what would she need to hide from me? Would it be triggering? Is she... I don't know. I don't know.

I need a shower. I need one now. I stop mid wipe and trail into the more than needed shower. The water's hottest setting barely soothes the itch over my skin. Minutes pass and steam starts to revert my straight hair back to curly, and I can't seem to find a care. Not at this moment.

Stepping out after soaping up, I watch as the steam follows me through the bathroom as a whole. The mirror is completely fogged up, and water droplets cover the floor. Drying off, an eery feeling spreads across my back, and I rush out to the living room. Towel wrapped around my body but gripped together in my shaking hands.

I'm scared. At least I can recognize it now. Six months ago... Five months ago, I couldn't.

I have a routine. I follow a routine every night. It gives me control. I have control. My stiff back hits the wall beside the bathroom, wishing for protection that isn't there.

What if someone is on the other side of this wall? With a knife? What if they get me this time? What if they kill me—

I slam my eyes shut, shaking my head. Move, Juliet, move. I have to move or I'll be stuck here all night. Prying open my eyes, the light of the hallway flutters in my system. I don't look down the hall, I don't look toward the kitchen, just straight to my room.

I see the light green painted door and dart toward it. Hastily grabbing the handle, I yank the door open, then shut it behind me, gripping my towel to my body.

I'm okay. I'm safe. I'm okay.

Swallowing the fear left in my throat, I move through my room. I can never stay naked for long. Not unless I'm in the shower. I need coverage. Whether it be water or clothes, I need coverage. I need to be safe.

I'm alone, though. I'm not safe when I'm alone. I'm not safe? No. Stop.

I may be alone, but *they* are not here to hurt me. *She* is not here to hurt me.

I *am* safe.

A text comes through my phone, sitting on my nightstand. Curling my trembling fingers, I reach for it. Sliding to sit against my headboard, I open the text.

All clear.

Two words from a virtual stranger. I don't know who they come from, but they always follow an anxiety attack.

It's an unknown number, maybe a number I forgot to save? I don't know. I shouldn't even believe the text, or give it another thought, but I can't pretend it doesn't soothe my mind when they come. Almost like someone is watching over me, no matter where I am. That even if I am alone, I'm not.

Of course, it's not true. I'm the only person here, but it… helps. Getting lotioned and dressed in my coziest pajamas, I make my way to the living room. I'm able to move freely now after the text. I can relax. Calm down.

Sitting down on the couch, I click on the news. Being in the know is the one comfort I can give myself. I need to know everything. Any and all crimes, world news, wars. I need to know what's going on so I can see. Truly see what's going to happen. Watch my own back.

"The deaths of these four officers is a tragedy, and while it has been labeled a case of misfortune, some still believe this was a planned attack."

"Thanks for the update, Jim. Please keep the families of these officers in your prayers." The news woman stares at the camera, but the four pictures that come up shoot a bullet down my body, and I can't feel anything anymore. The pictures of the four officers who blew off my rape report that night come across the TV screen one by one, and I can feel the tears I constantly hold back drop one by one. Josh Panko, Kyle Montery, Lewis Karplie, and Orlando Jones are dead. Since when? Dead? All four? On the same night?

Oh fuck.

Oh.

Fuck.

Diora.

Chapter 28
Diora

The bar is crowded, which I would normally hate, but tonight, I need it. Careful laughs and twinkling lights make me all too aware of the kind of establishment Yara Holdings wanted to meet me in tonight.

She thinks I'm an author writing a book on America's most powerful women, and I wonder if she truly believed my cover.

I'm alone on this one as far as I know. Elliot never texted me, and I'm getting fed up with his hot and cold attitude.

I don't need him. He was never part of my plan. I was always meant to do this myself.

I find my target sitting alone at the bar. The black countertop shines nearly as brightly as her jewel earrings. Her brown hair is tucked into a slicked back bun with carefully placed curly pieces decorating her slim face. She has a beautiful side profile with smooth skin and thin lips.

Too bad this will be the last night anyone sees it. She wears incredibly fitted dress pants and a blouse that has to be made of expensive silk.

She probably can afford that blouse from selling my sister's body.

That's all it takes to solidify the kill tonight. One of us will be dying, and I am dead set on it being her.

"Ms. Holdings, so nice to meet you," I say, tracing my hand on her back to her shoulder as I sit down beside her. All she has is a martini glass in front of her, and I can appreciate her choice for her last meal.

"Please, the pleasure is all mine. I must say, you have an outstanding backlist, Mrs. Landcast," she says in a voice that purrs all too smoothly. Having Elliot help create my persona meant putting up fake publishings that date back within the five years.

"Thank you. I only sell to a selective crowd now, if you know what I mean," I say. Darcy Landcast is an author turned personal intel collector for US government officials, and anyone with deep enough pockets, who want to know who is on the come up.

"Well, I must know who this next book is for?" Yara asks, smoothing her hands over her lap. The first and only sign of nerves on her part.

"Ahh, I think you know," I wink and turn away, waving the bartender down with eye contact and a nod. I order a Coke and turn back to Yara.

I lean over her, my black sleeves crossing the front of her chest as I hold her head and caress her hair as if we were lovers. As my right hand goes to hold her cheek, I slip some finely crushed up foxglove in her full, dark drink. "Max Coldwell has been asking about you," I whisper in her ear.

Her eyes widen as who I'm talking about registers in her mind. Max Coldwell works for the senate, but in the background, and has major influence over those who vote for the majority leader position, which Yara is gunning for. If she could get him in her pocket now, she'd secure her spot there in the future.

She's looking for dirt. Something that will have the man with the most influence on her side.

It's why she pimped out my sister. To later have dirt on the mayor of Michigan and all his little goons.

Too bad her strategy will be her biggest weakness.

"What does he want to know?" she asks, her voice dripping with need.

"Anything I find out," I whisper, leaning into her energy.

"I'll tell you everything," she breathes, as the light in her eye intensifies. "As long as you can get me one meeting with him."

"No." As if I really know the man, saying yes too early will alert her that something is wrong here.

"Come on, one meeting."

"No," I say, sitting back down on my barstool but keeping close to Yara.

"How much?" she whispers.

"How much?"

"Don't play dumb. Name your price and I can have it to you by morning." Yara tries again, and this time, I look at her from the side of my eye. Letting her think I'm giving in. Except I don't want her dirty money. I want her skin to lose its light and turn gray.

I want her dead more than anything.

"Let's talk somewhere more private." I let the words linger on my lips as her lips smile, and I think I may have her.

Her eyes become dull and her fingers fidget. Foxglove doesn't kick in this fast, not the amount I gave her. I tilt my head as she stares. She must be on something else. But what? I don't recall any addictions in the file Elliot and I drafted up.

She mindlessly nods her head, and I grab her hand as I lead us out of the club. Rule number one of staying alive is to never let someone get you to a second location. She broke the rule in a fifteen-minute conversation.

Yara stumbles, and I wrap her arm around my shoulders. What the hell did she take? Is it reacting to the poison?

I drag her next door. Popping the door open with my hip, I push Yara inside. Her pitchy laugh scratches my ears as she stumbles in. I quickly close the door behind me, and suddenly, Yara whips around to face me, and her drink is warm and sticky as it lands on my face.

"What the hell?" I spit, stepping back and wiping my face.

"You tried to poison me, you fucking bitch," Yara yells as she runs at me. She has a knife that comes out of nowhere. I dodge her swing, rolling on the floor and popping back up behind her. Thank fucking god I've been training with the Dogs.

"You killing my fucking team? Is it fucking you and these weak ass drinks?" she mindlessly yells as she keeps coming at me with her knife. I don't know if it's my months of training or what, but it's easy to dodge her.

Fear must control her motions. She's wild, weak, and scared. She must feel how Juliet felt that night. How Juliet's felt every day since.

"It's not a nice feeling, huh?" I ask as she runs into a dining table, trying to land that ridiculous pocket knife in me.

"What the fuck are you talking about?" she screeches.

"Being haunted. It's not fun being on the opposite end, is it?"

"I'm getting tired of your damn riddles, bitch."

"But I'm having so much fun," I say, tilting my head to admire the split in the wood table. She's weak, but her knife still went into the table. I giggle, turning to face her.

Her brows furrow as the fear clouds her eyes.

"Crazy fucking bitch," Yara yells, and this time, I let her get close. It's a risk, letting her get this close, since she's obviously not drugged and was faking the symptoms before. This was a risk we'd known would be there, but we'd take, anyway.

She swings, and I hit her wrist, and the knife drops out of her hand. She quickly swings her other hand, landing a blow across my face. My head snaps to the side, and a laugh slips past my lips as Yara stands frozen.

Her brows furrow as I nod a singular time and bring both my hands to her shoulders and headbutt the fuck out of her.

We stumble away from each other. That shit hurts, but the pain on Yara's face makes it worth it.

She doesn't make it far before her arm is in my grasp again and I throw her against the wall. She's got a few inches on me, but I've got shock working in my favor. I slide my own knife, a butterfly knife I found in one of the training rooms, against her throat. Scratching her skin, but not pressing deep enough to make her bleed.

"I've been waiting to do this since September twenty-third."

"September?"

"The night you ruined Juliet Moss," I whisper in her ear as she tries to buck me off of her. Her body suddenly stills at the name, and she tries to look back at me, but I've got her locked against the wall.

"You could've done so much with your life. You could've become the most powerful woman in the world, but you won't."

"Help!" she yells, realizing she's met a beast scarier than herself.

"You won't become the most powerful woman in the world because you hurt the *one* person I care for."

"Please. I'm sorry. I'm so sorry. I won't do it again. I'll never talk to Juliet again."

"You're right, you won't," I say, as I slide the knife into the side of her neck. Blood slowly slides out between the knife and her skin, covering my hand and her blouse. She screams and screams as her body gets weaker in my hands.

"Goodbye, Yara," I say as I let her body drop from my grasp. Her weight slides off my knife, and I smile at the satisfying pop sound it makes as her body disconnects from the knife.

It's done.

It's finally fucking done.

Chapter 29

Elliot

I stare at her text for a moment. I am missing our date, killing Yara Holding, the woman who hurt Juliet Moss almost a year ago. I've never cared about who I kill, not like Diora. She has a mission, a goal. I do what I want based on a feeling.

This feeling comes from the henchman stabbing a knife through my Little Crane's hand.

My Little Crane.

Now she has that scar on the back of her hand, and it's all I can fucking think about. The two men responsible for the scar are bound to metal chairs in my apartment in downtown Litchfort.

I have surveillance of both the bar Diora is at and the second location, where Yara will die. I need to see her, even if I'm not with her. Breaking into the surveillance cameras of both establishments was easy enough, and putting the cameras on loop was even easier.

Uploading the real footage to my app on my phone was even easier.

"You of all people know we can't say no to Mrs. Jay," henchman number one says as the sweat drips from his forehead.

"Yeah, man, come on," the second one agrees. He's scared, and that's when things begin to unclick for me. This fear, this emotion, isn't genuine. Not coming from them. They are entirely too relaxed in their bonds, and I wonder if Mother warned them. Maybe they think she will come to save them.

If that's their thought, they wouldn't have survived much longer in this world.

Dear Elliot,

last warning.

Mother's text comes through on my regular phone. I wonder why she's switched. That must solidify the opposing teams we are on now. Mother versus me. Totally didn't see this coming. I roll my eyes as I throw the phone on the table with my computers.

"That was your savior messaging me," I say as I drag a dining chair in front of them and straddle it to face them.

"Good, did she tell you this is ridiculous and to let us go?" henchman number two asks, raising his brows.

"Yeah," I say simply, with a lazy shrug. In not so many words, but yeah, that's what she was getting at. "But I'm not going to."

"Elliot, man, come on." Watching them struggle in their restraints is funny. Watching them nearly topple over is even funnier. I chuckle as I rise from my chair and drag them back to their places. The white tarp under them wrinkles under my footsteps and their shaking chairs.

Their eyes track my every move. It's not nearly as pleasing as Diora's stare, but my excitement is building, nonetheless. "Let's play a little game."

I lay out my choice weapon for tonight's game—daggers—and listen as their tussling becomes louder.

"Whoever survives the longest gets to live," I say, picking up the dullest one.

"What if we both live?"

"Then we keep going until one of you doesn't," I say, throwing my first blade at the one who stabbed their knife in Little Crane's hand.

Diora Moss is my crane, but I'm not hers. I don't bring good luck to her; all I've done is gotten her hurt.

I clean up the bloody mess; both guys are dead as I planned. Their limp bodies hang from their chairs, with knives of all kinds protruding from their bodies. Rolling my shoulders, I sigh as I take in the sight.

I missed seeing Diora for this. Instead of seeing my Little Crane kill, here I am, punishing these two henchmen for touching what's mine. Solidifying the target on my crane's head by angering Mother.

It's probably better if I don't see Diora again.

This has become a shit show, and it's all my fucking fault.

History repeats itself, and once again, I have a choice to make. When I was young, the decision was easy. I killed my foster parents for molesting the girls. It was plain as day why I chose to kill them, but now, twelve years later, the same decision isn't as easy to make.

Both of my foster parents deserved to die in my eyes. While the father was the one committing the crimes, the mother let him. She looked the other way. She'd remain silent when the kids tried to tell the social workers, and every single person was letting the crime slide.

That was when the urge to kill manifested.

And now I'm in the same fucking predicament as when I was fourteen.

This time, Mother is the foster father and I'm the fucking foster mother, letting her commit the crime. Oliver Longstead would've killed me for what I've been doing. Except life is not as simple as it was when I was fourteen.

Still, I know I can't let Mother live. I know this, yet a shower of dread covers my bones and my thoughts run toward the one person I cared about for so long.

My phone rings and Enyo's name comes up on the screen. I picked the phone up while wrapping the bodies in the tarp, so I can dispose of their bodies.

"Hey, man," I answer the phone and silence greets me for a beat before the rush of words assault me.

"Hey, we need to talk."

"Talk about what?" I ask, squatting next to the bodies on the floor.

"About you and Diora."

"Nothing's there, so don't worry about it." The less we knew about each other's personal agendas, the better. That's how it's always been. We don't want the other to have information that Mother can beat out of us.

It happened one time, and after that, we vowed to never let it happen again. One of us had a girlfriend. Enyo was in love with Elena Monte, fresh from high school.

He became her stalker for two years, watching her every move. Every time I called him, he was watching her. I'll never forget the first time he asked me to install cameras in her family's home, so he could "keep her safe". I said no, of course, but he convinced me after two months of endless begging.

It was too late by then, though. Mother had caught wind of an emotional flair for someone outside the corp. Once she found out, she pulled me into her room. The torture had intention behind it. A purpose behind the beating. It took all my will to resist. She knew I knew about Enyo's girlfriend and wouldn't tell her. She beat me until Enyo found me three days later. He broke and told her everything. She killed Elena the next day.

We aren't even allowed to date people who are part of the Society. We aren't allowed to love anyone outside of Mother, and she used Elena Monte to teach us that lesson.

Regret isn't something I experience often, but the day Enyo found her body in her bedroom, with a knife wound in her neck and chloroform residue on her cheek, I felt it.

If I'd put the damn camera in her room, maybe he would've been able to save her. Maybe if I forced him to stay away from Elena, he wouldn't have gone through the depression he did.

I don't like to play what-if games. In this world, there is no point. But from then on, I vowed to protect him. I'm a protector, and I'll protect Enyo, mentally and physically, for the rest of my life.

Her death put him in a depression for two years, and I'd rather see him dead than like that ever again.

"Let's skip the denial and think of a game plan to protect her against Mother."

"No, Enyo—" I begin to say. He can't get involved. He knows this, so what's changed?

"I know this is different than Elena. Diora has killer instincts, but Mother *will* beat her if we don't have a plan."

"A plan for what?" I ask, playing along with his game. There is only one plan that would save Diora. Save me. And that's—

"We have to kill her."

"What? Kill who, Enyo?" I ask, dropping the knife I pulled from the wood floor. Enyo doesn't want to kill Mother. He can't.

"Mother. We have to kill Mother. History will not repeat itself, Brother. Another love will not die at the hands of her jealousy. We deserve more."

"I—" If he knew the truth, would he still want to kill her? If he knew she was his birth mother.

Fuck.

Sighing, I sit down at my desk. I should tell him. No, I can't. I shouldn't. Maybe I can die with this secret and he'll never have to know.

"We're not waiting this time. She will not hurt us anymore."

"Is there someone else?" I ask as my brows furrow. He may be fighting for Diora, maybe for me, but there's something more going on. There has to be. Killing Mother is not a light thought. As much as I hate the woman, she... she raised us when no one else would. I—We can't pretend she didn't.

"No." His answer comes too fast and snappy. I snort as his side goes quiet. He could never lie to me for some reason, though I know the man *knows* how to lie.

"Who?" I ask, trying to think of anyone he's interacted with in the last six months.

"This is about you, lover boy. We need a game plan." He spins the story and I could laugh. Enyo's hiding someone again. That's why he's ready to take down Mother suddenly.

This someone, he's willing to kill for. When this man is ready to kill the one person who saved him from a life in the system, she must have dug her claws so deep he can't move without her ripping his skin.

He didn't even want to kill Mother after she killed Elena Monte. Who is this mystery woman?

He's as trapped as I am.

"Don't worry about it. I got Diora," I say, knowing the words are a lie. I'm out of control with Diora. She holds too much meaning to me. I'm damn near ready to do anything for her.

Anything but betray my brother.

"No, Elliot. Mother is already working on a plan." His words land like bullets in my chest. Is it too late? Is it too late to save her?

"What do you mean?" I ask.

"Mother already knows. She wants to get rid of her."

"When?"

"She wouldn't say."

And there's another decision I have to make. One I've dreaded making since the moment I laid eyes on Diora Moss. One that may not even have a "correct" choice.

To distance myself from Diora.

Or to keep her close.

All in the name of keeping her alive.

A pounding sounds at my door, and I jump. Twisting my chair to face my desk, I click on the security footage of the apartment.

I see her. Little Crane. Banging on my door.

"Open the door, Elliot." I hear her voice, but I remain frozen in my seat. I can't... I don't know. I don't know what to do.

"Enyo, how much... how much time do you think I have left?" I ask with a shaken voice I wish I could hide. As a killer, I should have my fear indicators in check. No one should be able to read me better than I can read myself and yet, I'm dissolving under the pressure that is love.

"Days."

"How do I... How can I keep her alive?"

"Elliot!" her voice yells, and there's an edge of desperation. The same edge ringing in my ears.

"Are you asking me for advice? Wow, I never thought I'd see the day."

"Enyo, be serious for two damn seconds," I snap.

"I already fucking told you, we have to kill Mother."

"What if I stayed away from Diora, made her seem unimportant to me?"

"That's what got Elena killed. Don't be stupid," he whispers, and that's when I shoot up from my chair. I land my hand on the door handle, and I'm about to open it when Enyo's voice comes back through.

"What if I can't protect her?"

"You can't keep playing the defense, Elliot. It's about time you come on the offense," Enyo says, trying to be... encouraging?

"We kill Mother first. Then we get the girl."

"Then we get the girl," he confirms.

I hear her sobs from the other side of the door, but Enyo is right. I have to deal with Mother first. That will be the only way to protect her. Once we deal with Mother, I can be with her. Freely. Undoubtedly. Hers.

"I have to go. Meet me at the headquarters in thirty minutes. I have something I need to tell you. Off the phone," I say and hang up.

I will not fail her.

I will not fail her.

I can't.

The pounding on my door gets quieter and so does her hoarse voice. It takes everything not to whip open the door and bring her into my arms. But if I do, I'll trap her in here, and knowing Diora, she wouldn't stay put. I have one day to make my move and kill Mother.

I only hope Enyo will forgive me.

CHAPTER 30

Diora

I may be done with my mission, but it doesn't feel like I'm done. Yara Holdings' dead body is being cremated at the Haven Headquarters, and yet I don't feel... done? Accomplished?

I tried to get Elliot to show his damn face. I went knocking on his apartment door again. I could've broken the damn door down, been more prepared this time, but... I'm fucking tired.

He wouldn't open his door, and we are back at square one. If this is still about the damn scar, I think I'm going to lose my mind.

He has to get over that. I'm a killer. More than that, I'm bad, evil. I'm going to get hurt.

The white metal door of my little greenhouse in the woods creaks as I step inside. Surrounded by my lovely flowers and herbs, I'm almost at peace. Almost to a point where the drag of the burn in my chest doesn't hurt. Yet the fire is still there. Lighting the fire, never letting it go out.

My workbench lights up under the lamp. Fighting the darkness that threatens to swallow it, and I just can't fight anymore.

Elliot Jay, you're one annoying piece of shit. Did he ruin my sense of accomplishment? Do I feel this way because he left me?

Checking my phone, not a single notification has come through since I sent that text before I left. All I wanted was you. I don't need you to protect me. I just want you.

I pick up my shears, the heavy shiny metal in my hands, and grip them hard. A tear falls down my face, landing on the shears, and I honestly could laugh. Truly.

A sob escapes my lips as I swing my arm aimlessly, throwing the damned things across the room. Next is a glass vase, and then a pair of pliers, a cup of dirt.

I tear up the foxglove stems with my bare hands and throw them. A flurry of pinks, purples, and whites blur my vision as I keep ripping.

Same with the elephant ear plants, my daisies, my oleander. My hands burn, and I can't stop destroying... destroying everything. I move across the room, ripping whatever my hands touch, and I fall in front of the one tree in here. Angel trumpets hang off the small branches above me, and I wish they'd shower me with their poison. I wish they would wash away the pain in my chest with a pain I'm familiar with. One I know how to heal. My knees hit the floor as the sobs wrack through me.

All the memories of Mom, Dad, and Juliet flow as Elliot's rejection stings through my veins. How could I be so stupid?

Why would he choose me? We both may be killers, but that doesn't mean he'll accept me. My... my love. My love.

I love that man.

Oh my god, I love Elliot Jay. Shit.

I turn around, away from the tree, a lash of anger scorching my senses.

My greenhouse is a mess, and yet it isn't messy enough. My gloveless hands rip apart my remaining plants. I throw anything I can grasp and kick around the boxes too heavy for me to pick up. This fire won't die.

It won't die.

Covered in sweat, dirt, and tears, I plop to the ground. My knees burn at the harsh contact with concrete and I stare at my mess. My masterpiece.

Emotions are a funny thing.

They take over when you least need them to, and what's even funnier:

Once you turn them on, you can't turn them off.

"Diora," Juliet calls as soon as I shut the door behind me and set my keys in the bowl next to the door. I can't fight the relief covering my face. Maybe things really are how they are supposed to be. I have my sister. My targets are dead. Maybe I can live in this world, where good and evil can mix, and I can fit right in.

Maybe I don't want Elliot, after all. Maybe I never needed him, or Mrs. Jay, or Haven Corporation. I need my sister. I need the one person who loves me and that's it.

"Juliet?" I ask, moving into the living room to find her. I haven't seen her for a while, now that I think about it. I've been so wrapped up in everything, I haven't noticed her hiding in her room again. Fuck, I'm a heartbroken, terrible sister. She stands in the middle of the living room, tense. "What's wrong?"

Only now do I register the tear-stained face and the swollen eyes. I see the subtle shakes in her fingers and the volume of her hair, high and slightly poofy, from her wet fingers running through it. I sigh as my eyes stray from hers.

I don't have to guess what's gotten her so emotional.

I don't have to add another person to the hit list.

Unless that person is me.

My eyes stray to the TV, that is still blaring. The news channel is on, and the host rambles on and on about something I can't compute in my brain. All I know is the deep sense of dread filling my stomach.

She knows.

She knows about the killing.

"Why, Diora? Why?" Her voice cracks and breaks, and she's coughing. I can't move. I'm cemented to the couch, and all I do is stare. We stare at each other, her with disgust and me—it's like someone cut open my body and put on a show of people staring at my insides.

Except, the show of people is just one person. The one person I love more than anything. My big sister.

"Who told you?" I ask, knowing if it was a person and not her brilliant mind, she wouldn't tell me. Not because she thinks that someone betrayed me, but because she's afraid of what I'll do to them. Seeing the TV on, she probably figured it out on her own, but I—I'm not ready for her to know.

"No one had to tell me. The connection wasn't hard to make. Why? Why must you hurt me like this, Dee?"

I swallow hard and stare at her. I need to move, but I can't. I want to hug her, tell her everything is fine and go back to pretending. She's spent our whole lives pretending there wasn't something wrong with me. Why stop pretending now?

"Haven't I given enough?" she yells, and it sounds through the apartment and slaps me across the face. "Has my pain not been enough? It had to go and feed the little monster, too?"

"Monster?" My voice comes out as a whisper. That is the final crack. The final resolve in my armor. I can move now, and I do. Pushing off the couch, I head back for the front door. I stop when my keys are back in my hand and spin toward her, probably for the last time.

"Yes, monster, Diora. What kind of person goes around killing people? And don't you dare say it was for me, because we both know damn well that it wasn't." She looks me in my eye when she says it. She yells so hard she spits, and the tears from her eyes won't stop pouring.

Maybe I need this. This isn't Mom or Dad, or my therapist, or that damn politician who hurt her. This is Juliet.

Juliet is calling me a monster.

I'm a monster?

She's ranting, mumbling, I don't know. I can't process her words. But a monster? A monster? I heard that word loud and clear.

"Oh, baby. My little baby, Diora. You're a monster." My mom's voice rings in my ears, and I'm stuck in a time I try not to remember. It's like I can feel the knife piercing my skin now, the scar coming back to life.

Her rant stops, and silence fills the room. My eyes shoot to hers. I should feel bad for making her this way.

She's my sister. She's good.

She's always been the good one. Best behaved, well-mannered, best grades, and destined for an even better future. Juliet Moss is kind and sweet and because she is good, I don't have to feel bad about being worse than bad, evil. I am evil, and she is good, and I think we both know that.

She is the good to my evil, but the curtain has been pushed back and she seems surprised. Like she doesn't know. But she does. She has to. Her eyes pour hurt and sadness out of her body and onto her face. She's feeling everything. Yet, I feel nothing.

In this moment, she's a stranger. Just another person who doesn't understand. She's like everyone else, and I feel nothing. I'm sure my stare is blank and cold, because she shivers and her shoulders slump. She collapses onto the floor. Her sobs wrack her body, and she holds herself, her arms wrapped around herself.

Any other time, I would console her, as she's done for me since we were kids, but not this time. I'm a monster. I'm selfish. I'm evil.

I'm an evil she can't live with.

I turn on my heel and head for the door. She shouldn't have to live with a monster, and I shouldn't be where I'm not wanted. She calls my name, but all I hear is monster.

A monster to the best, kindest person on this planet.

I should've controlled myself better.

I should've picked different targets.

I should've left her out of it.

Mom was right. My brain is hard-wired differently, and that's why I should've stayed away from Juliet. Instead, I went off and hurt her. Badly. She can't stop staring at me. Watching my every move, my every breath, as if I had the capabilities to kill *her*.

My own sister.

The one person who never pushed me away because I was different... until today.

I can't be with good and be evil myself. I have to let one go.

This is one of those moments. One of those moments when life strikes the perfectionism that your happiness you were growing to depend on, only to remind you, you are but a mere human and that perfectionism doesn't exist.

"Go," Juliet mutters at what must be the ending of the rant. Her chest heaves as she points a finger.

"Go where?" My voice comes out small. Going against her is the worst feeling I've encountered.

"I don't know," she says. Sweat drips from her forehead as she storms past me and yanks open the door. "But I can't stay with a monster."

The word hits like a lashing and I gaze toward the door. I contemplate fighting her on this, verbally, but I... I'm so fucking tired.

"If that's what you wish," I mumble, fisting my car keys and walking right back out the door.

Walking down the hall, the elevator dings and the doors open to reveal Mrs. Jay. Her pastel purple tweed suit set is a blur as the tears that should've come moments ago arrive. Her kitten heels clack as she gets closer, and I'm moments away from falling to my knees.

I look at her face. She's smiling, with her arms open, and I can't help but wonder if I'm hugging the devil, *my true maker*.

I can't help but wonder if Mrs. Jay and I were on the same level this whole time.

Maybe I am a monster.

CHAPTER 31

Elliot

Fuck. Of fucking course. Grabbing my phone, I storm out the door of my apartment. Not bothering to lock it as I leave. A text comes through my Corp phone.

And that's all it takes to have me dashing to the damned office.

Mother has her. I see it on the damn surveillance of Diora's apartment hallway, but also, I can feel it. The dread in my stomach tells me Diora's in danger.

Mother has her wrapped in her arms, and I should've seen this coming. I should've known Mother had her in her sights, and I should've known she'd sweep in like the fucking hero.

I've never been so stumped, so stupid before. I should've opened my fucking door. Let her inside. What the fuck was I thinking?

A woman has never made me so irreversibly attached that every move I make is determined by her wellbeing. Enyo appears at my side the moment I step into headquarters, the daylight shining through the goddamn windows, and his sunny persona dies the moment he sees me.

"What's going on?" he asks as he falls into step with me. Mother's office comes into view, and I stalk in and start digging in her desk.

"Enyo, I can't right now," I say, swiping through papers, notes, anything that could tell me where she is taking her. Mother has her. This can't be fucking good.

Enyo wraps his hand around my forearm to grab my attention, but I can't focus with him here. I twist out of his hold and shove him away.

"Elliot, what the fuck?" he shouts, his face twisting in anger.

"I don't have time. She has her!" I shout, moving away from her desk and moving to her filing cabinet.

"Who?" Enyo shouts.

"Mother."

"Who has Mother?"

"No," I say in desperation, making my head hurt. "Mother has Diora."

His face turns to stone as his brows drop and his lips flatline. I huff as I watch him. I've left him out of the loop for so long, and now I'm noticing that I shouldn't have. For a moment I can't afford, I watch the war in his eyes. He has a choice to make, as I have the last six months since I found out Mother was trafficking Strays. Is he on Mother's side or mine? Who is in the wrong: his mother or his brother?

"I'm not as good as you are, Brother," he says. "I don't know everything you do, I don't look for everything you do, but you're my brother, and I choose you every time."

"And she's your mother."

"Yeah, but—"

"No, she is your real mother, Enyo," I say and stare at his face. Watching for any sign of recognition, or disbelief, anything. He gives me nothing, which is miles worse.

"No, she's not." He shakes his head, and I watch as he steps back. Like the sentence pushed him.

"It's why I kept you out of the loop. She's your mother, and now I *have to* kill her," I say as I walk past him and out of the room. I have to find where she and Diora went. I disobeyed Mother too many fucking times, and Diora is going to pay the price.

I let this go too far, and I don't know if I'll be able to stop myself from killing Mother if I find Diora hurt.

"She can't be." He shakes his head, and as much as I want to comfort my brother, I have to save my girl.

My Little Crane is in danger.

He grabs my shoulder and whips me around to face him, swinging a punch across my jaw with his opposing arm. Spit and blood fly from my mouth, but I don't have time to swing. I have to find her.

"I don't expect you to forgive me. I don't expect anything from you, but at the very least, I need to save Diora. After that, you can do—" He cuts me off by wrapping his arms around me in a hug.

"I figured out she was behind the skin trade," he says, and I freeze, even as he lets me go.

"When?" I ask.

"After our punishment. Only when we messed with her money has she acted that way. Then I found..." He pauses as he shakes his head.

"Found what?" I whisper.

"Found the wire transfers and lined them up with the missing trainees, the newer Strays."

I know about the wires. The new custom-made suits made of vicuna fabric, a fabric valued at six-hundred dollars per kilogram. A fabric we shouldn't have been able to afford, despite being hitmen.

A fabric she had access to, with no trace of payment anywhere. Not cash, credit, nothing.

For someone who does her books, she sure forgot how obvious she can be. Maybe she wanted me to know. Maybe she didn't. I won't ever know.

I won't give her the chance to explain.

"Diora could be next, or she could be dead. I have to go."

"Let's go, then," Enyo says, though we don't get far, because a text comes to both of us on our Corp phones.

"They're at Mother's house."

CHAPTER 32
Diora

I never trusted Mrs. Jay. I can admit I was weak when I saw her in the hallway outside my apartment after Juliet kicked me out. I was weak when I ran into her arms. I can admit that, while my heart was being crushed for the second time in my life and for once, I wanted to feel a motherly love, to be taken care of, she was there. That must be how she gets the Strays' devotion. She gets you when you're weak.

Still, I'm not the dumbest person alive. I may have followed the lion into its den, but I didn't come unprepared.

"Diora, make me some tea, please," Mrs. Jay demands as she sits on the couch. She took me to her home. "I have eyes on the back of my head. No funny games, please. I'm tired."

Even better. You're tired. That works for me.

She points a lazy finger toward where I assume her kitchen is as I stand at her front door. Mrs. Jay lives pretty modestly for someone who wears tweed suits. Her two-story house is in the far suburbs of Litchfort. In the part where neighbors are about half a mile apart.

It doesn't surprise me that her closest neighbor is so far away, and it doesn't surprise me she'd brought me here.

What I can't figure out is *why* she brought me here. Am I here so she can kill me or sell me? According to what we found at the ring, I'm on the cusp of being too old to be sold, and even if she does want to sell me, she probably wouldn't get very much.

So, she must want to kill me.

Sighing, I round the entry hallway to the kitchen. She has a pristine white kitchen, where even her fridge is white, and it makes my skin crawl seeing all the white. Is this a doctor's office? Walking toward the one steel-colored appliance, her stove, I search for something to heat the water up in. She uses a kettle. I smile to myself as I carry it to the sink to fill up, and I turn it on. Dirt drops onto her pristine white marble countertops.

I'm sure that'll piss her off, but I guess it won't matter, 'cause I have a feeling only one of us is walking out that door tonight. The teapot warms up, and I know we have about twenty minutes until the water will be ready, so I walk back into the dining room where she sits.

The dining room is where Mrs. Jay played with the decor. She has a beautiful dark wood table and cushioned chairs with matching wood accents on them. In the center, there is a gray rug, and her walls are covered in artwork.

"Are we gonna pretend I don't know why I'm here or...?" I ask, leaning against her wall.

"Get off my wall. You're getting it dirty," she snaps with a tired glare. I smile as I stop leaning on the wall and come to sit across from her at the dining table.

"I guess we are pretending, then."

"I want some tea first, darling. We can get this show started after I've had my tea and once my boys get here."

"Boys? Elliot and who?"

"Enyo."

"Oh, Enyo," I say, as his name brings a slew of thoughts to my head.

"You can't have forgotten my Sons?" she asks in disbelief, and I shrug. Of course I know Enyo. I hadn't thought about the ramifications with him after I kill his "Mother" tonight.

Will he care? Will he seek vengeance? He's a wild card I should have considered, but honestly, it won't change anything.

Elliot is enshrined in Mrs. Jay's trap, and the only way to free him is to do the thing he can't do.

Kill Mrs. Jay.

I'll do anything for the people I love, and whether he likes it or not, he's become one of those people. The selfish bastard.

Enyo may kill me, he's definitely strong enough to do it, but Elliot will be free, so that isn't a deal breaker for me.

"You don't hate me for selling those Strays. Tell me, Diora, before my Sons get here. Tell me why you hate me." Mrs. Jay asks, leaning closer from her spot across the table. I see the genuine curiosity in her eyes, and I wonder if she truly does not know.

Sure, seeing those Strays put a nasty taste in my mouth and a fire in my heart, but that wasn't her only offense.

"I think you know, Mrs. Jay."

"Please enlighten me, darling."

"Your Son, Elliot."

"What about my Son?"

"I love him."

"Okay?" At this, I roll my eyes. I sigh and raise a brow as she leans back into her chair. She smirks. "Oh."

"Yeah. I love him and you've hurt him."

"I saved him. I save them all."

"You took advantage. It's fine, no need to lie."

"Perception is all it is, dear. I save them, take advantage. It is all the same."

"Sure," I say, knowing that "perception" is what is killing her tonight.

The kettle rings, signaling it's ready, and I get up from the chair to make our tea.

In the kitchen again, I take my weapon of choice out of my pocket. Wrapped in a white napkin, a white angel trumpet lies on the counter next to the kettle. I have ten petals. Completely lethal. Foxglove takes time, patience, care. Angel trumpet is quick, painful, and in a hurry. I won't have time to waste with Mrs. Jay. She's an older lady, but quick and smart.

I can't put this in her tea. She'll know. It's the only move I've played to her knowledge. I have to be smarter.

The front door opens, and two sets of footsteps come crashing in. "Where is she?" Elliot's voice rings out, and I can hear the panic in his raised voice. The anger in his underlying notes. How did he know I was here?

"She's fine," Mrs. Jay says as Elliot comes crashing into the kitchen, swallowing my presence up with his body shadowing over mine.

"Did you eat or drink anything? Are you wounded?"

"No, I'm making her tea."

"Why the fuck are you making her tea?" he asks.

"Because she asked me to." His brow furrows as he looks over the counter.

"Let's go." Elliot pulls my hand away from the counter, but Mrs. Jay clicks her tongue and ticks her finger.

"No, no, darlings. We need to talk."

"Let's not do this here, Mother." I hear Enyo's voice, but he must be in the dining room with Mrs. Jay.

Meeting Elliot's brown eyes, I softly shake my head no. This isn't a time to run. I carefully grab the white trumpet from the counter, making sure it doesn't touch my skin, and show him what I brought.

"This ends tonight," I mouth. He shakes his head, but it doesn't change anything. Setting down my poison, I gingerly bring his hand up to my lips and press a soft kiss to the back of his hand.

"You deserve a happy ending, Oliver," I whisper against his hand. "I'm going to give it to you."

"Diora, what's taking so long?" Mrs. Jay snaps. "Everyone, meet me at the dining table."

I quickly turn around, Elliot's hands on me as I move. I grab the neat stack of napkins from Mrs. Jay's counter and two cups of tea.

Elliot helps me with the other two cups as he strides into the room.

"Let's not do this—"

"Stop, not until we sit," Mrs. Jay snaps. Elliot's eyes dart to me. I can feel the pressure of his gaze on the side of my head, but I can't lose focus.

I hear him sigh. I set Mrs. Jay's cup down in front of her and one in front of me. She sits at the head of the table and directs me to sit to the left of her this time. Enyo sits on her right. Elliot pays no mind to her as she tries to guide him with her hand to sit next to Enyo, but he sits next to me.

It's the four of us again. Here in the same room. Angst and animosity brimming the air. Just like when she called us in after we took down her million dollar trafficking ring. This time, there are no guards, no Strays to hold any of us back.

It's time to deal with our issues. I snort as the thought floats by. How did I get twisted up in this family affair?

"Diora, please," she says, lifting her cup toward me. I nearly chuckle as I grab her cup, bringing it up to my nose, sniffing the warm black tea in her cup. I watch as Enyo's eyes widen as I take a sip. They assumed I'd be so obvious in trying to kill Mother?

"Thank you, darling." She gracefully takes her mug back and takes a sip of her own, smiling as she realizes there is truly no poison in her drink.

"Yes, of course," I say, taking a sip of my own tea, looking at my dinner mates. "Anyone else?"

"No, thank you," Enyo says while drinking his, as if to prove he... trusts me? I'm not sure how to interrupt Enyo Jay. He's the one I'm most worried about.

"So, everyone knows?" Mrs. Jay asks with a slight frown on her face. I watch as her face wrinkles around her frown and her eyes dim as the topic comes up. It's like she's truly out of the loop at her own organization.

"No, we are the only ones who know about the trafficking. Well, us and the Society," Elliot says. Her eyes go wide, and her head whips to Elliot in shock. "You thought you could do anything without the Society knowing?"

Her drink slips from her momentary lapse of control. Almost sliding out of her hand, spilling on herself and the table. She takes the napkin I'd set beside her and wipes her fingers before dabbing her lips and then the table. "So, what are you going to do about this? This obviously still bothers the lot of you."

"You were trafficking kids. Who would be okay with that?" Enyo asks, furrowing his brows.

"The buyers were fine with it."

"Now you want to play a cute mother, really?" Enyo snaps back, and Elliot clears his throat.

"We were never good people, but morally, we're different, and it's time to separate."

"And leave my Sons?" Mrs. Jay asks, and this is when I feel out of place.

"You've done it before." Enyo scoffs with a faux amused on his face. I look over to Elliot, who watches Mrs. Jay like a hawk.

Mrs. Jay's head snaps again, this time to Enyo. She tilts her head in question and smiles. "So, you know?"

"That you're my birth mother who left me in a dumpster but then came back when I was fifteen to start your little killer organization? Yeah, I know."

"Are you upset? Surprised?" she asks, like the heartless bitch she is. I scoff this time, but that's when the realization hits me.

I'm not just killing Elliot's tormentor. I'm killing Enyo's mother. His real mother.

Shit.

It's too late, though. The work is already in motion, and it's far too late to stop it. Not that I think I would. I guess I'll never know.

I watch her, as I always do. Her wrinkles are deeper than when I first met her four months ago. Her eyes appear sunken in, despite the worry clouding them now. Her fingers shake with each rise of her cup. This last sip has her coughing. Her cheeks begin to grow a reddish flourish while she tries to sip down her drink.

I'd put a lot of angel trumpet on her napkin. Incredibly poisonous to the touch.

"What's wrong with me?" she rasps, looking at me. Like she knows it was me. The only possibility being me. There being absolutely no way one of her Sons could try to poison her.

She's right, of course. Knowing that she is Enyo's mom, he couldn't do it, and I couldn't let Oliver kill another parent. Even one as evil as her.

I had to do it.

"I didn't lace your drink with anything," I murmur, continuing to sip mine.

She coughs, her hands gripping the table as her confusion settles in. Her brows furrow and her eyes close, probably as the photophobia starts to affect her.

Sweat dribbles at her forehead, and once I know she is too far gone for any of the boys to do anything, I speak.

"I crushed an angel trumpet in your napkin, poisonous to the touch, deadly by consumption." I lick my lips as she falls back in her chair.

Her breathing slows and her skin appears dry on the backs of her hands and high points of her cheeks.

"You won't hurt another kid, Mrs. Jay." I shrug as she tries to glare at me. I watch as her eyes narrow and her nose twitches. I can't help the glimmer of happiness I have covering my skin. "You can't now."

Mrs. Jay isn't someone I ever thought I'd have the skill to kill. The fact that she's dying in front of me, at my hand, is unreal. So unreal, that it seeds in my mind that maybe... she wanted to die.

"She has minutes left. If you have anything to say to her, say it now," I murmur while drinking my tea.

"Sons," she cries. I watch Enyo first. I watch as his shoulders remain stiff and squared as he watches his birth mother die. I don't find a sign of anger, regret, or vengeance from him. In fact, I sense close to nothing. Nothing besides the tilt of his head. The soft tilt to the left as he watches the mother he never truly knew die.

Elliot doesn't watch Mrs. Jay. He watches me. I think he knows this isn't just about the trafficking. I think a sliver of him knows I did this for him. Like Juliet, Elliot is a part of my family. A person I would do absolutely anything for, including killing the person he calls Mother, if it means he will have freedom.

His hand is resting on the back of my chair, and his eyes are glued to me.

"Diora." My name falls off his lips and leaves him speechless. I watch as his brown eyes light as his newfound freedom washes over him.

I grab Elliot's chin and pull him closer, gazing into his honey brown eyes as his Mother dies beside me. "I hope you know, when I say you're mine, I mean it." I kiss his cheek and lightly slap his face. Smiling. Mm. Protecting my man feels fucking amazing.

I hear Mrs. Jay's head hit the table, but I don't flinch or jerk away from Elliot. I don't look at the new threat in the room that could have feelings about me killing his mom, despite the hate he seems to have for her.

"Well," Enyo says, and I snap my attention to him. His buzz cut is slightly grown, and he rolls his lips as he tries to think of something to say.

I lick my lips and tuck a stray, frizzy hair strand behind my ear. I'm so tired. I'm so fucking tired.

"So, what do we do now?" Enyo asks me, raising his brows. His shoulders are loose and so is the rest of his body language, so I don't sense a threat, but I can't quite be sure.

"What?" I ask.

"What's the rest of the plan?" Enyo asks, like I'm the slow one.

"Diora doesn't think that far," Elliot chuckles, shaking his head, but I find nothing amusing. "Let this be a message. Call the Strays in the clean up department. I'll call the Society to let them know of the deceased member, and Diora..."

"I'm going to take a shower," I say, walking upstairs.

Killing two people in one night is exhausting.

Chapter 33

She did it. She did it for me. For me. I watch as she goes up the stairs, and I look back to my brother. Well—

"She's not *Mother* anymore," I mutter, staring at the dead woman at the dining table. I've sat at this table so many times. Except my scars aren't scars at the time. Instead, they are wounds—fresh, bleeding, bruised. Unshed tears lock behind my eyes, and I have a stomach full of regret and anger.

"We're still brothers, though," Enyo says, locking a hand on my shoulder and yanking me into a hug. It's an odd feeling, something we've never done before, but I wrap my arms around my... my brother. I pat his back twice and we let go.

"We're still brothers," I confirm. Enyo was the only person I cared for, wanted to protect, wanted by my side for so long, and now... now I get to build my own family.

And so does he.

"We're free," I say.

"So is everyone else," Enyo says, referring to the Strays at the Corporation. Mother collected them when they were desperate, alone, with no one looking for them. They were free now, too, though I don't think they'd go anywhere.

I'm not.

I've never hated the Corp, and I've never hated Strays. I hated the torture. I hated the manipulation, the blackmail. I didn't like turning innocent people who have no one into killers.

"I don't think they'll leave. A few might," I say with a half shrug. "But not all."

"I guess Haven is like a home. A home for hitmen, huh?" Enyo scoffs. "How iconic."

"But let me make something clear, Brother," I say, looking my brother in the eye.

"That's my woman in the shower. She's mine. You can't try to get retribution for Mother—"

"Don't worry about it. I'm glad we didn't have to do it." Enyo sighs as he opens the door for the Strays who flood in to "clean up". Enyo points to the dining room, and we listen to the gasps.

"Mother!" one of them, a younger boy around the age of seventeen, rushes in and starts stammering.

"We know," I say. I stroll back to the living room and take a seat on the brown couch. I have no idea how long Diora is going to take in the shower, and I probably shouldn't leave the Strays here, either, so I might as well get comfortable.

"And let it be known, we don't deal in skin. Ever. No matter what level you are at," Enyo says and directs him to get back to clean up. "I'm going to headquarters. We have a will to draft and a funeral to plan."

"A funeral?" I ask. We normally dump bodies and move on, since none of us are known people. We set up our lives to easily disappear, so there isn't a need for a funeral.

"Well, she had friends in government," Enyo says, rolling his eyes. Ahh, right, I forgot about her greed for power in the Litchfort government. Well, I'll let him deal with that.

"As first Son, I'm sure you've got this under control," I say, turning the TV on.

"Elliot," Enyo says, hand on the front door as he stares at me. I turn my head to look at him, raising my eyebrows.

"Good luck with her. You're gonna need it," he says and dodges the throw pillow I throw at him by dashing out the door.

Yeah, like I don't know he's got the hots for her sister. He'll have fun getting past her serial killer little sister, that's what I know.

Turning down the TV, I listen for the shower, making sure she's still here, as what went down tonight flashes through my brain. I read the digital clock on Mother's fireplace mantel, it reads three a.m.

Diora Rose Moss killed for me. She killed the one person I didn't think I could kill, and she did it without knowing whether I would be mad. She didn't care.

She saw a threat and just... eliminated it.

Running a hand over my hair, I can't help the heat coursing through my body as her words play like a loop in my mind.

I hope you know, when I say you're mine, I mean it.

Fuck. I launch up from the couch and follow the sounds of the shower to her. I need her. I love her. And I need her to know that. To feel it, to breathe it. I press my hand on the door and find it unlocked. What the hell? Scrunching my eyebrows, my head darts around the hallway, as if anyone here would try to come into this bathroom with my little killer in it. Opening the door and sliding into the steaming hot bathroom, I shut and lock the door behind me.

"Anyone could have come in here, you know."

"I was hoping *you* would," she says, smiling at me through the glass shower door.

"What if it wasn't me?"

"I doubt you'd let anyone else see me naked, handsome," she says, her voice dripping with want. "This body's all yours."

I play right into my Crane's hand. My eyes track the water droplets racing down the curves of her body. Between her swollen breast and down her smooth brown skin.

My cock takes well to this view, hardening as I stand at the door. I haven't even touched her yet. But I want to. I need to so fucking bad.

Diora Moss is a crane in this house of dogs.

I am a puppet whose strings have been cut free. As much as my freedom may taste good, I'd gladly give her the ends of my broken strings if it meant staying with her.

It's an odd feeling, being the one protected. That's a job I've always had to do for myself. No one's ever protected me. Not in the way Diora has.

Not Mother, Not Enyo, not any of the other foster kids, and damn sure not my birth parents.

Diora Moss is my crane. My good fortune. She's my protector as much as I am hers.

I could laugh. A woman being my savior is not the most manly reality, but I get to have Diora, and that's not something I'd change for the world. She came into my world and flipped it on its axis, and she did so mindlessly. All in all, it's just who she is.

I fucking need my Little Crane.

She stands naked under the warm shower water with her arms crossed over her stomach and her hip jutted to the side. My impatient bird raises both her eyebrows in waiting with a smile on her lips.

Charging the shower door, I tear my clothes off and join her. The glass door slams open and the hot steam attacks my face as my hands find the sides of her face and my lips capture hers.

The water streaming over us makes her slippery in my hands, so I grip her harder, more desperate to keep her to me as the taste of her lips consumes my every thought. I drag my hands from her face down her body. My fingers dig into her thighs as I sandwich her between the wall and myself. I lift her slightly so her pussy meets my cock, but I don't enter, and by god, do I fucking want to. I grind once into her, eating her moan into my mouth as reward.

"Diora," I whisper against her ravenous lips. "My Little Crane."

"Hmm," she rumbles, and the sound runs through her chest into mine.

"I love you."

"Do you even know what love is, handsome?" she asks, and while there's a note of playfulness, I see the worry in her face, in the way her cheek drops and her brows come together.

I smile at my love. "Let me show you," I say, moving my lips over her cheek, down her neck, to her collarbone.

Following the lines of water running down her body with my lips, tasting her skin on my tongue before getting to my favorite prize, I kneel before her.

"Let me show you for the rest of our lives, Little Crane."

Wrapping one of her legs over my shoulder, I watch her face flush with heat. She throws her head back as I press my lips in a kiss against her.

"Handsome, please," she moans as her hands find their place in my hair. She loves running her hands through my hair and I fucking love when she does. Her touch does something to my soul, lights me up, encourages me, loves me. I crave her touch as much as I crave the rest of her.

I lightly drag my fingertips over her cunt, watching as the moan in her builds from her throat up to her lips. I could watch her do this for hours.

"Come on, Little Crane, let me hear you again." I curl my finger in, getting her slicked up so my tongue can get a proper taste of her. I watch as her stomach rises and falls at a steadily increasing rate, and the leg she's standing on trembles. Bearing most of her weight on my shoulder, I heave her closer, letting her whimpers of pleasure fill the shower.

I'm sure the Strays downstairs can hear us, but I don't care. All I care about is loving my woman.

I work her with my tongue and my fingers, and far too soon, she comes on my tongue. I lap up as much as I can before the stream of water washes her cum away. Leaning back slightly, still holding her leg in one of my hands, both her hands snake over my shoulders to cup the sides of my face, gently guiding me to gaze up at her.

My bird smiles at me, and I love the look of her above me. I love when she stares down at me. There is so much... it's not... It's power. It's grace and care, and I am so damn lucky to have a woman such as Diora Moss look at me like this.

"I love *you*, too, handsome."

I love you.

Words I've never heard spoken to me until I met the woman in my arms. I wasn't meant to hear them, not until I met my Little Crane.

These words were meant for her.

Those words were meant for *me*.

Her eyes melt into mine, and the need to be inside her surges me up, lacing her lips with mine as I line my cock up to her entrance. Pushing my hips forward, I slide inside her to the hilt, feeling her suck me up. I groan as she kisses me again.

I hook both her legs around me as I thrust into her, angling her closer to me. Pounding into her under the hot stream of the shower.

Her thighs spread as I fit between her, her heels digging into my ass as I drive into my Little Crane. She moans as her hands slide off my face to curl around my neck, digging into my skin.

Fuck. She is everything.

I spiral as pleasure washes over me, covering every inch of my being as her pussy grips me. Her muscles tighten, and I feel her orgasm cover my cock. Letting out a shuddering breath, I let myself come, watching her come down from her high. I keep her in my arms, needing another moment to hold her weight, her presence, with me. Leaning my forehead on hers, I peck her lips.

"I finally get to clean you how I want, Little Crane," I mutter against her hot skin. I slide out of her, much to her dismay.

Lathering shampoo between my hands, I wet her hair. Her curls lengthen under the water. Silky smooth now, compared to the frizz she had earlier. I run my hands through her hair, from root to tip, as she leans into me. Moaning, still, this time from my hands on her scalp.

We step out of the shower, and I dry her body and wrap her hair in a soft towel. I lotion her skin and dress her in my t-shirt.

"It's clean this time." She giggles as the shirt slides over her otherwise naked body. We don't have clothes here, but that didn't matter. Not when I have her and she has me.

"Diora Rose Moss," I say, grabbing her hand in mine. I run my thumb back and forth over her hand. I stare at her hand. Her left hand.

"Whipping the full name out on me, huh?"

"I love you," I say, meeting her eyes. I watch as her smile softens, and she grabs my hand back. Her dark brown eyes stare into my soul as she processes my words.

"I love you... too... Elliot Jay."

Chapter 34
Diora

The shower sex didn't help me forget the hate my sister has for me. Neither do the days that follow. The utter silence in the apartment. These feelings are constant. I'm always waiting for Juliet to appear and wishing she never found out.

"She needs time, Little Crane," Elliot says as he lays down on my bed next to me. I've resorted to hiding in my room, too. To say I'm scared of facing how Juliet sees me is an understatement. It burns almost as bad as the need for her acceptance.

I don't need her forgiveness. I don't regret what I did. I'd do it again, and I have a feeling we both know that.

"But how much? How much time is a normal amount of time for her to be mad?" I ask. I'm pacing by the door of my room. Listening for a sound, any sound, from Juliet's room. She'll come to me, right? Will she come to me if Elliot is here?

I look over to him to find him already staring at me. "I'm not leaving."

"Hmm." I swallow the spit in my throat, trying to calm down. Nerves haven't cracked me like this before. My cuticles have never been in a worse state. A light sheen of sweat lines my hairline, and I'm sure I smell.

"What if she doesn't wanna be my sister anymore?" I whisper as I carefully sit next to him. He's been awfully attached to me since I killed Mrs. Jay. I don't know if it's in appreciation or fear that Enyo may change his mind and come after me for killing his mom, or maybe... maybe it's just his love. I don't know, but I like it.

"That's not how being siblings works," Elliot says with a chuckle as he sets his phone down and leans back on the bed.

I snap my head toward him with a snarl. "What do you even know?" I scoff.

"Don't be mad, Little Crane. She loves you, and more than that, science can't deny you guys are sisters," he says, tracing patterns I can't decipher on my arm. "Love is loyalty. Love is the warmth in my chest when I look at you. The security I feel when I can physically see you. I feel love for you. It's not quite the same, but it's similar for families."

"If that's love, then yes, Elliot, that's what I feel."

"For her?"

"Yes," I say, moving to cup his cheek in my hand. Feel the soft skin under mine. My lips turn upward as I gaze into his eyes, watching the color move in them. "And for you."

A knock pulls me away from him. The slow creak of the door lets light into my room from the hallway, creating a glowing halo over Juliet's peaking head. She's here!

"I'm sorry, I'll come back later," she pips as she tries to back away from the door. But I'm faster. My hand stops the door from closing, and I'm relieved she's here. I'm sure she can see it all over my face. I've been much more expressive since meeting Elliot.

"Please, no, stay," I say. I reach for her hand, her warm brown skin a comfort to me, but I stop. Maybe she doesn't want to touch a serial killer. I don't... I can't make her dirty. I stop, and I try to keep my face neutral as my eyes meet hers again.

Looking back at Elliot, I sigh. I have to do this alone. I know I do, and yet I want to drag him with me. Juliet would be shy, though. She might even know he's a killer, too, and get angrier. I don't know.

"Let's go to the living room," I say as I close my bedroom door behind me. I hover my hand over hers and lead us to our favorite spot: the couch.

The silence eats at us, at least at me. I have the urge to fill it, but I resist. I don't want her to lose her momentum; I need to hear what she has to say.

I need to know if she accepts me as I am.

Mom and Dad never did. Or maybe to better phrase, they tried the best they could. I don't blame them for wanting to rid the bad in their lives, in Juliet's. I'm not them. I'm not good, but I am a person. A person people can love.

Taking a deep breath, I wait as something crosses Juliet's face. Her brows scrunch and unscrunch as she wrings her fingers in her lap. She's scared.

I don't want her to be scared. Maybe if I show her my empty hands, she won't be scared. I try to relax my posture and place my hands open in my lap. It's a bit odd, but if it will help, I'll do anything.

She curls her legs up against herself as she sits on the couch. "Diora, you kill people?" she asks. Her eyes peer into me. Like a puppy who wants the truth to be different so badly.

But it's not. This is the truth. A truth our parents spotted miles away. A truth I have to accept and live with.

A truth Juliet doesn't have to live with.

She could turn me in, and I'd let her. I don't know if Elliot would. I would have to stop him, but Juliet, I'd let her turn me in if it made her feel better.

It chips at my heart to disappoint her. It feels shameful to meet her eyes. To want to hold her after I hurt her.

"Yes." The word falls from my lips and hangs in the air. I see her face drop for a moment as she stays quiet. She sighs before meeting my eye again.

"Why?"

"Because... I want to. Because I can't help it. Because you deserve so much better. Because you deserve freedom."

"But that's—"

"And so do I, Juliet. I deserve freedom, too."

"But what if you get caught? I can't, Diora. I need you, I love you, I want you to be safe—" My heart nearly pounds out of my chest to hear that. Is this acceptance? No, I can't celebrate too early. Shaking my head, I stop her rambling.

"The chances of being caught are slim, and even still, I'm not alone. I have Elliot. I have protections in place—"

"What if they don't work?" Her tears stream down her face as she moves to sit next to me. The closest we've been since she found out. She grabs both my open hands in hers.

"They ruined me, Dee, and I'd hate to think they ruined you, too." She sobs into my shoulder, grasping my hand. I lay a gentle hand on top of her curly head, and instead of flinching, she curls into me more. "I'm so sorry, Dee."

"You were right before, Juliet. It's not about them, it's about me. It's about who I am. I wasn't going to last much longer without satisfying the itch," I say, trying to put words to something indescribable. It's not something I can explain, and it's not something she'll ever understand. She doesn't get the itch in the way I do.

Her itch is soothed by cleaning. Mine is by killing.

"Don't get caught, ever, Diora. I need you here with me forever," Juliet says as she cries.

"I won't," I say as I lay my head on top of hers. I smell her strawberry shampoo and her frizzy hair tickles my cheeks, but I am so happy. Just as happy as I was when Elliot told me he loved me for the first time. The happiest I've been in my whole life. I kiss the top of her head again. Tears prick my eyes in relief. I could sob. I've never cried so much.

"And I'll make sure she never leaves you." Elliot's sudden voice makes Juliet jump in my arms. She sniffles and leans out of my embrace as Elliot sits on the other side of me.

"I'm assuming you're like her?" Juliet asks, nodding her head toward me. She watches him like she watches me. She doesn't know him, but I hope she knows he won't hurt her, either.

Elliot nods his confirmation and flashes a small smile at her. "But a whole lot more experienced."

"Whatever," I mutter, chuckling as I grab one of his hands and pull it into my lap.

"We'll be okay," I say, smiling again. "And more importantly, you're truly free, Juliet."

"They're dead, but my memories aren't," she whispers.

"For now, but that's a battle you'll be able to fight without them haunting you in the real world, too."

I stare at my little group on the couch.

As comfortable as I am here in this little home, there is still one thing I have to clean up.

Chapter 35

Diora

Walking into Haven Corporation is different now that Mrs. Jay is dead. I'm sure word has spread about her death. What I'm not sure is, if they know it was me. They don't mind me as I walk along the red carpets of the building, riding the elevator to the top floor to meet with the Top Dogs for a special meeting. Called by Enyo, of course.

I attempted to dress nicer today, in a pretty pink sundress that swishes at my calves. Sure, my hair is still a frizzy mess, and the dirty stains from being in the greenhouse don't exactly scream princess, but the dress will still have the desired effect. These Dogs won't care, but my man will. Elliot fucking loves sundresses.

"Diora." Enyo's voice booms in the office room with only a long meeting table and a whiteboard in it.

"Hi," I say politely as I stand by the door. I haven't talked to Enyo since I killed his mom. My purse is clenched under my armpit, and I try to think of any weapons I may have on me. I'm not naïve enough to think that he's totally cool with me killing his mom, even if she was a human trafficker who haunted her "Sons".

There is a knife in my purse, but if he advances on me, I'm not fast enough to reach for it. He's probably faster than me, too, so there is no outrunning him, either. If he leaves his neck unprotected, I could jab him there, buying myself time to run.

"I haven't had the chance to talk to you," he says, gesturing to the seat beside him. It's to the left of him, of course, the right side saved for his right-hand man, but why... Why does he want me on the left?

I play along, moving across the room with the huge table and many desk chairs, to sit in the one directly to his left. He smiles, but that isn't unusual; he's always smiling. The one time I haven't seen a smile on this man's face was at Mrs. Jay's house.

Before I can even sit, he's grabbing my hand, kissing it, but he isn't looking at me. He's looking past me. Turning my head, I spot the blinking red dot and roll my eyes.

"Elliot must be watching?" I say, fighting a smile. "Kiss my hand again."

"He's always watching you. Wherever you are, he is tapping some sort of camera to watch you. You might want to talk to him about it—"

I shake my head, my smile breaking through my face as Elliot comes to the forefront of my mind. "I like it."

His eyebrows raise in shock as he lets my hand go, and he chuckles before settling in his seat. "I do have something I wanted to discuss with you, though," he says, and my heart races.

"Mrs. Jay?" I ask, and he nods. "I'm sorry, Enyo, for the hurt I caused you."

A sorry is not going to cover killing his mother, but nonetheless, I am sorry for killing someone's mother. This kill was different. I didn't even turn this one in to the Society. This one impacted someone close. I may not be close to Enyo, but Elliot is, and by extension, I don't want to hurt him. In fact, me killing her was never about him. It was about Elliot and the Strays she trafficked.

"You're not sorry for killing my mother?" he asks. His voice is level and his posture is relaxed, but I can't tell if it's to throw me off, to make me think I'm in the clear. I can't forget he's been a trained killer for probably over a decade now.

"No, I'm not sorry for killing your mother." Honesty is the best policy and all that. "I know she was your mother. Elliot didn't want to kill her for that reason alone, but she hurt him, she hurt those kids, and would continue hurting them both. The solution was simple to me."

"What if I killed your parents?"

"You wouldn't hurt me doing that. You'd hurt Juliet, though, and that, well..." I smile as I remember Yara Holdings face as I killed her. I kill for Juliet, even if she wishes not to accept that, I do. Killing my parents would hurt Juliet, and in turn, I'd have to do to Enyo what I did to Yara. Well, at least die trying to. Enyo's much stronger than me.

He chuckles and leans back in his chair. "Elliot and I were on our way to kill Mother ourselves, Diora. So, consider it a favor owed. You only get one, so use my favor wisely."

"Well, since I have you here," I say, pulling out my phone and opening the screenshots I took from Juliet's phone late last night.

"Why are you texting my sister... when she already has your number?" Humans confuse me. I can admit, I don't always follow their lines of thoughts, but this... I can't figure this one out. "You gave her your number at Sadie's Flower Shop. Do you not remember?"

"Nah, I remember," he says, but doesn't answer my question.

"Are you playing her?" I ask, tilting my head as annoyance tickles my shoulders. Am I going to have to kill Elliot's brother, too?

"No, Diora. God, no. Jeez, turn those murderous eyes off. No, I just... It's a simple act of kindness."

"Kindness?"

"Yeah, ever heard of it, psycho?"

"You calling my woman a psycho?" Elliot's voice streams in from behind me.

"How the hell are we going to run a hitman company if you two are constantly working my last nerve?" Enyo jokingly says, pushing his desk chair away from the table and standing up.

"When are you going to keep your crusty lips off my woman?" Elliot snaps back, not nearly as amused.

"So, she's officially your woman now?" The Top Dogs fly into the room, laughing and talking, as if nothing is different. I guess for them, nothing is. I turn in my chair and face the crowd.

"So, sleeping your way to the top, huh?" Hank, the medic of the group, cracks, earning a laugh before Elliot shoots daggers at him. With his eyes, this time.

"You know you wish you could do the same," I say, winking at Hank, which earns me a grunt and hopefully a bite on my ass later on.

"So, I'm sure you've heard that Mother is dead." Enyo starts his speech and the Dogs quiet down. Elliot goes to stand to the right of Enyo.

I should be on the left of Elliot, not the left of Enyo.

"So, who's in charge now?" Tom, another Top Dog asks.

"We are," Elliot answers.

"The three of us," Enyo says, and I freeze. Three. Three of us? Three who?

"Three of whom?" I ask, coming to a stand with furrowed brows.

"Me, Elliot, and you."

"Why me? I—"

"Are trustworthy, and we need a tiebreaker."

"What makes you think I won't just side with Elliot?" I argue.

Enyo's face drops, and he tilts his head. "So, when you killed Mother, were you 'just siding with Elliot?'"

"She killed Mother? How?" Jones asks in disbelief. But I don't mind them. I've got bigger issues at hand. Like running a business I have no claim to.

"I've been here for less than six months."

"Are you accepting or rejecting?" Elliot interjects. His eyes meet mine. I watch him, waiting for any indication of what he wants me to say, but he gives me none.

Biting my lip, I gaze around the room. I look at the Top Dogs, and I think about the Strays that are here.

We're lost. We're the blind leading the blind, but we're together. I have never been a leader, and I didn't want to be.

"Accept. We still need a feminine touch," Tom not so quietly whispers, and I chuckle.

Elliot knew my answer before we even got here, and maybe that's why he didn't bother asking.

"Yes."

Chapter 36

Elliot

"Okay, so what's our first order of business?" The Top Dogs have left, as we still have assignments to carry out. Diora and I sit in front of Enyo's desk in his new, better office, as we lay the new groundwork for Haven.

"First rule: we don't trade skin. We kill it," Diora says, waiting for Enyo to type it on his computer.

"Solid, solid. What else?" Enyo asks.

"What are we going to do with new recruits? Or the people who wanna leave?"

"Let them leave," Diora quickly answers, like it's the most obvious answer in the world, and while I may agree that we should let them leave, it's not that simple.

"What if they rat?" I ask.

"Then we kill them."

"That simple?" I ask with raised brows, wondering if she's thought this through or not.

"That easy, handsome," she says with a half shrug. "Well, that ends this meeting."

Diora stands smoothing in her little dress. I know she wears them to rile me up, but I also know they make her feel pretty.

Little does my Little Crane know, that giddiness she has over her dresses is what actually riles me up. Seeing my little bird happy is all I ever want, all I could ever wish for, and now I can give that to her unabashedly.

"We have a showing to get to," she says, staring pointedly at the both of us. "Let's go."

Diora said she's never had a dream like she did a few nights ago. She dreamed of a huge house where she and Juliet could raise their families. Two wings, with a center for big family celebrations, and while she may have never thought she'd have kids, she knows Juliet will, and she wants to be a part of that.

She wants a family home.

A place where the people she loves can call home. A safe place.

So, I need a home fit for my woman's dreams, and we're changing the Haven Corporation into what the name implies. A Haven. A haven for those who are lost, a haven for those who aren't normal. A haven for people like us.

"We're being called, Brother," I say, getting out of my chair and following Diora. Of course, family also means Enyo. Why he agreed to live in a house with Diora and her sister is a mystery to me.

He's always loved his space. He kills in his home in Litchfort, which will *not* be happening in this new home, so why he agreed to live with us is confusing to me. But he's a grown man who can make his own decisions.

Living with my brother again isn't something I'll argue with, either.

Walking beside me, Enyo laughs as he puts his computer in his bag.

"Have you heard from the Society?"

"Nothing besides a simple 'good' after I sent them the message that Mrs. Jay is dead."

"Do they care that much about human trafficking?"

"Maybe, but maybe they were doing something else that we don't know about that the Society doesn't want members to know about." I shrug as we load into the car. The Society may have put me on to Mother, thinking I'd be able to kill her, but I'll never know the real reason.

The Society isn't a group you ask questions to. You don't even ask them about themselves. Ask the wrong question, and you'll find yourself at the bottom of Lake Michigan.

I'm just glad they didn't ask me to kill someone I love. 'Cause if I couldn't kill Mother, I damn sure can't kill Enyo or Diora.

"So, this is a ten-bedroom house."

"Mansion," Enyo coughs as we walk up the pathway to the front door of what I'm pretty sure is going to be our new home. It's a modern build, with black trim and a cream exterior. The house is expensive and going to be hard to keep fucking clean, but the gleam in Diora's eyes makes it all worth it.

The agent goes on and on about the house, with Diora stone-facing her the entire time, but I can tell by the twitch in her fingers she loves it.

The house has a greenhouse in the backyard, more than enough room for me, Enyo, and Juliet to have at least two rooms each. It's got big windows, and it has a pool.

This is the family home of her dreams.

The agent leaves us to discuss in the kitchen. The kitchen has nice white marble countertops and tall black cabinets, with an island with a chandelier over it.

"So?" I ask, circling my arm around Diora's waist as she looks around.

"We're gonna need some rules," Enyo says, raising his brows. "First rule: no fucking in common areas."

"Rule number two: no promises." Diora winks, circling her arms around me. The only one missing is Juliet, who is currently signing up for classes at the local college to start her new handmade soap business.

If anyone of us has made progress, it is Juliet. The PTSD, and maybe undiagnosed OCD, still plagues her, but instead of it taking her life, she's found something she's passionate about—soap. Cleanliness is her all day long, and maybe a house this big will make all her cleaning dreams come true. Though I don't know if feeding the monster is the wisest thing to do.

With caring for Diora came caring for Juliet, too. I want her to succeed as much as Diora does, so paying for her college, under the guise of a full-ride scholarship, is one of the many things I'd do for her.

"No fucking in the common areas. I do not want to see Enyo getting it," I say, kissing the top of Diora's head. She scoffs, but agrees nonetheless.

"Is this the one?" Enyo asks, showing his arms around, as if he's the one showing us the place.

I gaze down at Diora. My sweet, beautiful Little Crane, and I know before she even nods her confirmation.

"Juliet will love this house. Will you be okay sharing a wing with her?" Diora asks. "And I don't want no funny business, Enyo. If you don't love her, don't fuck with her."

"How do you know if you love someone before you even have a conversation with them?" Enyo says with a light smile on his lips.

I don't know the extent of their relationship, but I hope he knows I can't save him from Diora.

"I did. The moment I saw Elliot, I knew he was mine," Diora snaps back. I turn my head to hide the red that's coming.

"Okay, are we buying this damn house?" Enyo asks.

"We're getting this house," I confirm.

Chapter 37

Diora

I've never had my own office before. Nor did I ever think that I'd be running a company of serial killers and hitmen.

I also never thought I'd have a dream or a man who'd do anything, even spend twenty-five million dollars on a house, to make it happen.

I'm not the kind of person to get a happy ever after. Good things don't happen to bad people... yet here I am, in a sky high office, surrounded by the people I love, helping people who are like me.

Bad. Evil.

We kill people, and so do the many members of the Society around the world, and I still get to have my happy ending.

Even better, Mom and Dad were wrong. My badness didn't rub off on Juliet, even after she found out about it.

I came clean about what Mom did when I was six, the scar on my forearm not being me, or an accident, but a moment of weakness for Mom. I like to think that maybe, one day, my parents and I can come to love each other like a normal family, but I know, deep down, we aren't normal.

Plus, I'd take the life I have now over the life I could've had, had I been normal.

"You called?" Elliot slides into my office and shuts the door behind him. I watch as he glides to one of the chairs in front of my desk. A vision of me sucking him off at his desk in downtown Litchfort in his studio apartment flashes through my mind.

Hmmm.

"Yes, I did," I say, staring at my man. My handsome man. Mine. A shiver runs down my spine in excitement. I love being in the same room as him. I could live the rest of my life handcuffed to him. As it gets colder in the fall, he wears more layers. His crewneck sweatshirts are his favorite, and he wears one now, with a teddy bear embroidered on it.

Pulling back my shoulders, I flip my hair back and stare at him directly in his eyes. "I want your shirt on the floor."

"Oh, really?" he asks, smirking at me. I lick my lips as one of his eyebrows goes up. His shirt doesn't come off, though. "Is that why you brought me here? To demand office sex?"

"It's not demanding if you want to, too, right?" I ask, standing from my desk and circling it to stand directly in front of him.

"No, I guess not," he says, and his sweatshirt is off, but he has another layer on, too. A t-shirt. My smile drops and nod toward his still clothed torso.

"Oh, this, too?" And I know he's playing me. He knew exactly why I called him in here, and now he wants to be cute.

"No, it's okay. I got it," I say, and as soon as the words leave my mouth, the dagger from my pencil cup is in my hands and cutting a line straight down the middle of his shirt. Nicking his lower stomach. A thin drop of blood bubbles over the torn skin, and I have half the urge to lick it up.

But this is my office.

He needs to kneel for me.

"The office has a no fucking rule."

"When have we ever been rule followers, handsome?" I ask as I sit back on my desk, my legs hanging and my heels threatening to slip off. "Plus, are you really gonna tell me no?"

"Absolutely not, Little Crane."

I hook one of my heels under the leg of his chair, and with great strength, pull him closer to me. His chair doesn't move far, but I don't need it to.

Leaning forward, I see the amusement dance in his eyes as I cross my arms. My hair flies forward like a curtain.

I don't have to say anything before his hands shoot for my waist and he's pulled me into his lap, his lips meeting mine. My hands find his soft hair, and my legs straddle his as our chests brush each other. I love his skin against mine. The warmth, the blood pumping through his veins, the aliveness of Elliot Jay, is like a drug. I try to touch more of him, his cut open shirt giving me free range of his chest. Pushing myself closer to him, I accidentally tip the chair, and we go flying toward the floor.

I try to break free of his kiss to laugh and fix ourselves, but his lips remain on mine and his hands dig into my hips to get me to stay. I'm high off the rush of the fall, and if he wishes to stay, then so be it.

Kneeling, under, sideways; however Elliot Jay will take me, I'll let him.

His hands slip up my short dress and my bottom is bare to the air, feeling just how much he wants me through the fabric of his jeans.

"No underwear?"

"Not when you're here," I murmur. He smiles, taking the straps of my dress down and letting it slide down my body so it lays twisted up at my stomach. The dress also didn't call for a bra, which I'm grateful for, seeing the look in his eyes. He leans down to take a breast into his mouth. He licks my nipple before sucking, and I grind my hips against his thigh, needing the pressure, the friction.

I feel wild as I hump his leg with my breast in his mouth. He doesn't stop there and nips at the underside of my boob, which has me gasping for breath.

"God, Elliot." I groan, feeling the heat building in my core. I think I'm going to come before he enters me.

"Use me, baby, I'm all yours," he whispers in my ear and I nearly collapse. I love having an office.

I reach my hand between us, needing him more than I need my next fucking breath. Unzipping his jeans, he slides them down and frees his cock.

Gosh, my man is handsome.

I line him up at my entrance, ready to ride this frustration off, when I hear a hard knock at the door.

"Fuck," I sigh. I move to get off of Elliot, but he thrusts his hips up, entering me, and in that moment, I slam down, probably hurting him, but by his groan, maybe not.

"We finish what we start, Little Crane," he grunts and takes hold of my hips, helping me ride him to our end.

"Did you lock the door?" I mutter, meeting him thrust for thrust. My hands grip his chest to steady myself, but then he launches forward, leaving kisses and nips over my chest. I'm fully dependent on him in this position.

Like in many ways, I'm so dependent on this man. He holds the thread of my sanity, and the few moments I lost him, I lost my thread. I need my handsome man as much as he thinks he needs me.

"I did lock the door, but Enyo has a master key. We'll have to be fast, Little Bird," he says. His fingers find my clit, and I thrust with wild abandon.

"Juliet is here for lunch, Diora," Enyo's voice booms from the other side of the door as I hear keys jingle. I think the man is trying to buy us time, since I know there are three damn keys on his keychain.

"Oh, handsome," I mutter against his ear, no energy for much more.

"I got you. I always got you, Diora," he comforts. His golden brown eyes peer into mine, love and warmth spreading into his face, and I snap. I come as he kisses me again, and I wanna swallow the damn man.

"I love you, handsome." I fucking love those words, and I hope he loves hearing them.

"I love you, Little Crane."

Him coming inside me is the best feeling in the fucking world. I have to rush, though, because my sister is about to come in, and as morally questionable as I can be, Juliet seeing me have sex is not on that list.

Shooting off Elliot's lap, I pull my dress down my hips, and push stray hairs back over my shoulder. I speed walk around my desk, feeling Elliot's and my cum slide down my thighs.

I try to control my breathing as Elliot puts himself back in his pants and rights his chair as the door opens.

Enyo and Juliet will know what we did, since not only are we hot sweaty messes, but Elliot's shirt is cut open, down the middle, with a faint line of blood in spots down his chest.

Still, I giggle, as he raises his eyebrows at me and the crew walks in the door.

"I would hope you'd save the fun times for when you don't have something scheduled with your sister," Enyo boasts, barely holding back his laughter as he and Juliet walk in. Juliet's beautiful face is beet red as she grips the strap of her crossbody purse.

"I said I'd reschedule with you, but he was insistent on coming in," she excuses, pointing a finger at Enyo as she sits in the chair next to Elliot, who silently watches this exchange.

"You're throwing me under the bus, honey pie? I thought we were a team," Enyo says, clutching his heart as he gives Juliet a pained look, which has her face creasing with worry.

"She's on my team, and my team only," I say, leaning back in my chair, raising a challenging eyebrow.

"Well, it sure didn't feel that way when you left her waiting outside your door while you were fucking my brother."

"We were fast," I excuse, as Juliet chuckles. Enyo and I both smile at that, and I decide to let his annoying ass persistence of coming in go.

"Lunch?" I ask, grabbing my purse and nodding at the brothers in invitation.

"Of course. We're always hungry," Enyo answers, leading the way back out of my office. Juliet follows him, and I wait for Elliot, who pulls a clean shirt from the stash he keeps in my office.

"Ready, handsome?" I ask, holding out my hand for him to take.

"Always, Little Crane."

Epilogue

Diora

Five Months Later

"How are classes going?" I ask Juliet, as I sit between her legs on the floor. A movie plays on the TV, and the living room has been turned into a hair station.

I love the feeling of her hands in my hair. They're soft and gentle, calming. Her fingers slowly trace lines in my scalp, and while it is causing tangles she'll have to comb out, this relaxation is worth it.

Just like this house was. The fireplace is on, and the whole room is spotless.

"Good, I mean, I know I have the full ride, but I don't think I need a degree to run a business," Juliet rambles, and I nod as she explains how she decided to take certain classes, only the ones she thinks she'll need.

She goes on about a friend she made. A friend I've already vetted. She's actually a member of the Society, and I wonder if

Juliet somehow attracts serial killers, or maybe there is more than what meets the eye when it comes to my sister.

Maybe she's really as lost as the rest of us. She's not bad, she never could be, but lost, well, lostness doesn't discriminate, I suppose.

Her friend is younger than us, she's nineteen, and a serial killer. This I had an inkling about when I saw her and Juliet hanging out, from her mannerism, and her aura was off. So, I followed her a few times to an art studio. That's when I saw a courier come to her house. As much as I'd rather Juliet not hang out with serial killers, she's the one friend Juliet's made since trying to get back into society, plus she's a sweet girl and extremely protective.

I can't pretend I didn't see the girl kill a man because he insulted Juliet's soap business idea. She genuinely takes protection to a whole different level.

I like that in people. I like that about her. Juliet needs people who will protect her goodness.

"So, where is your date night tonight?" she asks while she's parting my hair. As much as I want her to continue the scalp massage, I know that I'm on a time limit tonight.

We have a kill tonight. We, as in Elliot and me. A real kill date this time. There will be absolutely no family members third wheeling us this time. I made him promise.

"We're going out to dinner, and something else, too. We'll be out most of the night," I say, trying to be as vague as possible. Elliot is prepping our prey as we speak.

It's odd not being with Elliot right now, but the prize waiting for me will be so worth it.

"Dinner? Are you going to a diner? You're dressed pretty casual," she asks, finishing one braid and starting on the other. I have on overalls and a long-sleeved shirt on. I don't need to look cute. I need to be able to move.

"Yeah, he's taking me ax throwing after, too, I think. I'm not sure. It's supposed to be a surprise." This earns me an excited squeal and giggle as she accidentally pulls my hair.

"Juliet!" I laugh, leaning my head back, trying to lessen the pull.

"Sorry! I... You guys are so cute, and I'm... I'm so happy for you, Dee," she says. I wish I could see her face, see the goodness pouring from her. I can practically see her smile radiating from the back of my head. This is the kind of happiness I wish for her, the kind of happiness I killed for her to have.

"Thank you, Juliet. I'm happy, too," I say the words I never thought I'd get the chance to say. I wasn't supposed to survive this long. Being a killer has its perks, but the risks associated with being a killer aren't ones I take lightly. I should've died after killing Juliet's demons. I should've died after killing Mrs. Jay.

But I didn't. And as my prize, I got *them*. My family.

Unlocking the metal door, I slide into my first greenhouse. The metal creaks as it moves, and it snaps the attention of the people in the room to me. Smiling, I close the door, locking it.

"Please, please save us. Please, I beg of you."

"She's just a girl. She's not gonna save us."

Their pleading voices drain any doubt I had about killing the Bensens. Most of our targets are lone wolves, single buyers who'd found Mrs. Jay's ring, but some are couples. The couples are always married, with a house most could only dream of and staff to fulfill their every command.

Even with all the help in the world, all the money in the world, the hired staff would never be enough for them.

Being hired, meaning being willing, and that is one of the attributes they wanted to change.

"You even started the tea for me, handsome?" I say. Elliot spent months rebuilding my greenhouse with his own hands, since I have weapons in here, after my breakdown. It's been a long five months of getting our lives situated, but now, life is... life is perfect for me.

I drop a kiss to his soft lips on my way to the kettle. Placing my cute new teacups down, I place four on the table, but this time, I only add foxglove to two of them.

I used to dose myself with foxglove, to feel an ounce of what my victims were feeling, but my gaze meets Elliot's instead. His golden hour colored eyes shine and his lips; he smiles as he stares at me. I can't hurt Elliot like I'd hurt myself.

That's not the way I saw it, but he did. He hated that I'd put foxglove in my cup and dumped my tea over the target's head. I can laugh over the scene now as it plays in my head.

Elliot isn't a fair man. Not in the traditional sense. He calls it his sick sense of judge, jury, and executioner. He's much more secure in this belief since I killed Mrs. Jay.

We're judges, jury, and executioners every time we kill.

I can't blame myself for being smarter and stronger—his words.

So, I stopped putting poison in my drinks. I don't need the punishment and I don't need to even the playing field anymore. Nothing is ever fair, and most of all, I deem these creatures worth the excitement of taking their lives.

I place each cup down in front of my party guests. Listening to their sobs and cries for help, knowing not a soul will ever hear them.

"Hi," I say as I turn around to grab Elliot. Before I can sit, Elliot grabs my hips and places me on his lap. His arms trace light lines on my arms, comforting me for a moment before taking my teacup and taking a sip.

Elliot trusts me, my words, and more so my actions, but the man likes to be one-hundred percent sure in every move he makes. I don't fault him for it. It's cute when he fusses over me. It brings a flush to my cheeks, and I almost shy away.

This is how I know he has my back, no matter what. It's not about right or wrong with Elliot, it's about me. Just me.

My eyes move to the couple here before us. The Bensens are *the* power couple who followed Mrs. Jay's trafficking ring everywhere it went, buying Strays for whatever they saw fit. If she was in Wisconsin, so were they. If she was in Texas or Paris or anywhere else, so were they. Desperate for their next hit.

You would think the buyers of a trafficking ring would be strong, able-bodied, powerful, but we've found they are weak-minded people with too much time and money on their hands.

It's a shame they didn't do something better with their boredom. Maybe it would've saved them from us. From me.

"You're right, you know. I'm not here to save you. Not because I can't, but I don't want to," I say, kissing Elliot's cheek once more before moving to sit in my chair. My tea table is out. The white metal frame has seen better days. The matching chairs are strong but wobbly. Elliot smiles as I sit; he enjoys watching me kill so much more than doing the killing himself as of late. I'm afraid he won't get his required number of kills to go to the ball next year.

I guess he'll have to be my date this time.

"I can pay you! I'll pay you whatever you want," Mrs. Bensen says, tears and snot streaming down her face. She is a beautiful woman, even as she's aged. Maybe it's the money, maybe it's the evil that settles inside her, but her brown hair still shines and her skin is smooth as porcelain.

Good people give. They give and give and give until they can't anymore, and that's why they need to be protected. They give their health, physically and mentally, and that's why evil looks so much better. So much more appealing to people, and yet, they forget about people like me.

I can't say I hate evil, because I don't hate myself. But I can say it pisses me off.

"If you can give me one thing, one thing of my choosing, I'll set you free," I say, hugging one of my knees to my chest as I lean forward. I even smile like I am telling the truth. A light flickers in the whites of both of their eyes.

"Anything," Mr. Bensen shouts. This game is my favorite of all. Pretending as if I am giving them a chance for freedom. A wish they think they can fulfill. Each and every buyer we've ever killed has fallen for it.

"I want Koby Jackson." Their faces drop, and that's when the true giddiness starts to take over. The itch crawls its way up my shoulders and around my neck as the realization sets in their faces.

Koby Jackson was nine years old when they bought him and eleven years old when they killed him. They abused him to death, and now he is resting in my greenhouse under my new angel trumpet tree.

The Bensens kept his remains in a jar, like a trophy, over their fireplace mantel. Such a bold place for the remains of someone they killed. I don't even know if they knew I stole it from them about three weeks ago.

"What?" Mrs. Bensen mutters as shock drenches her from head to toe. It started with the paling of her already pale skin, to the slight drop of her jaw and the now harsh tremble of her body.

"You know what? That's fine. Forget about Koby. What about Marcus? Marcus Stanley. Can you get me Marcus Stanley?" I say, lolling my head to the side, as if I'm asking a genuine question. I have to say, it's a shame they killed those boys, but this game... Man, is this game fun.

"Who the hell are you?" Mrs. Bensen snaps, her gaze turning cold at the mention of her victims.

"The real question is, how do you want to die?" Elliot snaps, his once smiling face snapping to one of disgust as he looks at our guest.

"The real question is, how are they going to drink the tea I prepared for them?" I ask Elliot. "Should we untie their hands?"

I can hear their breathing quicken as, once again, another chance to win our little game becomes a possibility.

But even as Elliot glares, I can see the amusement in his eyes, the slight tick in his jaw, and how a corner of his lips is turned upward. He's just as excited as I am.

"One hand, Diora, one hand only. They are our targets, not our friends," he says his line well, and I laugh. I get to laugh so much with him it makes my chest tingle.

"Okay, handsome." Launching up from my chair, I glide over to Mrs. Bensen's chair first. My fingers caress her forearm as my hands make their way to her hands, which are bound to the back of the chair. Loosening the fabric restraints, I let one hand free. I work at loosening one hand of hers, but leave both of Mr. Bensen's hands tied.

"You didn't think I was stupid, did you?" I whisper against Mr. Bensen's cheek. He trembles in his chair, shouting profanities as I back away from him.

"Help your husband drink his tea," I command, sitting back in my chair.

"No."

"No?" I ask, tilting my head to the side. "No? Did you let Koby say no to his punishments, Mrs. Bensen? How about Marcus, or Romeo, or Jules?" She trembles in her seat, the metal wobbling against the concrete floor. "Then help your fucking husband drink his tea."

"I can't."

"I'll kill him right now—" I yell, showing her the beast she's facing, but I don't even have to rise from my chair before she gives in.

"Okay!" she sobs. Her shaking hand grabs the handle of his mug and brings it to his lips. He doesn't open his lips at first, but Elliot jerks the table, scaring him, and his wife presses the cup to lips. Tipping it and forcing the liquid down his throat.

"How's that taste, Mr. Benson?" I sweetly ask. Of course, he doesn't answer me, and I'm fine with that.

"Let us go and maybe we won't hurt you." My head snaps to Elliot, and he smiles before he slides to stand.

"You won't hurt us?" Elliot's voice sends thrilling chills over my skin as I stare up at him. He laughs, and his favorite weapon is out from his back pocket before I can blink and around Mr. Bensen's neck. His wire cuts a beautiful line of red, bubbling blood. It digs deeper as he screams, and I smile at his wife, who screams at her husband's pain.

I guess I can understand her pain. I'm sure it's the same kind of pain I felt when the Strays stabbed the knife in the back of Elliot's hand. The thought makes my smile drop, and I look over to Elliot's hand, which is scarred now.

It's still there.

So is mine. So is Enyo's.

Sighing, I swing my gaze back to Mrs. Bensen, whose pleas fall on deaf ears. I can't hear her, nor do I want to. Our pain can't be the same. We're both monsters, in our own rights, but looking at her is not like looking in a mirror.

I'm a good monster.

That's what Elliot tells me.

I have bounds, limits, morals, and that makes me a good evil.

We're both good and evil, and that is okay.

Mrs. Bensen is a bad evil. She doesn't have bounds, limits, or morals. She'll hurt whoever she pleases because she can. She'll hurt the innocent, the bad, and the in between.

She is bad.

Swallowing the spit in my mouth, I lean closer to her from across the table. I take her loose hand in both of mine, and I look at her well-manicured fingers. Free of any callouses and scars, unlike mine. Her hands are soft.

I hate it.

Koby and Marcus and so many others are dead, and they don't carry a single scar? A single memory of the damage, the evil, she's caused? I take my knife that was taped to the bottom of my chair and stab it through her hand.

Now she'll scar.

She howls in pain as Mr. Bensen thrashes in his chair, practically sawing his own head off. My eyes stray to Elliot's. His warm eyes shine over me, and I smile.

I love smiling at him.

He always smiles back.

The chaos in the room sounds like lovely soothing music to my ears as I zero in on my man.

Elliot Jay.

Elliot Moss.

"Marry me," I say. As soft as the words may have fallen from my lips, over the screams and cries of our captives, he heard me.

"Marry you?" he asks, his tone as low as mine.

"Marry me. Become a Moss, handsome."

"Why don't *you* marry *me*, Little Crane?" he asks, but I'm already shaking my head. Confusion fills his brows, but I can't marry him.

"You're not a Jay anymore. You have to marry *me*, Elliot." At this, he laughs, throwing his head back, and I stare at him, awaiting his answer with my knife still in Mrs. Bensen's hand and the table.

He stares down at a bloody Mr. Bensen, who is nearly dead, and his hyperventilating wife, who has tears of sorrow and terror streaming down her face.

"Everything I do, with every breath I breathe, I will belong to you as you do to me." His eyes blaze into mine, as if I had any doubt of being unsure about my ask.

Didn't he know he was mine?

And that I wasn't asking.

I was telling him. He will marry me. Legally.

"You will be mine. Legally, illegally, and all the meanings in between, Diora Moss."

"Yes," my answer falls on a breathy moan as Mrs. Bensen sobs, staring at the knife holding her hand to the table.

"You'll give me your last name?" he mumbles, leaning back and cutting Mr. Bensen's throat for the final time before his head flops onto the table. Blood leaks from his throat and all over my table, but it looks… romantic.

"Of course. I'd give you anything, Elliot," I say, shaking my head mindlessly.

He thinks as he stares at Mr. Bensen's head.

"You could go back to your previous name, too, if you wanted. Oliver Moss." My words steal his focus. He is looking at me, yet his eyes fog, as if he is actually looking through me as his birth name leaves my lips.

"Oliver Moss," he tries out the name on his tongue as he wraps his bloody wire saw.

"But I met you when I was Elliot. I wouldn't have met you had I not become Elliot."

"We could meet again," I mutter.

"I'm Elliot," he says, shaking his head, focusing on me, my eyes, to tell him what he needs to hear.

"You're Elliot, handsome," I confirm, seeing confidence fill his eyes, his posture. He smiles. It's a soft, kind hearted smile, despite the blood dotting his face.

"You are Elliot Moss."

"Let's get married."

"Let's get married." I yelp with joy as Elliot drops his weapon on the table and wraps his arms around me. His arms snake under my armpits, lifting my head to his as he rests his forehead on mine, his hands in my hair, and I reach up to kiss his lips as he laughs into my mouth.

"Yes, Little Crane. Yes."

He doesn't let go of me. My handsome, soon-to-be husband doesn't let me down, and I hold his face in my hands. His soft, beautiful, handsome face.

"As my wedding gift, could you clean this up for me?" I ask, pecking his lips as I slip out of his arms. "It's a real mess we have here."

"Then you can't turn it in to the Society, Little Crane," he says, laughing as he picks up Mr. Bensen's head by his hair. Finally done with the night, I turn on my heel, a smile I can't control on my lips. I stand behind a tired Mrs. Bensen and yank her head back by her hair and stare into her eyes as I plunge the syringe of foxglove into her neck. She blinks for the last time as she slumps over, dead.

"I'm not the one who still needs their eight kills this year, handsome," I say. I grab some blood slides to record these kills. Elliot always gives me the kills. We do them together now—it's much more fun that way—but he always lets me take the credit, like a true gentleman.

Getting a drop of blood from each of them on separate slides, I package them up for a courier of the Society to pick up.

"We have a hit for Haven in the morning." I hear him sigh as puts the decapitated head into a black trash bag.

Haven is what it's always been: an organization of hired hitmen. When people with too much money need someone killed, they call us, except it's not no questions asked anymore.

Our clients are fully vetted. We make sure there are no ties to the trafficking ring, or the selling of skin, and if there is, they become our targets.

Our clients haven't quite caught on to that notion, but they will soon.

"Fuck," Elliot mutters as he starts cleaning up our kills. "You know what, Top Dogs will do it."

"No, we said that last time," I say, sliding onto my workbench stool. "You didn't want to leave bed, remember?"

"No, I didn't want to leave you." I laugh as I prepare a potted plant for the Bensens' home. I leave Angel trumpets in our targets' homes, normally in place of their "trophies".

One thing about killers is, we all have our tells, our trophies. Mine are people who have wronged the people I love. Our targets happen to be the kids they destroyed.

"We'll go together," Elliot sighs. My head snaps to him, and I scrunch my eyebrows.

"Why do I have to go?" This mission follows two businesses in the car industries who are tired of competing. One company hired us to take out the CEO of the other. I don't like going on kills based on cash. It's pretty boring.

It doesn't bother me morally as much as it should, but I'm coming to the realization that is just who I am. I'd rather stay home than kill based on who pays us the most.

I'd rather be home.

Our home.

"No, Elliot," I plead, as I clean up the excess dirt around the pot.

"We're to be husband and wife. We stick together, Little Crane," he says, warming my beating heart with our new titles. In a world where legality is largely dismissed, having legally binding titles is just another way I can tie Elliot to me, and I love it.

"But you're the face of the company."

"So are you," he argues, wiping down my tea table. Dragging the table back, Mrs. Bensen's body falls to the ground with a thump.

"Oh, I forgot about that," I mumble. I forgot he and Enyo roped me into running the corp with them. It's the last thing

I ever want to do, but... but I like training the girls, the girls like me. That's the only upside, besides seeing Elliot at work. Oh, how I love seeing Elliot at work.

"You'll miss me?" he asks, his bloody hands trapping me against my workbench as I turn to face him.

"You know it," I say, leaning forward to kiss his neck. His skin is smooth under my lips, and I let my teeth nibble his skin.

"Kiss me," he mumbles, capturing my lips against his. "Kiss me again."

"I'll kiss you for an eternity, handsome. Always."

ENJOYED LITTLE CRANE?

Leave Little Crane a review at Amazon and Goodreads.

I would be so grateful if you left a review for this book. Leaving a book review is like buying the book a million times over and is a great way to support authors! One review could lead to more readers finding another book they love.

Your support is the lifeline for many authors. Reviews give us the chance to receive feedback on what readers, like you, are enjoying!

Thank you in advance for your support! A review left anywhere, like amazon, goodreads, storygraph, social media and beyond is incredibly helpful for authors and readers alike!!

Other Books in the Darkest Desires Series

Did you enjoy Little Crane? Then check out all these other amazing books in the Darkest Desires Series!

See the whole series on Amazon.

https://www.amazon.co.uk/dp/B0DGGMB42F

Forgive Me Father by Ryan Reeve

A serial killer priest and his tattoo artist companion team up with a lost soul to exact revenge.

-

Perfect Poppy by Casia Pickering

A therapist catches the eye of a mortician when she goes feral against toxic men.

-

Little Crane by Jorjor Battle

A poisoner and a professional assassin team up to take down a human trafficking ring in their town.

-

Her Lips to God's Hands by Aurora Light

A serial killer meets her obsessed fan, throwing her perfectly controlled life into disarray.

-

<u>My Little Disasters</u> Jorjor Battle
A painter, a guard, and a courier take on the mafia to protect the ones they love.

-

<u>The Sinners Gambit</u> By Annie Gray
A top surgeon is kidnapped by a lonely serial killer who is infatuated with her, uncovering shocking revelations

-

<u>Beyond Death</u> by Morgan Dale
A trafficking victim turned serial killer vows revenge on those who've wronged her.

-

<u>The Bludgeoner and His Little Monster</u> by Daffodil Rae
A former nightclub host recruits his boyfriend, a brutal assassin, and a black market meat dealer to exact revenge on the fiends of his past.

-

<u>Fatal Dates</u> by KD Michaels
A female serial killer who goes after men on dating apps who are cheating on their significant other.

-

<u>My Murderous Wife</u> by Abigail Hunter

A woman cuts out the hearts of men to gain memories of her husband, until a murder goes wrong, and the man who rescues her looks all too familiar.

ALSO BY JORJOR BATTLE

<u>Stained Series</u>

Stained Perception

Stained Fate

<u>Darkest Desires: Season 1</u>

Little Crane

My Little Disasters

About the Author

Jorjor Battle is a Michiganer pursuing her dreams of becoming a dark romance author. She'd prefer to fall in love in real life but, for the time being, accepts her unhealthy obsession with love in the forms of books, tv shows, and movies. A couch, a blanket, a gallon of hot tea, chips in a bowl, a tv remote, a pillow, her laptop, her phone, her dog, and a book is *all* she needs to have a good time ;)

Follow her on social media to hear about upcoming projects and all things about being a writer and book lover!

Instagram: @readingjorjor

TikTok: @readingjorjor

Pinterest: @readingjorjor

Read on for a Sneak Peak into My Little Disasters

Chapter 1

Pandora

Being pretty has never bitten me so hard in the ass before. I've had many advantages to being pretty. To some, paying off my family's debt by fake dating a Mafia henchman is a blessing. Especially since I haven't had to fuck him yet.

But it's not an advantage. It's not even like the Mafia henchman is attractive or protective. No, he's tall and strong, sure, but an ass and controlling. His self esteem is below hell and his insecurities guide every move he makes. I can't stand the fucking man. I like nice men and he is the furthest thing from nice.

Marcel Amos, the Mafia man I'm "dating" to pay off my dad's debt, finally pulls into my damn driveway after the longest date of my life. I hold the sigh I've been dying to let out. The bastard was going thirty-five miles per hour the whole damn ride and taking all the back ways to irritate the hell out of me.

My cheeks burn from the fake smile held during dinner and my high heels are cutting off the circulation of blood to my toes.

Marcel can hardly put the car in park before my door is open. One heel is on the concréte when I hear his weak-ass grunt of dissatisfaction. Rolling my eyes, I glare back at him with a snarl.

His smug, chiseled face turns to me with his finger on his cheek. He wants a kiss, but I want to stab one of my paint brushes through his cheek and watch him bleed.

I drop forward, giving him the fastest peck of all time, and dart out of the damn car. Slamming the door of his sports car, I pull my white fur coat closer over my chest as I make my way to the porch.

He rolls down the window of the passenger seat, not bothering to be a true gentleman by walking me to my door.

"Consider that 1k off your debt," he yells and that makes me turn on my heel and storm back to the damn car. Only 1k? Is he fucking kidding me? It would take forever to pay off my Dad's debt if one measly date was One-fucking-K.

"Two hours of my time is only worth 1k Marcel?" I snarl, leaning in the open window of his car. "Please, you know that was worth five thousand and that kiss wasn't free either."

"Like it knocks that much off your debt." He laughs at me, throwing his head back as my family's enormous debt is thrown in my face. I tell myself the blush on my cheeks is not from embarrassment and instead from the makeup I put on hours ago.

"Learn to count or I'm calling the boss."

"You a snitch?" he growls, but his bite isn't worth a damn cent.

"I'm a bitch too, so make sure you learn to count or I'm calling Daddy and letting him know his men are pussyfooting around.

I wonder what that will do for his reputation," I say before walking to my porch.

My hand hovers over the door handle. I wait to hear his wheels screech as he whips out of my driveway. Taking a deep breath, I turn away from my house and start walking towards my art studio.

Litchfort is a small town outside of Detroit, Michigan that stays away from the crazy shit that a city brings. The town is filled with people who "made it out," including me and my Dad.

Except we didn't make it out. Not really.

The fall air chills my bare legs. My short dress isn't doing anything to keep me warm and neither is my jacket. Pulling out a cigarette, I light it as I walk. Litchfort is one of those towns from aesthetic girly tv shows with little shops lining the streets and sidewalks absolutely everywhere. There are tons of small businesses, and greenery that is sure to have cost the town a pretty penny, but I'd say is well worth it.

It's why I make sure my cigarette butts make it in the trash and not all over the damn garden beds.

We moved here because this was the furthest suburban town we could afford to live in. Except, we couldn't afford it. No, that's where the Mafia comes in.

They offered my Dad a loan with rates illegally high and that was my Dad's only option to get us somewhere safe.

Dad had a real chance of paying off the debt eventually, but now that the new leader of the Mafia took over, our interest rate tripled and, in hand, changed the trajectory of our lives.

I have an art studio about four blocks from my house where I paint... amongst other things. I pay the rent with the profits from paintings and any other cash I make goes to the Mafia.

Not that I make a hell of a lot but, but anything is better than nothing.

Running my tongue over my teeth, a smile grows on my face. I have a prize waiting for me at my studio today. Two prizes, in fact.

One is named Marko Mayfield. He's hanging by his hands from a chain bolted in my ceiling, shirtless and ready for my art.

The second surprise is on his way to my studio. Kohen Harthwarn is my second treat of the night. While he's not on my kill list, he is definitely on my fuck list. He's... well, he's a nice guy packaged into the sexiest man I've ever seen who comes at my beck and call.

Walking up the stairs on the side of the building, I step into my studio. Locking the door behind me, I see Marko Mayfield. His stomach is heaving as if he's out of breath, maybe from screaming his head off for the past hour or so.

He has no idea why he's here, I'm sure. No one ever does. I always set them up to wake up in a serial killer's den. Confused, scared, and exhausted from the hours I leave them hanging for.

"Un-fucking-tie me," Marko demands as I walk in. I stop at his harsh command. The words spit at me as his glare sharpens. Is this how you ask someone to save you? I take in his extremely athletic body. It was nearly too heavy for me to drag here. His sweat glistens over his abs, and for a moment, I appreciate his body. Abs are hot, what can I say? Though, in my appreciation, I noticed the subtle shake of his weakening body.

His glare stays strong on little old me. The viciousness of his eyes lands on me and I'm not too cocky to admit this reaction surprises me. He doesn't know why I'm here. Maybe he doesn't care.

That's... interesting.

He will, in a minute, but right now he thinks he's in control. The fact he's glaring at me instead of begging is one sign and another is his eyebrow. It doesn't waiver, it's completely normal. No scrunch, no raise, nothing. He's not scared. Besides the slight tremble in his body, which could be due to body exhaustion instead of fear, I'd have no indication he was fearful. His belief in himself is astonishing.

"Why would I do that when I spent so much time getting you here?" I ask, sliding my jacket off. I'm left in a short black dress with the prettiest flouncy skirt. It makes me wanna twirl with glee.

Seeing a girl in a short dress leads my victims to believe women get dressed with them in mind, a man in mind, and this would be the only time they'd be right.

Only they're not the right man. My short dress attire is for Kohen.

This line of thinking, that women dress cute for men, is exactly why they end up stuck here with me.

I've had targets think this is a kink exploration or something. As if there was no other possibility for a girl to have them hanging from her ceiling. All that ego dies when they realize this is actually their deathbed. Death site? Death... studio?

"Fuck that, let me down and I won't hurt you," he spits, and I scrunch my eyebrows. Hurt me? I take a hit of my cigarette and cover my laugh with a cough.

"You don't look like you're in the position to be hurling threats, Mr. Mayfield," I say, picking up a clean pallet and a paintbrush.

"When I get down—"

"Does the name May Harley ring any bells for you?" I ask, cutting Marko's lame ass rant off. The name definitely rings a bell for him. I made sure of it.

I'm an art student by day and a serial killer by night. A death angel taking out students at Litchfort University for seemingly no reason.

No one has connected the sexual assaults these men have committed as a motive for their murders. The reports, if there is a report, have been buried under dirty money and favors.

That's fine. There are other, more effective, ways to deal with these kinds of people.

I committed my first kill about a year and a half ago. A football player got handsy with me. He didn't get any further than his body over mine, but the instinct to kill him took over all my senses.

I said no. I said no multiple times. I screamed. I even cried and he wouldn't stop.

So I killed him with a trophy that was sitting on the nightstand. Bashing him over the head until blood covered my vision.

His blood was everywhere. Red painted my pretty dress, my face, everything from the waist up. It was a mess.

I didn't mean to kill him. I was only saving myself, but no one would have cared.

I killed a man, and I got away with it. Well, with Kohen's help. He's such a nice guy. He saw me struggling with the dead body as I tried to throw it out the window of a frat house. He was walking by and saw me. My prince charming.

See, being pretty helped me out there too. What are the chances a stranger would help me out if I was ugly? Probably slim.

I'll admit I thought I was busted. Panic coursed through my body like the blood in my veins. I kind of liked it. That rush.

Kohen didn't snitch. He's not like that.

He's actually like me.

Something about his eyes when they met mine told me he knew the rush I just experienced.

Ever since, I've craved the rush of killing. So I did it again. And again. And again.

Not long after, the Society contacted me about admission into their cool little club of people similar to me. Kohen works for this Society. Maybe he put a good word in for me, I don't know. I joined and now, a year later, I'm a more skilled serial killer with connections all over the world.

Switching my paint supplies to one hand, I remove my cigarette from my mouth, exhaling the smoke, and gaze up at Marko.

He glares down at me with his light blue eyes. Sweat drips down his tanned face, and his jaw is clenched, but he has no fear. Now that I'm here, he thinks he's safe? Is it because I'm a 5'5" girl, he's not scared?

"Who the hell is May?" His voice is rugged, but scratchy.

"Oh, we're playing this game," I say, burning the butt of my cigarette on his chest right above his nipple. His body jerks back as he hisses, but he doesn't get far because of the chain he's hanging from. "Oh, did that hurt?"

I smile as his face twitches in pain. He does his damndest to hide it, but even his best isn't good enough. Shocker.

"No, please, stop, stop, please don't do this to me," I scream like bloody fucking murder in his face. His eyes widen as he stares at me in shock. "Remember May now?"

The color from his face drains resembling a blood bag after a vampire sucks it dry. His jaw can't help but drop the slightest bit and the anger that heated the room before dissipates. He pulls on his chains and now is when he truly realizes the trouble he's in.

I giggle as I toss my cigarette in a nearby trash can. "So you do remember. Good, now we can get started."

May Harley was a student he raped four weeks ago at a fucking frat party.

I was at the same party with Marcel. Of course, that fucking looser wanted to go to a damn frat party. I saw May after Marko hurt her. In the bed. Frozen.

My face twitches as the frozen image of her plays in my head. Anger bubbling up in me at the memory.

I was going to the bathroom and I walked past the room with the door cracked open and May Harley lying there. Frozen, hopeless, scared.

I took her to the hospital and they made a report, but the school made it disappear.

So instead, I followed my natural instinct, and decided I'll make Marko Mayfield disappear. It's only fair.

Picking up some paint from the pallet, I paint his stomach red, the acrylic coming out chunky. It's not my favorite paint but it does the job.

I much prefer dreamy landscapes and oil paints, or even gouache, but for this, acrylic is perfect.

I start with dots. Each touch makes him flinch. He tries to kick at me, but he can't. He's been hanging here for so long his core isn't strong enough to lift his legs up.

Screams, spit, and all the waterworks begin as I paint his skin, but once I'm in the zone, it's too late.

I'm as dead to the world as he will be.

"Who the hell are you?" he yells. This question I do hear. I stop my art on his body and gaze up at him.

"Oh man," I say. His brown hair is wet with sweat and he's crying. His arms must be killing him. Good. I gaze up at him through my lashes and pouting my lips. "I ran out of paint."

"Is this for fucking show? Are you trying to make an example out of me? I swear she wanted it. She's lying. She's a lying whore–"

I let his rambling fall on deaf ears as I break the tip of my wooden paint brush and stab it into the center of his stomach. Blood splatters as he howls in pain. Pulling it back out, I watch as his blood drips on my palette.

This time, his screams are from pain and I smile. I smile so damn hard as he realizes I'm here to hurt him. This smile isn't fake like earlier. The rush of what's coming covers my skin like a blanket and I'm sure my eyes are glittering as I stare at the blood.

I cackle as his eyes widen. "Oh no! I don't think this'll be enough," I say and stab him again, this time ripping upward to create a bigger hole in his stomach.

"Stop! Please stop. Oh my God, stop."

"Did you stop when May begged? Pleaded? Did you?" I ask, digging deeper.

His eyes bleed into mine as I lean close to his face, close enough I feel the urge to try to rip his nasty lips off his fucking face with my teeth.

His nose might be easier.

"No?" I gasp in fake surprise. "Hmm, how unfortunate for you." I lean back to paint the rest of his body with his blood.

Covering every inch of exposed skin, I layer the thick liquid over the acrylic. Moving around his body, I do his back and I feel him go slack in his chains.

Between the bleeding wound and the strain on his body from hanging, he isn't too far from death. Which is perfect because his body is covered in paint and blood and now that the canvas is covered...well. There's not much left to do.

Knock. Knock. The sound has me snapping my head to the door and I nearly skip to the door, my four-inch heels clicking against the floor as I go to open it. Setting my palette and brush on the side table by my door, I straighten out my dress, making sure my boobs perk up against the lace trim along the strapless neckline.

My courier service is here! Which means Kohen is here. Fucking finally. I swing open the door and the moment my eyes meet the wrong brown eyes, I growl.

"Where's Kohen?" I ask the man at my door who is missing his partner. Turning on my heel, I stomp away from the door. The Society has a rule when it comes to their courier service, which is that any Courier must be accompanied by a Guard to ensure no one tries to hurt them.

Kohen always comes with his boyfriend, who happens to be the most annoying fucking Guard ever. Eros grew up with Kohen and they fell in love somewhere down the line.

So my crush has a boyfriend. I never minded sharing.

Eros Warm smirks as he walks into my studio. I let my eyes drop down his body. I'm not petty enough to say he's ugly.

Eros Warm is pretty fucking hot with deep tan skin and brown, molten eyes. That sharp jaw, lean waist, and strong broad shoulders. I swallow the drool in my mouth as he turns to face me. I'd let myself have a crush on him too, but the man fucking hates me.

Maybe because I call on the Society a lot? Maybe because he knows I'm trying to get with his boyfriend? I shrug. Who the hell knows?

"You know he's not dead yet, right?" Eros's voice comes out rugged and like sex on a damn beach, but I scowl.

"You think I'm fucking stupid or something?" I say, taking a dagger from one of my drawers around the room. I quickly jab it in Marko's neck, all the way to the hilt, properly killing him. "Now, where are my slides?"

The Society tracks our kills with blood sides. We don't have to log all our kills, but once we get to eight, we get an invitation to the annual ball in June. I didn't make the cut last year since I didn't get enough kills before June, but this year, I'm making sure I get my kills in.

Marko will be my seventh kill this year, and it's only August.

"Ring?" Eros asks and I sigh, pulling the gold ring with a skull on it off my finger so he can scan it. Each member gets a ring and this holds all our information, and the Couriers, as well as the Guards, use them to identify us.

He does the scanning thing and puts the blood slides on one of my desks. He cracks his neck as he leans on one of my tables, getting entirely too comfortable in my space.

"You can leave now." Taking a blood slide, I open it up and get a drop of blood, not mixed with paint, and close it before handing it back to Eros.

"I could, but we have to talk." He uses my momentary lapse in awareness to draw me closer to him by bringing the slide closer to him. I look up at him, confused.

"About what?" I spat.

"The Mafia," He says, and I roll my eyes.

"It's handled. They won't find out about The Society." The Society must be kept absolutely secret. It's been a secret for over a century and no one knows more than they are allowed to know about them, even the members. Its official name is Mortes Ostium, Death's Door in Latin, but I refer to them as the Society. Their whole goal is to connect serial killers together and give them a space to be, well, ourselves.

"That's not what I'm worried about and you fucking know it." I scoff, clenching my jaw as I look away from his sharp brown eyes. He must not like that since he yanks my jaw forward to stare straight at him.

I know what he's talking about now. He's talking about my "special assignment" from the Mafia. The one thing they asked me to do and if I accomplish it, they'll erase my debt and keep my Dad safe.

The whole reason I don't attempt to kill the whole damn Mafia is because of my Dad. If I can't kill them all fast enough, or all of them together, and they could try to get my dad and I can't afford that kind of risk.

So I do what they say. I play the part of a Mafia girlfriend until the debt is paid off and we're free.

That is, at least, until they spotted Kohen dropping me off at university one day after a kill in the studio. I was being fucking stupid. I called him because without a ride I'd be late to class since my kill session ran over time. I was lying about running late. Obviously, I only wanted to see him. But that little lie got my Kohen on the Mafia's raider. They somehow spotted his smarts from a mile away and decided they wanted him to work for them.

"They won't touch him," I say, and I mean it. I'd rather pay off this debt by acting as a girlfriend and keep Kohen away from it all.

Kohen isn't pure by any means, he works for the Society. You'd have to be some kind of crazy to do that, but Kohen isn't like anyone I've ever met. He smiles at me. Truly smiles at me. He knows about my void, my killer tendencies, and he still smiles at me.

He's warm, and kind, and that fucking smile, God. That smile. He listens when I ramble on about my art, even when he is supposed to leave to cater to some other serial killer. He stays. He understands. He's special.

He has to be mine. It may be selfish, but I love the way he makes me feel. He's the kind of guy you want to dress cute for. Not because you have to, but because he makes you feel so special when he stares at you.

No one has made me feel that way before. It's more important to me to keep someone like that safe. I'd do anything to keep him safe.

"Then it looks like we're on the same page, Princess," Eros says and backs away from the bubble we're in. I let go of the slide. I swallow as I watch Eros leave my studio.

Between me and his Guard, no one will get their hands on Kohen.

MY LITTLE DISASTERS

Want to know what happens next?
You can find My Little Disasters right here on Amazon!

BLURB

The Mafia wants him, but she wants him more.
Motivated by her twisted sense of justice, Pandora Melrose
has stumbled upon a problem that a dead body can't fix. The
Detroit Mafia have caught Pandora's father in deadly debt, and
the only way she can free him is by surrendering her body to
the Mafia's right-hand man Marcel Amos. She was willing to
pay any price if it meant protecting her father, until the Mafia
touched something they shouldn't.
The Mafia has their eyes on Kohen Harthwarn, her college
crush But Kohen's boyfriend has skills of his own, and getting
through Eros and Pandora might just be the thing that destroys
their empire.
They've opened Pandora's Box, now let's see who lives to tell
the tale.